MANTA RAYS AND MARGARITAS

— *Tropical Travels to Dive the Oceans* —

by Karen Begelfer

For my Little Mermaid, my King Prawn
and my favorite Sea Cucumber

TABLE OF CONTENTS

Chapter 1 Bora Bora: Shaking My Coconuts and
Other Pleasurable Activities · 1

Chapter 2 Moorea: Land of Well-Fed Sharks and Tantalizing Tikis · · 19

Chapter 3 Caribbean Cruising: She Who Lacks Undergarments
is a Popular Girl Indeed · 37

Chapter 4 Australia: Down Under the Waves, Down
Under the World· 57

Chapter 5 Bahamas: The Art of the Chicken Bag · · · · · · · · · · · · · · 73

Chapter 6 Mexico: Parasites in Paradise· 91

Chapter 7 U.S. Virgin Islands: Duty Free Rum, Lack of Rhythm,
and Other Indications You Might Be a Tourist · · · · · · · · 109

Chapter 8 Hawaii: The Gods of Sun, Sand, and Retail· · · · · · · · · · · 131

Chapter 9 Aruba: The Goats of Wrath · 155

Chapter 10 Federated States of Micronesia: "You want to go where?" · 173

Chapter 11 Republic of Palau: Land of Day-Glo Sumo Clams · · · · · · 191

Chapter 12 Belize: Patience is a Virtue, Whale Sharks are a Vice · · · · 211

Chapter 13 Cayman Islands: Hammerheads on Harleys · · · · · · · · · · · 235

Epilogue · 255

CHAPTER 1

Bora Bora: Shaking My Coconuts and Other Pleasurable Activities

As the plane descended, paradise peeked through the clouds like a bejeweled dream, an emerald island amongst a sea of sapphires. The captivating Bali Hai mountains slowly came into focus. An extinct volcano dominated the center of the island in the form of two romantic 2000 foot peaks, Mount Pahia and Mount Otemanu. The fringing reef became visible, its puzzle-like growth promised a maze of untold secrets of the underwater world. We were about to touch down in Bora Bora.

"Hold onto your flower leis and say a prayer. We're landing soon," shouted our Captain over his shoulder on our nineteen-seater plane. The Twin Otter airplane, the 1960's Volkswagen Beetle of the aviation world, did not instill much confidence in us. Our Atlanta flight connected to the relic in Tahiti, where an airport worker had to fiddle with one of the two propellers before it would start.

The craft produced in-flight noises that modeled digestion-oriented bodily functions and the Captain kept tapping at the altitude and fuel gages as if willing them to work. A prudent person would have been concerned or at least planning to request a ticket refund, but my primary emotion was excitement. I had traveled extensively, but always to popular, well-visited tourist destinations in the U.S. and Europe. This was different. French Polynesia was exotic, unknown, and mysterious. This was the first true adventure of my life; prudence be damned. I was going to step off the beaten path and learn to scuba dive, an activity which promised to be new and exhilarating. I was ready.

French Polynesia is the vision of an idyllic, exotic paradise, with more palm trees and less annoying co-workers than at home. But, the island of Tahiti, my flight's destination, is also the most polluted, and industrial of the territory's 118 islands. Better to wait at the airport to catch another, even smaller plane, and head for a different island. French Polynesia, approximately the size of Europe, is actually made up of five island groups: the Society, Marquesas, Austral, Gambier, and Tuamotus, each with its own unique topside and underwater character. Some features, however, are consistent across the islands. Sharks are more common than people, with black-tips, white-tips, greys, and lemons making frequent appearances. Traditional tattoos decorate the bodies of many of the islands' inhabitants. The topography is magnificent; the dramatic and varied land formations continue down into the depths of the sea. My husband, Michael, and I chose to spend our time on two islands in the Society Island group: Bora Bora, a Leeward Island and Moorea, a Windward Island.

First stop: Bora Bora. "Old Man" Otter touched down surprisingly gently, then taxied across the miniscule runway to a small hut, all on a bump of sand surrounded by water; I mentally prepared to swim to our hotel. Could I use my suitcase as a flotation device? Now I understood why the reservation agent insisted the hotel pick us up from the airport. We boarded a well-polished, wooden boat and zipped through the lagoon toward our hotel on a small offshore island. The crystal-clear water magnified the reef below as we sped towards our accommodations.

As my gaze left the water, I found myself staring at our hotel, a teak and glass dream straight off of the cover of "50 Places to Visit Before You Die or Go Bankrupt" magazine. The architecture stunned us. The lobby stood over the water on stilts through which hundreds of tiny multi-colored fish shimmied and sought shelter. Carved into the middle of the floor of our room, also on stilts, was a large Plexiglas window offering a voyeuristic view of the habits of aquatic creatures below. Of course, the fish had those same viewing privileges, which sent me into a fit of self-consciousness that limited my use of skirts for the week. Our balcony's short set of steps led down to a landing on the water's surface. If so inclined one could roll out of bed and into the ocean in one motion.

Access to that magnificent water for scuba diving purposes was our sole impetus for going to French Polynesia. Scuba diving training is made up of two parts: study sessions in a classroom and a pool followed by four dives in open water. We recently had completed the classroom and pool portion of the training back home in Atlanta. A zealous dive instructor had taught us the curriculum developed by PADI, the Professional Association of Dive Instructors. PADI divides the training into ten useful sections, including: equipment, how to plan a dive, impact of diving on the body, and identification of items that will eat you underwater. The pool practice focused on the gear: how to apply it, use it, and most importantly, how to avoid dropping the thirty-plus pounds of equipment on one's foot. All this training leaned heavy on theory, but light on actual practice, thus the need for the four open water dives. Most would-be, land-locked divers usually head for the nearest water-filled quarry to finalize their certification, which we found to be a mundane prospect at best. The open water requirement gave us a perfect excuse to travel somewhere exotic, so we pulled out our world map and chose a place we had yearned to visit for a long time.

With our destination decided, we chose a Bora Bora dive operator based on internet advertising alone. My theory on choosing dive companies via the internet is simple: if the pictures of divers have happy expressions and there is at least one photo of an ocean-loving dog on the site, the dive shop has to be good. The chosen dive company picked us up at our hotel, a real plus since otherwise we would have had to hire an expensive and inconvenient water taxi to bring us to the main island. The castaway experience of our hotel's location on an outer island was certainly a tropical novelty, but not very practical when needing to go back to the mainland.

We waited in the hotel lobby for the dive company representative to arrive. Much to our dismay a small, rusty boat came into view. I wasn't sure it would make it to our dock from the time we caught sight of it; I was even less convinced it could bring us back to the main island without involving a good swim. The driver, Christophe, invited us to jump in, but not too energetically lest we poke a hole in the bottom of the boat. With a shutter and a puff of black smoke we pulled away from the dock.

The loud engine sounds left no opportunity to talk with Christophe. We arrived at the dock partially deaf and potentially suffering from black lung. Christophe passed us to Philippe, the instructor who would monitor our four dives and eventually, hopefully, certify us. He was a small, lithe, chain-smoking man with piercing blue eyes.

"So why do you want to dive?" he asked in a French accent so thick he made Inspector Clouseau sound like he was from Ohio.

I had not contemplated that specific question before. I guess it was because I loved the ocean and thought it would be fun. My mental inner voice told me that this sounded shallow.

"Because the ocean covers two thirds of the world. I think I should get to know it a bit better before global warming covers the rest." I said. Ha! So much for sounding shallow.

"Good. Most people just like the ocean and think it would be fun. They don't always do so well once they get underwater," he said. *Great.*

Our first certification dive took place at a reef called the Aquarium, no deeper than twenty feet, an easy depth for a certified diver. As we geared up, my heart pounded in my chest. The sun radiated heat; my gear felt awkward and constricting. Michael and I were the only people on the boat obtaining a scuba certification. The other divers had passed that initiation long before we even considered taking the plunge. They kindly let us and our instructor off the boat first, perhaps remembering their own crazy selves that emerged on their first open water dive.

One large step, a "Giant Stride" in scuba terms, took us off the back of the boat and into the water. Full of air, our vests bobbed us right back to the surface. So far, so good. The instructor checked to make sure we were okay, then gave us the hand signal that starts every dive: one fist clenched, thumb extended, pointing down. It was time to descend. We deflated our vests and slowly started to sink. The waterline eased past my neck, my chin, my mask and finally the top of my head. Breathing underwater was a pleasant surprise though I knew, theoretically, that was why the tank of air was strapped to my back. Suddenly, my decent came to a halt. I floated vertically, but about a foot below the surface, bobbing like a buoy. The instructor indicated I should continue my decent, but I could not seem to drop anymore. He pointed to my vest, suggesting I had air still trapped inside. I pushed the deflator button, but no additional bubbles came out of the escape hatch on my shoulder. Philippe swam over to me in order to assist. He pushed my deflator button, and then enveloped me in a full body hug in order to squeeze out any remaining air in my vest. His efforts, though effective, made me feel like a porn star, enduring full body thrusts with a mysterious French stranger behind a mask. I looked around for the underwater video camera.

As luck would have it, the other divers' entry into the water coincided with the illicit hug. Their looks of shock and awe pretty much solidified my porn star status. One

> **"The expanse of the ocean is seldom seen by the novice with indifference."**
> - James Fenimore Cooper, *The Pathfinder*

even pointed to us, using obscene underwater gestures that indicated he not only had seen this adult film, but had memorized the ending. The group began to laugh uncontrollably, sending a case of champagne air bubbles effervescing through the water. I sank quietly to the bottom, coming to rest on the sand between boulders of coral, hoping I could simply blend in like a flounder and disappear.

Finally, my husband and Philippe joined me, and the other divers headed for deeper water. Having regained my calm, I began to look around and quickly became entranced. The sun threw mesmerizing beams of light through the water, projecting the curves of the waves on the sand. The sea floor glowed pink, then cream as the light played against its fine grains. With the surface acting as a ceiling above our heads and the surrounding boulders as walls, I felt like we sat in a small, brightly lit room.

In the distance the water appeared turquoise, but there in our room, it was crystal clear due to our shallow depth. Best of all were the thousands of small, tropical fish that filled the space with a rainbow of color and movement. The kaleidoscope of fish made me dizzy.

Philippe had each of us practice our underwater skills. I found the equipment retrieval drill and the drill to share air when one diver's tank runs empty to be fairly easy. We also practiced communicating with various hand signals, a useful tool when one needs to make a statement underwater. Thought there are many scuba hand signals, a few stand out.

Highlights of Underwater Communication

Signal: one hand, fist clenched, thumb pointing up
Meaning: I want to surface now because I am: tired, hungry, low on air, bored, needing a margarita, or I just don't like diving with you anymore.

Signal: hand held flat, palm down, making a sawing motion across the neck
Meaning: I'm out of air. Unless I sprout gills I'll be dead soon.

Signal: hand held flat, fingers pointing up on the top of the head like a shark fin
Meaning: A shark fin. Rest of shark attached. Swim fast.

Signal: hand held flat, palm touching mouth
Meaning: I am low on air. I am about to rip your air regulator out of your mouth so I can use it. Or, you can pass it to me. Your choice.

Signal: index and middle finger touching the mask, then pointing outwards at an object
Meaning: There is something very interesting that you must see. Ha, ha, I saw it first.

The difficult part of the skill practice was removing and reapplying our masks. The purpose of the drill was to become comfortable with putting one's mask back on if it comes off underwater or clearing the water from the mask if it floods. In theory this is a good drill in which to excel, but in practice it leaves the diver's eyes burning and her nose filled with water. I had to fight the urge to rocket to the surface as I reapplied my mask. The feeling of panic was not pleasant, but learning this skill was important. We would practice this drill twelve times over our four certification dives.

Being new to the sport we were greedy with our air, sucking down the entire contents of our tanks in about twenty minutes. Michael wasted half of his air before our descent, having laughed it out during my silver screen debut. We slowly ascended and got back on the boat. The adrenaline and the excitement had taken its toll. I felt exhausted, although we still had another dive to do that day. I slumped onto the front of the boat, waiting for the rest of the dive group to return. Fortunately no one mentioned my attempt to make the home movie version of *Karen Does Bora Bora*.

After a brief rest, we moved onto another dive sight named Toopua. The dive was beautiful and mercifully uneventful other than the periodic bursts of panic when we were expected to remove and replace our masks. Again, the beauty of the underwater world took my breath away, and with confidence I found my concentration slipping from Philippe to the amazing sea world. I had learned that I could survive underwater and even enjoy the sea life around me. I had come a long way in just one day.

Our hotel offered a unique break from diving, a *motu* picnic, which we eagerly embraced. *Motu* is a Polynesian word for Gilligan's Island, or a "small sand bump with palm trees." Our hotel would drop us off on a small, deserted isle with a lunch basket, then pick us up several hours later after the feast. It was the Robinson Caruso experience of which everyone fantasizes with a little city slicker fear factor thrown in considering no one, except the hotel, would know of our whereabouts or pick up location. One forgetful front desk clerk and we could be the Professor and Mary Ann forever.

We approached the *motu* in a small motor boat captained by one of the hotel bellman. The regular captain was out on another errand, but the front desk clerk assured us that the bellman was sufficiently adept. When we were near the *motu*, we hopped over the side of the boat and waded the last fifteen feet to shore, our picnic basket and swim paraphernalia held high above our heads. With a wave and an assurance he would return in three hours, the bellman left with the boat. Blessed silence replaced the drone of the motor as it retreated into the distance, leaving us with a peaceful but excited feeling at our impending castaway experience.

We decided to plant our belongings and go exploring. The *motu* was approximately the size of a football field with sandy fringes. Lush green palm trees and leafy foliage covered the island. A basic, wooden shelter stood on one end with a table and comfortable chairs; the perfect place to escape the sun. The owners also had considerately strung hammocks here and there between the trees, each with a picture-perfect view of the majestic mountains of the main island soaring in the distance.

The word "paradise" did not sufficiently describe our surroundings. It was beyond our dreams. I wanted to hold that vision in my memory forever, to make it the happy place in my mind to retreat to on rainy, cold days. It was so quintessentially tropical. It was so breathtakingly beautiful. It was so...buggy, I noticed, as I squashed a mosquito on the back of my arm. *Hmmm.*

"Let's go for a swim first, and then eat," Michael suggested. We put our bags in the shade of a mound of scrub, then grabbed our snorkels and masks and waded out into the shallows. Little fish abounded, flitting between the nooks and crannies of the ocean bottom. The reef mimicked a giant aquarium with us as the headlining fish in the tank. We circumnavigated the island like Columbus and his first mate, making sure to stay relatively close to the shore so as not to drift out to sea. Before we knew it, an hour passed. My stomach told me it was time for lunch.

"You grab the bag and I'll set up a nice place for us to eat," I offered. I walked down the beach to the shelter and arranged the seats next to each other, facing the ocean. The shade was a welcome relief from the early afternoon sun. Two more mosquitoes became preoccupied with my legs. I made a dash back to the beach to see Michael's progress.

"I can't find the bags," he said. "Do you remember where we put them?"

"Under the palm tree, next to that scrub."

"Do you remember *which* palm tree and *what* scrub?" he emphasized. They did all sort of look the same: green, tropical, beautiful, and all potentially bag-eating.

We set out in different directions, scouring the island. In an effort to hide them from the sun we had inadvertently hidden the bags from ourselves. After much futile searching, I heard Michael shout from down the beach, indicating success. Another thirty minutes in paradise was gone, but at least food was on the way. When he returned with the bags in tow, I grabbed the one with our towels and clothes first, hoping to wipe off the salt residue that had formed on my arms and legs during the search party.

"Well then!" I shouted, as a family of hermit crabs scuttled into the folds of cloth when I opened the bag. They had climbed in, apparently thinking the bag was "finders keepers" after no one claimed it for an hour. I spent the next ten minutes picking through item after item, removing the crustaceous squatters from my personal affects. The mosquitoes capitalized on my diverted attention and bit me repeatedly. Clearly the island residents had learned to work together.

By the time I sorted out the zoological aspects of the island, Michael had unpacked the designer picnic basket provided by our hotel. The kitchen staff got points for presentation, which included linen napkins and a large bottle of water kept cool by an insulated sleeve. Several containers held a variety of foods and a large piece of French bread. Conspicuously missing, however, were silverware and cups. Well, we would just eat with our fingers and drink from the same bottle. Did hermit crabs and mosquitoes care about bad manners?

By then we were famished. We each grabbed a container and explored the contents. Inside mine was a white oval with green vegetables and a white sauce, while Michael's had a similarly shaped oval, with rice and a black-flecked brown sauce. The other containers, we learned, all held similar mystery foods that involved significant amounts of sauce. This was going to be messy.

"I could carve a spoon out of a piece of wood," Michael said in his best "confident outdoorsman" voice. He doesn't even mow the lawn at home. I knew his carving skills were not up to par.

"Let's just each pick up some and try it," I said. "I don't care if it is a mess, I'm starving!" I pulled a part of my white oval off and took a bite. Michael did the same with his brown oval. "What do you have?" I asked.

"Fish. With a brown sauce. How about you?"

"Fish. With a white sauce." We both reached for the French bread, hoping it would mask the lingering unpleasant taste.

Container number three also held fish, as did containers four and five. To the hotel's credit, they did manage to find a different color sauce to put with each, although it all sort of tasted the same to me. After sampling the fare from each fishy container, we closed them all up and packed them away, mostly uneaten. We like fish, but not five kinds, with no utensils, in ninety-degree heat. Perhaps we were not cut out for deserted island life after all.

As I moved to the hammocks to rest, the mosquitoes moved with me, their captive victim. The rustle of the palms and the crash of the waves quickly sent me into a napping state. The gentle sway of the hammock was the final straw, practically requiring me to fall asleep. I drifted off peacefully, slapping my arms only once or twice for good measure to dissuade the resolute bugs.

"Honey, wake up," Michael said. "I think they forgot about us!"

I slowly opened my eyes, visions of a muscle-bound Polynesian god receding back into my dreamstate to wait for another time.

"How long have we been here?" I asked groggily. It didn't seem like that long.

"The captain said he would pick us up in three hours, but it has been almost four. I fell asleep like you. Maybe they came by and thought we were gone."

"Yes, perhaps we swam the miles back to the island, or perhaps a giant sea squid ate us. Really now, where would we go?" I asked. I really didn't think our ride had been there and gone like an impatient grade-school kid when the ending school bell finally rings, but it was possible they had forgotten us. That would be bad. We argued back and forth debating what happened, then eventually turned to the "what if" scenarios. What if they did not come pick us up? Did we have enough food and water? What if nighttime came? Would exposure be a problem on this unprotected bump of sand? What if the Mosquito King showed up and deemed me worthy of the all-you-can-eat bug buffet? It felt more and more like *Lord of the Flies* and less like *Gilligan's Island* by the minute.

A motor boat's drone suddenly broke through our voices. Our faces flushed as we realized how silly we sounded planning for Armageddon. The original bellman had been replaced with a real ferry captain. He waved and smiled as he moored the boat.

"Where have you been?" Michael asked.

"It's a four-hour tour. I'm back right on time."

"But the bellman told us three hours," I said.

"Oh, he don't know nothing. I'm the one that runs the boat out here. He just picks up bags," the Captain said.

Ahh. We began to see the root of our issue. We boarded the boat and sped back towards the hotel with a new version of paradise in mind, one that included a fully stocked restaurant of food and mosquito screens.

A 4x4 is required to traverse the main island of Bora Bora, the exception being the one main, paved road that follows the curvaceous contours of the island's shores. Taxis, though rare, do exist, but cost more than a Hollywood starlet's Gucci spree. To get anywhere most people walk or take Le Truck, the government-run public transit system. "Le Trucks," which are truck-bus hybrids, have bench seats, open sides, and a decidedly island-like flair. Some are painted a demure khaki or green, the color of the surrounding foliage. Most are blindingly vibrant, more like the parrots in the trees.

We wanted to explore the main island's major settlement, Vaitape. Although we could see the city from the dock on which the water taxi deposited us and could have easily walked, the Le Truck drivers were determined to give us a ride. With the tenacity of a randy high-school prom date each driver would ride up perilously close to us and motion for us to jump into the cab. The drivers interpreted our "no thanks" as "why yes, what a great idea," honking and pulling up even closer in case we had problems seeing them. With such assertive sales tactics they could well be top sellers of Amway products in their spare time. The third Le Truck "welcome" attempt finally crushed our will; we hopped on the vehicle for the five-minute ride to the capital.

> **The English word 'tattoo' actually comes from the ancient Tahitian word 'tatau.' Tattooing has always been an integral part of Polynesian culture embraced by men and women alike. Historically, tattoos indicated one's wealth, rank, and sexual maturity. When European missionaries arrived in Polynesia, the art of tattooing was almost wiped out entirely. Only in the last 40 years has it seen resurgence in the French Polynesian culture.**

To call Vaitape a city stretches the truth a bit. A few streets housed several two-story buildings, a dusting of tourist shops, snack bars, and a government building or two. St. Pierre Celestin church, a white edifice with a bright red cross on top, stood out from the rest. Though small, the humble building looked regal, its simple colors practically glowing against the lush green mountains behind it. In general, the clean town appeared to have all the normal trappings of modern humanity: running water, electricity, and a video shop plastered with David Hasselhoff posters.

I am not a shop-a-holic, but I love to see the locals' perception of the tourists based on the products they offer in their stores. One glance at the price tags of the black pearls in Vaitape told me the shopkeepers thought I was made of money. I settled for a simple, pretty, green sarong from an unassuming shop that stood slightly off the road, partially obscured by some tropical trees and scrub. The proprietor, a woman in her twenties with rich dark hair, spoke French to a young girl behind the counter as I inquired as to the price. She charmed me with her accent, made genteel by an island lilt.

The French did not always dominate the island, of course. The Polynesians landed there in the fourth century. Captain James Cook set the first pair of European feet on Bora Bora's golden shores in 1777. In the 1840's, Admiral Abel Thouars aggressively collected neighboring islands like seashells in the name of France. In 1842 France made Bora Bora a protectorate, and the French language and culture became prevalent. Now Bora Bora is part of the Society Islands of French Polynesia. Although French and Tahitian are the main languages spoken by the inhabitants, some people, especially those in the tourist trade, speak English. Vaitape grew from an unusual, but well-balanced mix of Polynesian and European influences, a fertile combination of old-world sensibilities and island flair.

After our brief shopping excursion, we continued down the road in search of a snack. Several one-story buildings appeared to have living quarters in the front and family-owned, sit-down restaurants in the back, along the water's edge. One, in particular, caught our attention. The large fish painted on the front indicated to our trained eyes that it was a seafood restaurant. The words "Fresh Fish Served Here" on the door were another good indication. We approached the building, but could not see anyone inside. Going around the back we found a handwritten sign sitting on one of the tables that read in several languages "Out fishing. Open later."

It was a profound statement of island supply and demand: "When I catch some fish I will come back and sell it to you." There is no more straightforward an economy or fresher fish than that. We made note of its location, planning to return for dinner.

Along the same street several local entrepreneurs set up stands selling various island foods. Some, like the "fresh fish lying in the sun" vendor and the "stinky green lumpy stew" vendor, were clearly planted there by the Pepto Bismol people in order to keep the medicinal trade brisk. Others, however, displayed tantalizing fruits, vegetables, and flowers that forced me to slow my pace to browse. Unable to curb my enthusiasm, or my hunger, any longer, I approached an aged man with a tarp covered in an abundance of bananas, papayas, and coconuts.

"Qui c'est?" *Who are these*, I asked in my sad attempt at French, pointing to the coconuts. The vendor frowned, and then lit up with a giant grin when he surmised I had not been a very diligent language student. I assumed at that point that whatever the price had been, it was now doubled.

"They're coconuts," he said in English. "I didn't give them each names." Make that triple the price.

"I meant who do these belong to? Did you grow them?" I stammered.

"They grow on my land and my friend's land. They are top quality," he added proudly.

Michael sized up the bananas, his favorite fruit. I reached for two coconuts, wanting to feel the smooth husk and was surprised by their heft. I had no idea what I would do with them once I got back to the room, but perhaps our accommodating hotel could turn them into a nice beverage. I seemed to remember Ginger and Gilligan drinking from them with a straw on one memorable episode. I once read that if the liquid could be heard sloshing around inside, the coconut was fresh. So I shook one. Big mistake.

"What are you doing?" the vendor shrieked, his face turning red as tried to grab the nuts away from me. "I just picked them! Why are you touching the fruit?"

"I just wanted to see if I could hear the juice inside," I said, slightly embarrassed by his increasingly loud tone. Michael abruptly left me with the raving vendor and headed for the video store across the street, suddenly remembering a lost fondness for David Hasselhoff. *Chicken.*

"Are you saying I am selling old fruit?" the old man questioned, his voice now rising above the din of the town. People started to turn their heads and look at me. My head sank into my shoulders, willing my whole body to disappear. Abruptly, the heat of the afternoon began to feel oppressive; the hot sun mocked me. I was a long way from home, where feeling up the fruit was a necessary step in my supermarket routine.

"No. I...just..." I stammered. "We'll take these two. And two more. And some bananas."

The vendor loaded my fruit into two enormous plastic bags, questionably recycled from some prior, non-consumable use. He glared at me, but took my money and made change. The reasonable price, a little less than five dollars, made me feel bad for having offended him. I thanked him and slithered off before I did any more damage to cultural relations and my own pride.

"Wrap them good before putting them in your suitcase," he called after me, sounding a bit more understanding than before. I had to stifle a laugh. Did he really think I was bringing them home as souvenirs? "My friend went to Bora Bora and all she brought me was this lousy coconut." Since I had four I could bribe the Atlanta airport customs officer with two and still have two left for a pina colada when I got back home.

"Thank you, sir. That's good advice," I said sincerely, as I walked off into the sunset, my bags of souvenir nuts in tow.

Bora Bora is surrounded by a lagoon ringed by a barrier reef. Only one navigable pass exists between the inner lagoon and the outer open ocean. Such limited access for humans and sea life reduces the number of large predators and makes the lagoon a basin of tasty nutrients, perfect conditions for harboring manta rays year-round. Our fourth dive, the last one to meet our diving certification requirements, was to see these graceful but mammoth ocean dwellers. If we survived the rays we would officially be Scuba Divers.

To us novice divers, meeting these fish was a thrilling, but frightening prospect due to their enormous wingspan and large mouths. In reality, however, manta rays are filter feeders, straining microscopic plankton out of the water. Nothing larger than a pencil eraser intentionally passes through their jaws, and last time I checked, I weigh a bit more than that. I had a greater chance of being swept out to sea, dropping a tank on my foot, or starring in another porn flick with Phillipe.

The Pass and two different sites, Toopa and Anau, were the three main places to see manta rays in the lagoon. Our boat took us to Anau, as manta ray sightings were relatively predictable there. Anau has a shallow zone and a coral drop-off of thirty to seventy-five feet. A large sandy zone exists up to the beginning of the drop-off. Mantas use this sandy area like high school kids use a mall: a little exercise, a little food, and a whole lot of flirting.

Once again our dive boat contained a group of more experienced divers and us, the lowly newbies pulling up the back of the pack. The moment the others hit the water they disappeared with their divemaster each in search of his or her own adventure. Phillipe briefed Michael and I on the less than ideal diving conditions: low visibility due the enormous amount of plankton in the water and a strong current. Mantas loved these conditions, but scuba fry like us might not do as well. Despite the circumstances, we forged ahead; divers spend their entire lives hoping to see an aquatic phenomenon as amazing as a manta ray, and here we were completing our certification with the animals. We were really, really spoiled.

With a giant stride off the back of the boat I entered the water. The lack of visibility was apparent on contact. The cloudy water looked like a glass of watered-down milk. The current flowed at a marathon-winning pace. It dragged us along as we descended through the water column, heading for the bottom. Every five feet we had to stop our descent and equalize our ears against the water pressure so that we would not pop our ear drums. The sideways-pulling current made ear equalization more difficult. I hoped our boat captain could follow our bubbles, since we would be surfacing a long distance from where we started.

I struggled to keep an eye on Michael and Phillipe in the cloudy water. If I lost sight of them I could become easily lost and would have to surface on my own so that the boat could come pick me up. I did not want to punctuate this amazing adventure with a disappointing finish. Even though I knew the bottom was only about forty feet down, I could not yet see it, which was disorienting. With all my focus on trying to see where I was going, breathing correctly, equalizing my ears, using my gear properly, and keeping an eye on my partners in crime, a manta would have had to bump into me to get my attention.

Finally, the rocky bottom came into view, little by little, as I sunk farther down. We were still moving along, but the current weakened near the bottom, as is usually the case. Phillipe had us hover and steady our breathing. In the exertion and excitement of descending I used up half of my air tank, so if I did not calm down I would be returning to the sunshine in short order. I took out my basic underwater camera, a gift from my dad better suited for snorkeling than diving. I avoided using it throughout the underwater adventures because I wanted to focus on the proper way to use my gear. Now, the camera acted as a focal point, a way to calm me down and divert my nervous energy. Cheerleader pom-poms of coral growth dotted the rocks in cheery lumps of purple, pink and green; perfect, stationary subjects for my beginner underwater photography skills.

A shadow passed overhead and Phillipe's amusement turned to wonder, then to wild gesturing. I looked up to see the wing of a manta passing about ten feet above my head. It quickly faded into the milky water. Then, silence. We each held our breath, a big no-no in scuba diving, at the sight of a magical manta that quickly vanished, like an aquatic illusionist. I began to doubt if I had really even seen it when it suddenly returned, swooping and gliding above us. Another manta joined it and together they performed an aerial show above our heads, keeping us guessing by disappearing into the haze, then reappearing from different directions. I wondered if they even noticed us, or if we were just voyeuristic seaweed watching their game of tag. I took picture after picture of the graceful animals until I finished my roll of film. We ascended to the surface soon after that, our reserves of air running low. We were now officially scuba divers, a joyous coming of age event that the whole boat celebrated all the way back to the dock.

The creator god Ta'aroa appears in many Polynesian myths. For the people of French Polynesia, Ta'aroa is the supreme creator from which all things on earth originated. The name Bora Bora comes from the island's ancient name, Pora Pora, meaning "first born," from legends describing it as the first island to rise when Ta'aroa pulled it out of the ocean which he created with his own tears. I like the idea that from Ta'aroa's own efforts came this new, exciting place, because in many ways it is similar to my own pursuit of scuba diving. My efforts to learn the sport of diving produced a new, exciting pastime, one that promised to produce opportunities for travel, education, and fun. I couldn't wait to dive in again on the second part of our French Polynesian adventure.

CHAPTER 2

Moorea: Land of Well-Fed Sharks and Tantalizing Tikis

I woke to the sound of waves lapping against the stilts that held my bungalow above the water. The peaceful white noise comforted me. Above the gentle splashing of the water rose the sound of a woman's voice singing an ancient Polynesian tune of the dawn. A fellow guest must have ordered a traditional breakfast, delivered by outrigger canoe, an indulgent form of room service. Fortunately, anyone awake nearby could partake of the vision of the local woman in her flower-covered breakfast ferry paddling the meal to its destination. As she passed by my bungalow, I thought *how does she do that without spilling the coffee?*

We had continued on to Moorea, the second and final stop of our French Polynesian adventure. Unlike the Leeward Island of Bora Bora, the Windward Island of Moorea sat on the eastern end of French Polynesia's Society Islands, quite close to Tahiti.

Aimeo I Te Rara Varu, the island's ancient name, roughly translates as the Place with Eight Mountain Ridges, reflecting the geographic characteristics the island still possesses today.

The melodic name Moorea, meaning "yellow lizard," only came to be used for the island in the 1800's when a powerful high priest had a dream at a sacred site on the island. In the dream a native couple had a yellow lizard as a son. The strong French Polynesian currents washed the lizard up on the shore of Aimeo, thus forever altering the name used by the natives to reference the island. Every place I had ever lived had a nonsensical name or had egotistically been crowned with the founder's moniker. I found it refreshing to visit a place where legends and terrain had a profound and lasting effect, even if lizard boy was a little sci-fi for my taste.

Depending on one's inclination – love, books, or food – Moorea's geographic shape looks like a heart, the letter "W," or a fork. Two nearly symmetrical bays, Cook's Bay and Opunohu Bay, carve the island's north side. The Society Islands evolved from a tectonic plate moving slowly across a hot spot deep beneath the sea floor that produced volumes of volcanic lava. This earthly indigestion belched forth a mountainous Moorea somewhere between 1.5 and 2.5 million years ago. Since then, wind and rain rounded off the jagged peaks and a thick layer of green foliage spread like velvet over the entire island, producing a picture postcard perfect vision from every vantage point.

The view from our hotel room was no exception. We were again fortunate to be staying in an over-water bungalow through the miracle of hotel points I earned during prior business trips. Many nights I fell asleep in hotel rooms in U.S. cities like Nowhere, Idaho and Forgettable, Utah dreaming of using those points for a trip to beautiful French Polynesia. The view from our room exceeded my expectations, with turquoise blue water surrounding us and lush, green mountains rising in the distance. A Plexiglas window in the floor of the bungalow's living room enabled a voyeuristic view of passing sea life, a view that I encouraged daily by throwing bits of bread off the balcony.

But the islands were not always viewed as picturesque. From 1960 to 1996, France built its nuclear capabilities by testing bombs in the Tuomotu group of French Polynesian islands. While their warheads grew, French Polynesian tourism stagnated, although in reality the testing sites were 1,200 miles away from Tahiti, roughly the distance between New York and Miami. Then, in 1996 after worldwide outcry at the practice, the nuclear testing ended and hotel construction began. Developers recognized the draw of the islands' beauty and exotic reputation, incubated over hundreds of years by the likes of famous people such as explorer James

Cook, scientist James Darwin, and painter Paul Gauguin. Tourism in French Polynesia blossomed first on Tahiti, the island that contains the nation's capital, the highest per capita of inhabitants, and the best plumbing. In the wake of Tahiti's popularity, Moorea developed into a hot bed of tourism as other French Polynesian islands began to lure visitors. After Moorea, Bora Bora's tourism began to take hold. Though further afield, a one-hour plane ride from Tahiti, Bora Bora's extreme beauty and remoteness just could not be denied.

This evolution of tourism across the islands explained the various states of our hotel rooms. Our remote hotel in Bora Bora, sitting on a small motu in the waters surrounding the island, was brand new, the faucet chrome shining, the decorations ultra-modern, and the staff clueless as to how to make a proper pina colada. In Moorea, our slightly older hotel sat on the mainland, our over-water bungalow accessed by a worn wooden walkway that sat on stilts above the surf. Since our hotel was located on the main island, we felt more connected to Moorea's activities and culture than in Bora Bora, where we had to take a long boat ride to connect with the local way of life and daily rhythms.

Though French Polynesia's alluring ocean originally attracted us to the region, we quickly observed that the dry parts of the islands were just as fascinating. After arriving, we felt compelled to take a closer look at Moorea's dense, mysterious jungles and remote island culture. Based on a recommendation from our hotel's doorman, I hired a native guide with a 4x4 jeep to educate us on the island's highlights. Too often on past trips we opted for self-guided tours, only to go home with pictures of pretty rocks, nice mountains, ancient things, and absolutely no idea what we had actually seen.

The next day our guide picked us up at the front door of our hotel. His tanned skin and long dark hair hinted at his Polynesian heritage, but his name, Vinnie, sounded more like he came from the island of Manhattan. He prepared his jeep for island touring, removing the roof, doors, and all the windows except for the bug-spattered windshield. A spare tire attached to the hood doubled as a snack holder, filled with fruit grown locally in Moorea's rich soil.

"Ready to go?" Vinnie shouted then smiled. His genuine enthusiasm told me he really enjoyed his job. We climbed into the back of the jeep, eager for our tropical adventure. With a rev and a jerk, the Pineapple Express pulled out of the hotel drive and onto the main road.

Moorea's circumference is thirty-seven miles, similar to my home city of Atlanta, but with infinitely less traffic. Its manageable size made it easy to see most of the island in only three and a half hours. The tour started at Belvedere Point, a high promontory overlooking Mount Rotui with Cook's Bay to the right and Opunohu Bay to the left. Sweeping island vistas graced the majestic view. We could see the blue ocean stretching out to the barrier reef and beyond. Our hotel was a tiny speck on the shore below.

After snapping a few pictures, we descended from Belvedere through the lush Opunohu Valley. The famous Moorea stone road markers in the heart/"W"/fork shape of the island lined the drive. Each monument had chickens pecking below like poultry sentries on duty. They eyed us warily as we continued on to our next destination, the ancient marae, stone or coral constructions with platforms on which religious sacrifices were made. Vinnie gave us a brief background on the way to the first site.

"The marae are religious sites where people came to pray and give offerings to the gods," he said. "Unfortunately, when the Protestant and Catholic missionaries came in the nineteenth century a lot of the marae were destroyed as the islanders were converted. Over time we've tried to fix them, build some of them back to look like they did before." Hopefully they were not including human sacrifices in the renovation, I thought.

We arrived at the first mare and climbed out of the car. A large, square clearing stretched out in front of us, the site lined with palm trees on three sides and the dirt parking lot on the forth. A jumbled group of lichen-stained rocks sat in the center. I know we were supposed to be experiencing something profound, but the former glory of the site proved hard to envision by looking at the haphazard pile of stones.

"This is Afareaitu Marae," said our guide, pointing to the site. It is one of the oldest on Moorea, maybe 1000 years or older. The stones would have been built up in a rectangular shape in the center." The spot was peaceful and shaded, with a glint of ocean sparkling through the trees on the opposite side. Though the mystical feel of a truly religious place was lost over the years, I could still see the appeal of the site. We continued our marae visits, stopping at several more locations including reconstructed Titiroa Marae, where Polynesian chiefs not only worshiped, but also practiced archery, an important and revered skill in ancient times. After touring several more piles of stones, we had a great knowledge of historical religious practices, and an even greater need to move on to the next part of our tour.

We built up a sweat hiking around the marae, so the long air conditioned drive to our next stop provided a welcome break. While Michael and I poked around the last marae site, Vinnie cut up some pineapple, which we munched greedily as we drove on. We off-roaded into the jungle down a dirt path in search of another lookout point. We drove in silence for awhile, not passing anyone along the way. Palm

> In French Polynesia, the wearing of flowers behind one's ear indicates dating status. A flower behind the left ear means the person is taken. A flower behind the right ear means the person is looking for love. Best of all, a flower behind both ears means the person is taken, but is open to a little something interesting on the side.

fronds reached into the sides of the jeep and pot holes jostled us as we traveled. Through the trees, I glimpsed delightful little waterfalls and vast green meadows. I felt like I was in the Land of Oz, though I hoped the creepy Lollypop Guild wasn't going to sing for us.

With each passing minute, my anticipation increased, knowing that something worthwhile must be at the end of the rainbow. Suddenly, we burst through the heavy trees into a clearing. On one side, cliffs dropped away to the sea and on the other, the south rim of the ancient volcano that made up Moorea's mountain range rose in green splendor. We climbed out of the jeep and admired the view in both directions. One green mountain with a hole near the top stuck out from the rest and piqued my interest. I asked our guide about it.

"The pinnacle there with the hole is called Moua Puta, which means 'split rock' in Tahitian," he answered. "Pai, a son of the gods of Polynesia, made the hole with his spear. He was warned that Hiro, god of thieves, wanted to steal the sacred Rotui Mountain and take it home to the neighboring island of Raiatea. The warrior Pai threw a spear from Tahiti that pierced the top of Moua Puta and the noise woke up all the roosters on Moorea, who crowed so loudly that the thieves were forced to flee." Vinnie shrugged. "Or, that part of the rock just eroded over time. You decide." I stuck with the story of the gods. I don't hear a lot of deity stories describing my backyard at home.

We continued on our journey, next heading to a plantation. I'm definitely not a horticulturalist, having killed every houseplant I've ever tried to grow, but our guide assured us it was worth the stop to see some of the indigenous plants of the region. We took his word for it, but I assumed he would enjoy a kickback of pineapples for bringing us to the farm. My skepticism evaporated when we arrived and I learned that the ranch was an educational, not-for-profit commune trying to reestablish traditional plants and agricultural techniques in the islands. We were introduced to Mike, one of the directors of the program. A native Polynesian, Mike attended school in Hawaii then returned to Moorea to work on the plantation. His well chosen words and well calloused hands indicated a strong work ethic with books and soil alike.

"We grow a variety of agricultural products here, including cotton, coffee, sugarcane, and pineapple," he explained as he led us on a tour of the property. "We try to farm strains of the plants that are native to the Society Islands, but of course some common plants here were actually brought by explorers." Well-worn dirt paths connected a variety of fields and terraces filled with plants of all shapes and sizes. Here and there I could see people working the farm with hand tools; a small, red tractor stood out as the lone piece of machinery.

"We're really trying to bring back the practice of agriculture that has begun to fade away on the islands most impacted by tourism," he added. "Some people have left the fields to work in the tourism industry where they can make more money, but then we have to import more products to live and thus prices go up. Soon people have to work more to afford what they need. It's a vicious circle."

"We're combining traditional farming techniques with modern science here, studying the impact to the plants and to the environment. We've got some great results. Our pineapples are sweet, our coffee rich, and our whole operation sustained by selling what we produce here," he said proudly as he reached for a fistful of soil, warming it in his hand before letting it slowly trickle through his fingers back to the ground. He exuded energy and enthusiasm. It made my own employment activities, which involve mostly poking at a keyboard with unconvincing fervor, look pretty weak in comparison.

Mike led us to a section of the farm that contained large vines, each held upright by a five-foot wooden post. Each plant had stems branching out from a main vine. Long green shiny leaves covered the stems, some decorated by small, greenish-yellow flowers. The rows and vines were well taken care of, with the earth below free of weeds.

"These are our pride and joy," said Mike, pointing to the vanilla orchids. "Growing them is extremely labor intensive and requires lots of patience. You have to wait three years before you can get even one bean off a plant. We have to pollinate them by hand, soon after the flowers open, or a bean won't grow. Once it starts growing, it takes almost nine months to mature on the vine. Then, we harvest the beans by hand as well," he said, his brow knit as if re-living the long, hard process.

"No wonder they're so expensive at home," I offered.

"Exactly. Tahitian vanilla is known worldwide as a high quality product. It's costly to grow, but we can charge a good premium for it. We're experimenting here with ways to curb the cost without lowering the quality. What's interesting is that the vanilla orchid is actually native to Mexico. It didn't arrive on these shores until the 1800's. There's something ironic about a product originally imported that is now helping our exports," he said. I liked the irony in that. It reflected what I had been observing all day throughout our tour. The Tahitians seemed to be a passionately flexible group of people, making the most of their history, but also embracing new opportunities, like tourism, as they came along. I stopped in the small plantation store on the way out, buying a pack of dried vanilla pods to improve my own flexibility and my crème brule when I returned home.

In French Polynesia common items can be blindingly expensive, especially if they're for tourists. I knew that before we began our trip, but could not help but have sticker shock when I ran out of sunscreen and needed to buy more in Moorea. The hotel wanted $35 for a tube so small it should have been made of gold. I did not fare much better at the local market, where a similar size cost $25. I reluctantly coughed up the funds, choosing to save my skin instead of my money.

French Polynesia's main industry is tourism, with copra farming and fishing a distant second and third. Copra farming involves collecting large volumes of coconut husks in the hot sun and selling them for pennies. Fishing involves more hot sun and, well, fish. It's easy to see why tourism ranks highest on the list, but the trade depends on wealthy travelers spending lots of dough.

Like many tourists, I went to French Polynesia intending to purchase Tahitian black pearls, the best known product to come from the islands. But in Bora Bora I found that in order to buy a string I would have to sell my house. And my car. I hoped that Moorea might have more affordable pearls, so I checked out a few of the local stores. To my dismay, the prices were the same. I decided to find out why.

One of the shops I visited had no other customers, the sales lady looking quite excited I had picked her store. Here, I thought, I could find answers. I expressed my interest in learning more about not just her pearls, but also the pearl industry. Judging by her ready answers, other visitors had asked these questions before me.

"Well, all of the black pearls we sell are cultivated on our islands. They come from the black-lipped pearl oyster," she said as she showed me a wooden bucket full of gaping bi-valves. "There are several large farms that supply most of the pearls, but a few individuals still cultivate them. Pearls appear naturally in oysters without the help of farming, but only one in 15,000 natural oysters will have a pearl in it, so a little science is a must."

"What drives the cost?" I asked. "Some of the ones you have look alike to me, but they've got very different prices."

"It can take a long time to grow a pearl, five years or more," said the shopkeeper. "Out of every fifty grown, maybe only one is top quality. And, the size, shape, luster, and color are all important."

"I like that one," I said, pointing to an oval-shaped pearl hung as a necklace pendant.

"Ahh, you have a good eye," the woman said with a smile and the gleam of a dollar sign in her eye. "We call that purple and green color a 'Peacock' pearl. It's fairly rare." Leave it to me to pick the expensive one with a fancy, exotically named color. Why couldn't I have been attracted to the pigeon of the bunch?

"And of course there are taxes..." she said, almost as an afterthought. I thanked the clerk, then left, opting to keep my house and car and leave the pendant in the store. I saw similar pricing in other stores in the village. It wasn't price fixing, but it was close. The prices all fell into the "exorbitant" range.

I acquired the rest of my education on the high cost of everything in French Polynesia through a little research. The government applies a one-two punch of import costs and tourist tariffs that drives costs sky-high. Tourism keeps the country afloat, and so they leverage it as much as possible. I didn't begrudge them their need to earn a living, but I decided to let my travel alarm run out of power instead of buying those $40 batteries.

Emboldened by our newly minted scuba diving certification cards, we decided to partake in a specialized dive in Moorea: a shark feed. It sounded exotic and exciting and more than a little stupid, but what a topic to put on a postcard! We couldn't say no.

The dive shop associated with our hotel took groups out on shark feeds only once a week. Our timing was perfect, as the next one would leave that afternoon. We paid our money, signed our life away in accident waivers, and boarded the boat with our gear in tow. We were accompanied by four other divers, all of whom had recently been certified. I eyed each diver up, judging weight, height, and the ability to defend themselves underwater. I felt confident that if the sharks decided to eat one of us, there were other divers that appeared tastier and easier to consume than me.

We made small talk on the thirty-minute boat ride to the diving spot. Two of our fellow divers were newlyweds from the U.S. After brief pleasantries with us they escaped to the front of the boat to play kissy-face for the rest of the ride. Having established the boat bow as their boudoir, we migrated to the back of the ship to talk with the other passengers. The remaining two divers were scruffy-looking guys "on holiday" from Scotland hoping to return home with tales of high adrenaline diving and exotic Polynesian babes. Unfortunately, they just achieved scuba certification the day before and hadn't had any luck meeting available women during their entire trip despite a variety of "sales" tactics that they generously pantomimed for us. I empathized with their disappointment and wished them good luck, silently wondering at their sharing of TMI (too much information). It wasn't like I established a bare-all sort of relationship with them at the start of the conversation by exposing some highly personal detail. *Hi, I'm Karen, and I think my boobs are way too small.* I've since learned that dive boats create an instant diver camaraderie that produces a free flow of thoughts, hopes, and bizarre personal information not common among strangers in other situations. Sasquatch theories, pornographic media career aspirations, and third nipples are all fodder for dive boat conversations.

Upon arrival at the dive site, the captain anchored the boat while the divemaster jumped up on the boat's bench seat and prepared to deliver his briefing. The divemaster was long and lean, with flowing hair bleached blond by the sun. He appeared confident, even cocky, an attitude no doubt fueled by the successful execution of hundreds of shark feeds without any noticeable loss of his body parts.

"Okay, who has done a shark feed before?" No one raised their hands. "Okay, so who has gone diving in Moorea before?" Again, no one raised their hands. We were a really impressive group. "So, has anyone actually done any scuba diving anywhere?"

"We just got certified in Bora Bora," I said proudly, an admission met with congratulations from the other divers. The divemaster's face fell.

"Okay, so we will keep this easy. Descend directly to the bottom. I will show you where to go. Do not move around. Do not gesture or hold your hands out towards the sharks. Do not make erratic movements." Do not pass go. Do not collect $100. Do not feel bad about pushing the diver next to you towards the shark's open mouth if it looks like it is going to attack.

As the other divers suited up, I peered over the side of the boat into the bottomless cobalt abyss. The sky had clouded up, causing the water to appear murky and foreboding. Off the back of the boat I noticed fins breaking the surface, lots of them.

"What are those?" I asked the divemaster.

"Reef sharks. Small ones," he said. "They know they're gonna get fed, so they're waiting for us. They'll leave when the big guys show up."

This endeavor began to look less and less like a great idea. Clearly we were expected to jump into the water with the sharks swirling on the surface, like lobsters dropped into a boiling pot of water. I envisioned the sharks heating up some drawn butter in anticipation of our entry. We geared up, preparing to take the plunge. I lingered while putting on my scuba vest, cleaning my mask, and slipping on my fins in hopes of being the last diver to jump into the water. The shark "feeder," one of the crew members, donned a suit made of heavy woven chain designed to protect him from shark bites. The chain mail suit covered him from head to toe in medieval scuba chic. He looked like a tropical Knight of the Round Table.

The moment divers entered the water, the surface sharks disappeared. I took a giant stride off the back of the boat and instantly felt more relaxed as I soaked up the warm, 80 degree water. As we descended, the visibility improved and I realized the depth was only 35 feet. The sloped, rocky sea floor undulated with deep grooves like mini canyons extending out towards deeper water. The divemaster guided our group to a point at the shallower end of one of the grooves and gestured for us to stay

> **"I don't have to swim faster than the shark, just faster than the other divers."**
> **-Not so ancient wisdom from a Moorean Divemaster**

put. Holding a stationary position would be difficult, however, because the major waves at the surface created a surge of water down below. With each passing wave, we floated forward and back five feet. Despite our best efforts, we could not control it; the water moved each diver with a force that flailing arms and legs just couldn't combat.

I heard the splash as the heavily-weighted shark feeder entered the water. As he sank to the bottom about 25 feet in front of us, I noticed he held a large bag full of fish bits for feeding. A tsunami of small fish engulfed him, greedily eyeing up his bag of food as he prepared for the feeding frenzy. Sir Fish Head took a chunk of snack out of his bag and placed it on the end of a long, pointed stick, which could double nicely as a jousting lance later in the day if needed. Appearing suddenly from the blue, as if by magic, was a small black-tip reef shark.

It snatched the piece of fish then like a shot disappeared back into the blue. The surrounding small fish went crazy picking up the bits of fish flesh the shark left behind.

Although that early shark caught the proverbial worm, the rest of the shark flock was not far behind. Reef sharks started appearing from all directions, replacing the fish swarming around the feeder. The sharks were anywhere from two to five feet long, not huge, but impressive because of their sheer numbers. I counted at least 20 of them, though there could have been more. Sharks streaked in and out of view, grabbing, tearing, and stealing the bits of food offered, working their way into a true feeding frenzy.

The surge grew worse, and I could no longer hold myself upright and face-forward because of all of the water movement. I leaned at a 45 degree angle to my right, my left leg thrust awkwardly high in front of me like I was trying to clear an invisible, aquatic hurdle. The other divers were also having trouble. My husband floated on his stomach, his legs steadily rising up and threatening to flip him over. Another diver had already achieved the flip and stared upside down between his legs at the fish feeding spectacle. Our collective lack of underwater skills made us look like a deficient Cirque du Soleil troop knockoff. Our attention, though, was focused on the amazing display of power in front of us, our various acrobatics all but unnoticed.

Then, as abruptly as they arrived, all the fish and sharks left. The silence was eerie, no swishing tails, no crunches of fish bones. The only animals I could see were us awkward humans suspended in the water. Clearly the other fish knew something we did not. The divemaster pointed to the distance, behind us and to the left. Divemasters, in general, tend to be a jaded bunch, having seen almost everything there is to see underwater. If one points to something there is a high likelihood that it is something amazing and so it's wise to take a look.

An enormous shark swam towards Sir Fish Head who looked surprisingly at ease despite the pelagic dragon barreling towards him. No wonder all the other sea creatures left the area; this shark could have easily eaten anything that had previously been swimming around us. The ten-foot lemon shark bulged around the middle, having clearly indulged in a whole lot of fish. So corpulent, in fact, that I suspected one might find several masks and fins in its stomach and the gear owners digested. The brown-hued creature had yellow overtones and two large dorsal fins. It grabbed the proffered fish head without chewing; one gulp swallowed it whole.

A second lemon shark appeared, chunky as the first, but not as long. Sir Fish Head barely had time to pull another fish piece out of his bag before hungry jaws closed near his hand. I wondered what would happen when the fish bag grew empty. At the end of a meal I usually need a little desert. With all my gear I hoped I didn't look too much like a tasty wetsuit filled with rocky road ice cream.

My concerns were unfounded. The moment the fish bag was empty, the lemon sharks disappeared and small fish swarmed to clean up the scraps. The divemaster gestured to return to the boat, and we began our ascent. Unlike our water entry, this time I wanted to be first in line to climb back onto the boat. If the lemon sharks returned I didn't want to be the last scoop still in the bowl.

Our visit to Moorea grew to a close. During our entire French Polynesia trip we had managed to avoid the aggressively marketed Polynesian dancing shows, as they seemed touristy, exploitive, and more than a little goofy to us. However, several folks we spoke to in Moorea had mentioned a cultural heritage organization that produced a show, the proceeds of which went to the native population, rather than a hotel chain. The event included a sampling of local foods. It sounded like a fun way to embrace more of the culture, so we attended the show during our last night in paradise.

We arrived at the *tamaaraa*, the Tahitian word for a traditional feast, at the designated time of 7 p.m. The outdoor pavilion had a slightly raised stage at one end and long communal tables and benches at the other end.

Earlier in the day, the Polynesian grill masters dug a large cooking pit, a *himaa*, in the sand several yards away from the pavilion and then lined it with hot volcanic stones. The pit emitted smoke and a mouth-watering, meaty smell as our hosts began digging out the layers of food that had been placed in the pit to cook earlier in the day. Roasted vegetables and fish were removed first, followed by an entire roast pig at the bottom of the pit.

A long, buffet-style table lined one side of the pavilion. Local girls moonlighting as flower-clad *tamaaraa* attendants plated the hot foods from the *himaa* and added the steaming bounty to the cold dishes already placed on the serving table. The attendants then encouraged the dinner guests to grab an empty plate and choose their dinner from the buffet. My husband and I approached as a line started to form. Comfortable island décor adorned the pavilion with palms and candles. At the head of the buffet stood a five-foot tall, carved wooden tiki statue. It looked authentic and worn, like a true native decoration rather than a fake, plastic item placed for tourist pictures. I headed over to take a closer look.

Although it sported a headdress, the figure was decidedly male. A fierce grimace on his face gave way to broad shoulders and a muscled core. However, not until I edged closer, did his crowning glory become apparent: an enormous penis, proudly erect and extending to the same level as his chin. Knowing that statues such as this were usually stylized representations of the population, I could see why the people of Moorea were peaceful and happy. They had plenty to do in their spare time.

My husband made his way along the buffet line and inched up behind me. Handing me a plate, he steered me away from ogling the statue before I developed any more good ideas. The table overflowed with fantastic looking food. Salads of cucumbers, carrots, and beans were followed by freshly baked breads. A bright red bowl held *poisson cru*, a raw fish dish marinated in lime, salt, and coconut milk that we had also eaten in Bora Bora. Long platters of sliced pineapple, papaya, and other tropical fruits I couldn't even identify gave way to an abundance of grilled fish and meats towards the end of the table. The roasted pig completed the line of platters, its empty eyes disturbing, but the aroma seductive. We filled our plates and found room at one of the communal tables to enjoy the feast.

We ate with abandon, every bite better than the last. The pig gave new meaning to succulence, tasting richer and pleasantly gamier than any pork I could buy at home. My husband and I compared notes on what we thought the exact ingredients were for the *poisson cru* so that we could duplicate it in our own kitchen. By the time we were through the sun had fully set, darkness had arrived, and torches were lit all around the pavilion. The attendants cleared the food and plates in anticipation of the show about to begin. Relaxed conversation started up all around us until the dancers took the stage and a hush fell over the crowd.

The dance troupe came from a local village. The six women and three men wore vivid, blood-red traditional costumes. The women sported headdresses, modest tops, and rustling grass skirts. The men wore simple woven palm frond circles on their heads, wrists, and ankles, with their waists covered in red cloths that came half way down their thighs. Remembering the generously-endowed tiki statue I realized they must use a lot of bolts of cloth on the island. They danced in unison to a complicated beat of drums on the side of the stage. Their first dance was fast and more aggressively emotive than I had anticipated; it bore no resemblance to the slow, romantic hula Hollywood featured in tropical-themed movies.

A variety of traditional dances ensued, some faster, some slower, some involving the whole troupe, and some just the women or just the men. All the dancers were graceful, their steps well practiced. Two of the dances included music from a singer with a guitar, but most were to the beat of the drums performed as they had been for hundreds of years. The finale included the three men twirling fiery torches at a frenetic pace. Though I sat in the audience, I could feel the intense heat from the torches. I wondered how the men still had eyebrows. When the show ended, we applauded over and over for the dancers, displaying our genuine appreciation for sharing their talent and culture with us.

On the way back to our hotel I reflected on our vacation. Not only was it great fun, but also incredibly educational. More than just learning how to dive, we learned about the amazing kinds of places diving could take us. The trip was over, but I knew our travels had just begun.

CHAPTER 3

Caribbean Cruising: She Who Lacks Undergarments is a Popular Girl Indeed

The Ghost of Christmas Past must have visited the partners who owned my company, Ye Olde Accounting Firm, and scared them into giving us extra vacation. Bright and early one late December Monday, we received the good news via e-mail: the office would be closed the week between Christmas and New Year's Day. I ran out of official vacation days earlier in the year, so I planned on sulking at work during that time. Armed with the gift of a week of freedom, Michael and I began the search for a place to scuba dive.

Planning was easier said than done. With only a week and a half notice, the rates that airlines and hotels offered were exorbitant. Our saving grace came in the form of an e-mail touting "last minute savings" on cruises. I thought of cruising as a vacation choice for the elderly and their parents, but once I saw the affordable pricing and scuba-possible ports of call, Belize, Honduras, and Mexico, my opinion grew more favorable. A little research on my part educated me about the abundant reefs and healthy sea life in all three destinations, which outweighed the downside of shuffleboard tournaments with grandma in between ports.

Over the next week and a half I planned and packed; before I knew it we boarded the ship. Elevators whisked all of our fellow passengers up to their cabins. Since we booked one of the last available rooms, we were

> "Fish don't applaud." -Bob Hope (Commenting on why he cut his cruise vacation short)

required to enter the bowels of the ship, descending to the lowest deck passengers were allowed to go. Opening the cabin door, we were relieved to see a pleasant entryway; that is, until we realized that the entryway was actually the entire room. A three-foot radius around the bed was the only navigable floor space. A large mirror on the wall was meant to give the impression of spaciousness, but it only served to reflect our horror over the impending claustrophobia. Even the bathroom was the epitome of space-saving efficiency. Once I stepped in and closed the door, I could use the toilet, wash my hands in the basin, and take a shower, all without ever moving my feet. No wonder the room was 20 percent cheaper than others on higher decks and unbooked a week before sailing.

We escaped our shoebox and headed down the hall to explore the ship. We passed several large gathering areas with appropriately nautical names such as the Mariner's Theater, the Explorer's Den, and something like the Avoid The Iceberg Lounge. The central meeting place in the ship was a multi-level atrium, complete with a rotunda and a stained glass domed ceiling. As we walked through the hall I noticed mauve seating areas crammed into every nook and cranny, like the ship designers took advantage of a massive sale on 1980s-era chairs and then felt compelled to load our ship with them all. The intercom overhead piped in soothing Muzak as numerous elderly passengers shuffled in and filled the seats, giving the overall impression of a geriatric game of musical chairs. We escaped through doors at the back of the atrium onto a patio that contained a large pool and even larger bar. With its access to sun and adult beverages, I knew this would be the place we would spend most of our time.

With an eardrum-popping, hair-curling horn blast that took several years off my life, the ship left the port. A "The Love Boat" episode seemed to erupt all around me as a samba band started up and the vacation revelers threw paper streamers and toasted to their upcoming week of paradise. A gold lame shirt was all I needed to complete the 1970's theme. Several umbrella-clad drinks later we retired to our cabin to dress for dinner. Michael and I took turns sitting on the bed to give the other person room to function. We had requested to sit alone at dinner rather than be paired up with a table of strangers, hoping to avoid uncomfortable conversation and spend a little time just the two of us.

A stiff maître d', looking suspiciously like a penguin in his formal attire, led us through the dining room. He pointed to our table, which I had mistaken for a decorative pedestal meant for a flower vase. A *small* vase. Measuring three-foot by three-foot square, our setup occupied the space directly in front of the kitchen exit where waiters passed to deliver food.

"I know it is a bit tight, but we were told last minute that you wanted your own table. This is the best we can do," the maître d' said as a waiter bumped into the back of my chair with a tray full of water glasses. "Tomorrow we can move you to another table with other people if you would like."

"We'll stick with this one," Michael said, determined. He violently opposed any situation in which Grandpa could lecture him on the various types of incontinence undergarments. We enjoyed the meal of salad and succulent roasted lamb, though the bumping grew worse as the night wore on. By the end of my flaming baked Alaska desert I had heard a thousand "excuse me's" and had dinner roll crumbs and green beans slide down my back. This table did not work. The maître d' promised to find us a new location the following night, preferably with people within 100 years of our age. As we left, he smiled and waved with a knowing look that said "be sure to bring your knitting needles and plenty of yarn tomorrow night!"

We spent the next day "at sea" which is euphemism for too much drinking, too much sun, too much food, and way too much gambling at the casino. We signed up for scuba diving in Belize the next day, so we were determined to relax. All too soon our lazy day came to a close and dinner was yet again upon us. This time the maître d' proposed a new table.

"I think you will like this new spot," he said, but we were still skeptical. He led us to a table of four couples, surprisingly all near our age. Finally, we had found life on Mars. We introduced ourselves all around.

One couple had just started dating, one was newly engaged, one newly married, and the last couple had been married for a while. Our group provided a strange study in the lifecycle of a relationship. I wondered where the divorced couple would sit when the maître d' brought them to our table too.

Dinner progressed nicely; the conversation was animated and enjoyable. Ted and his fiancée Amy were also scuba divers and would be joining us on our dive in Belize. Newlyweds Vlad and Irena hailed from Russia, and kept the conversation lively, comparing weather, food, and vodka to those of their homeland. By the time the entrées came we felt like old friends. Michael and I were thrilled with our new seating assignment.

When a waiter arrived to replenish our wine, he knocked over a glass of water, causing half of us to jump from our seats. The splash was minimal, and so after a brief moment of patting the area dry, we settled back to eating. It was when I began to ask the newly dating couple what they did for a living that I realized a one-eyed monster had joined us. Apparently, when the woman jumped out of the way of the water, her braless breast had accidentally slipped out of her halter top. She had a petite chest and didn't notice the wardrobe malfunction, but I had to imagine she wondered where the sudden breeze originated. I stopped mid-sentence forcing my eyes down, suddenly finding my grilled salmon incredibly fascinating. I knew these people for less than an hour and already we were learning so much about each other.

I peeked around the table to my right and left, curious if anyone else noticed. Most seemed oblivious, but one guy had turned a telltale shade of red, his eyes staring intently at the bread as if memorizing every poppy seed. Had I known this girl well, I would have communicated the issue right away. Being a stranger, it didn't feel right shouting across the table. *Hey lady, your ta-ta is hanging out and people are starting to take aim at the bulls-eye.*

By now, all eyes were focused on the issue in question, attempting to telepathically will the private dancer to retreat. So, I decided to ask her to pass the butter, an action that would require her to stretch her arm. Although several people were closer to the butter, no one moved, having caught on that a bit of reaching might put the cow back in the barn. As she leaned in to pick up the pats, the pink petunia slid back underneath her shirt, provoking a collective audible sigh. It promised to be a fun week.

The dock in Belize did not exude the "jungle paradise" I expected. Before the cruise the thought of Belize conjured up visions of toucans, jaguars, and fierce Inca men with rippling muscles. In their place were yards of concrete, stacks of marine shipping boxes, and skinny dockworkers running around like ants trying to secure our boat.

Belize is located on the Caribbean coast, south of Mexico and east of Guatemala. The country has a 185-mile long barrier reef, the longest in the western hemisphere. Most diving is done near the cays, reefs, and mangrove islands off the northern half of the country. We found ourselves in Ambergris Cay, perhaps the most famous Belize dive area.

We piled into a minibus filled with fellow divers from the cruise ship, and were driven to the dive shop. There were ten of us in total, including the couple we met at dinner, Ted and Amy. Everyone appeared to be recreational divers except for two guys who looked like Navy Seals. They were tall, beefy men with crew cuts and an entire store's worth of scuba gear tucked into enormous black duffle bags. They looked like they were going to dive the deep waters in search of the Titanic rather than the shallow Belize shores. Their Armageddon-ready, weighty equipment listed our minibus to the left side the entire ride to the shop.

Once again we signed our lives away in accident waiver forms upon our arrival. I have always wondered why shops require divers to perform this task. The pens never work; the salt air instantly corrodes them. The counters are always wet, so the minute one puts the paper down to sign it, it turns into a soggy, inky mess. And, finally, there is never any place in a dive shop that is organized well enough to store something like the thousands of waivers that accumulate in a year. I am sure there are parrot cages all over the globe that are lined with these liability releases.

We boarded the dive boat and set up our gear. I knew the divemasters were assessing our skills based on our knowledge of the hoses, gauges, and straps that are involved in a scuba setup. I suspected they might insist I wear water wings after I tried to set up my tank backwards. Twice. I finally prepared the equipment correctly, and then contorted myself into my wetsuit, an activity I perform as gracefully as a fish ice skating.

The divemaster took us on a eye-opening tour of Terraces Reef, patiently pointing out large sea turtles and small decorator crabs. I acted like a paparazzo at each stop, snapping picture after picture of starlet starfish. Sadly, as I learned after developing my film from Bora Bora, fish tend to apply an especially vigorous burst of speed when I get my camera set. They are good at swimming, and so they do, frequently out of focus or out of the frame altogether. By looking at my photos, one would assume Bora Bora had a lot of empty water.

I was ready with my camera for the new and fascinating sea life that revealed itself to us on this trip. Most notably were the green moray eels, which spanned five to ten feet in length. Morays have very large teeth and dorsal fins that extend evenly from their head all the way to their tail, making them look like angry green vipers with full body mohawks. I saw moray eels in French Polynesia, but they all hid in the reef with only their faces and fierce-looking mouths exposed.

In Belize the morays were free-swimming, which is unusual since most types of eels venture out only at night. These long, green ribbons of muscle undulated through the water like Cruella De Ville's feather boa waving in the chilly breeze. Because of their notoriously poor vision, morays are not known for biting humans unprovoked, usually reserving this defensive tactic for a diver's intrusive hand or foot mistakenly lodged in their reef holes. Seeing the body power behind the large teeth gave me the creeps; their full exposure expanded their menace exponentially. Although the dive was fascinating, I was glad to end my time with those particular reef residents.

On the way back to the dock I struck up a conversation with one of the Kiwi divemasters who had been kind enough to point out numerous sea critters. He clearly loved his job and had a lot less stress than I have during my daily routine. I love to hear the stories of people in the dive industry, as their lives are often fun-filled and unpredictable, and their job is also their passion: diving.

"I had been traveling around the world with some of my mates and I just fell in love with Belize," he said. "The shop needed some help, so they took me on and taught me about the business." I wondered if they needed some more help; his vocation seemed more than a smidge better than my desk job. "It's cool diving here, but I haven't done much diving up north. I hear my company may open a shop in Puerto Rico. Maybe I'll see if I can go up there next."

I loved his carefree attitude toward his job. I wondered why the company needed to import help, however. More than 320,000 people live in Belize; surely some of them could become successful dive instructors. I noticed when we returned to the dive shop that most of the employees were ex-pats. I guessed this diversity mimicked the European-centric customer mix, but it was disappointing to see the dive proceeds miss the pockets of the natives. I vowed to ask about this when booking dive companies in the future.

When I think of Honduras, I usually think of Maya and that whole Sandinista/Contra affair in neighboring Nicaragua. One label I had never ascribed to this Central American nation is "popular tourist destination." It wasn't until we booked our trip that I learned there were diving sites there. But one look at the Honduran flag, which has three horizontal stripes (the top and bottom ones are blue to represent the Pacific Ocean and Caribbean Sea), it can be assumed that the country knows something worthwhile is going on along its coasts.

The day after we left Belize, we arrived on Roatan, the largest island off the Caribbean coast of Honduras. We were once again whisked by minibus to the dive shop that would provide our fearless divemasters for the day. Before I could blink, we boarded the dive boat and prepared our gear. My gear setup skills were improving: I set up the rig backwards only once this time. My new-found efficiency enabled me to enjoy more time with the other divers before the boat delivered us to the dive site. Fewer divers joined us on this excursion than on the one in Belize. Perhaps Honduras needed a more prolific scuba marketer.

As I sat back and watched the other divers getting ready, I noticed something interesting: divers have an unusual predilection for body art. Tattoos abounded in all shapes and sizes. The divemasters had the most art as well as the least inhibition as to where the pictures appeared on their bodies, including backs, fronts, and in one case, a neck. My fellow divers fit right in, exposing a fish tattoo here and a dive flag tattoo there as t-shirts and shorts were removed. Our newly engaged dinner companions, Ted and Amy, were no exception to the body art cult. He had a shark tattoo around his bicep and she sported a starburst on her lower back. I didn't recall the PADI certification requiring body art, but perhaps we skipped that lesson. As a group, our diving companions resembled an undulating caricature of the underwater world. I wondered what my inability to withstand piercing needles said about my future in the sport.

We arrived at the dive site, Melissa's Reef. The excursion planners scheduled only one dive that day; we hoped it would be a memorable one. The divemaster gave a perfunctory briefing that basically consisted of: jump in, follow him, and maybe we would see stuff. My novice skills made me prone to stupid, but potentially dangerous situations like running out of air and floating off uncontrollably. Hearing lackluster dive briefings like this one reduced my confidence in the dive operation and, specifically, in the divemaster. With a nervous knot in my stomach, I entered the water with the other divers.

The water was shallow, perhaps only twenty feet, with the sea floor gently sloping out to the ocean depths. Olive-colored sea grass covered the sandy bottom, its foot-long, green fingers waving back and forth in the wave surge. We followed the divemaster toward deeper water, heading out at a relaxed clip. My tension receded as I gained control over my breathing and buoyancy. I took in the scene around me and noticed a serious lack of fish. Had Poseidon given them the week off? Only sea grass and other divers filled my field of view.

As the divemaster led us further and further from the boat mooring site, I thought: *Hey, look at the sea grass.* We swam along the sea floor. *More sea grass.* We rounded the plateau and continued down a more sloping part of the sea bed that contained boulders. Still, the sea grass prevailed. The ocean contained a cash crop of the underwater weed. We continued along the rest of the dive seeing an occasional small, gray fish and plenty more grass. A lawn mower would have been more use than my scuba apparatus. Mercifully our dive ended thirty-five minutes after it began. I still had almost half a tank left, but was happy to conclude the botany lesson. Back on the boat, the divemaster swore that he saw turtles in that area "all the time." Perhaps they got bored of all the sea grass and swam away.

Since we completed only one dive, we arrived back at the scuba shop with several hours before our cruise was scheduled to leave. We decided to walk around town with our tattooed dinner companions. The town consisted of a partially paved main street with several smaller, perpendicular side streets. Plain, two-story buildings lined the curbs, their pale pastel façades faded from the constant sun. Tourist kitsch dominated the main drag; carved coconuts, wooden bead necklaces, and shell paperweights abounded in every shop like the marine flora in the ocean. Despite the touristy feel, everyone we met seemed genuinely friendly. Stooped backs and calloused hands told a tale of people who were used to hard work, from the shop keepers, to the men selling "a bit of grass" (decidedly *not* the sea kind). We were clearly not in Kansas anymore, but I felt safe.

The side streets hid buildings with more character; wooden shutters, stonework, and painted decorations provided a more lived-in feel than their stark main street counterparts. These small, dirt streets felt gritty under my feet, the dirt pasting a thin, grimy layer on the facades, but it only served to make the structures look more realistic. Stores selling products to the locals punctuated the side streets: a grocery offering canned products with unfamiliar labels, a law office, its open door displaying a prim receptionist dabbing sweat from her brow, and others.

We entered a store selling hand-carved furniture that spilled out onto the sidewalk. The pieces were mostly chairs and benches, although the proprietor assured us his "boys" could create anything we wanted. He led us through the back to an outdoor workshop where three men were busy working wood into various furniture forms. I didn't see many machines; most of the work was done by hand. As we left, we promised the owner we would consider ordering an entryway table. It wouldn't match our house at all, but we loved the idea of supporting the local artisans and decorating our home with an authentic, hand-crafted piece.

We walked on, the heat starting to overwhelm us. The next side street brought a welcome sight: an open-air bar with ample shade and a sandy floor. Best of all was the large, hand-painted sign: "Cold Beer." The owner looked up from his newspaper and smiled. Thus encouraged, we sat down in four mismatched chairs around a battered wood table.

"Amigos, what can I get for you today? Some beer? It is getting hot," he said. "Are you hungry? My wife has a few things cooked up. I recommend the conch soup." At home I am an adventurous eater, but when traveling I try not to eat anything prepared with sanitation standards that have no hope of being to the same level my stomach demands. I wasn't being elitist. I just knew that spending my vacation in a bathroom, especially one as small and unremarkable as ours on the ship, was not ideal.

We ordered four Imperials, the national beer of Honduras, and promised to think about the soup. Our friends were bolder than me. They were perfectly comfortable with suffering gastrointestinal distress in the name of trying something new and local. When the beers arrived they ordered a bowl of the soup, complete with four spoons in case we changed our minds. The owner assured us we would all want our own after trying just one spoonful.

The beer was ice cold, the perfect complement to the warm, dusty day. Two four-legged mutts sauntered by looking for a snack. The dogs were followed by a group of shouting kids with dirty t-shirts chasing a soccer ball. The scene felt almost surreal, a stereotypical vision of what a hot afternoon would look like in a small Honduran town. Ted picked up the Spanish-language paper from the bar to read the local news. Our limited knowledge of the language helped us understand that there was a used car sale advertised on page three, but not to actually comprehend any real news.

"Here's the soup," the owner announced, placing a large bowl of steaming stew on the table along with four spoons. "My son, he got the conch from the ocean himself," he said proudly. Although still skeptical about beastie parasites hiding in third-world kitchens I had to admit the bowl looked appetizing and smelled wonderful. I could see tomato chunks and conch floating in a sea of rich, brick-red broth punctuated with cilantro bits. Even thought it was ninety degrees outside, the soup still sent steam plumes into the air.

"So what are the headlines today?" Ted asked the owner, pointing to the newspaper we could not decipher.

"Oh, it's our mayor again. He's loco, you know. He likes the senioritas, especially when they are married to someone else. The newspaper loves to print pictures of him with the women," he said. "He is a good mayor, though. There are more jobs here now than ever before," he added before returning to his place behind the bar. It was interesting that the people of the town kept the mayor's personal indiscretions separate from his ability to lead the local government. I found it ironic that that social acceptance enabled him to be more honest about his extra-curricular activities than if he held office in the United States.

Our stomachs began to growl for the soup. I ate my spoonful with care, blowing on it beforehand to avoid a scalding. It tasted wonderful; it was rich, thick, and briny with just a hint of sweetness. In addition to the tomatoes and conch, I could identify some other type of root vegetable, perhaps potatoes or turnips. Just when I decided I needed my own bowl, I felt the first tingle. It started on my tongue tip, and then spread to the rest of my mouth in a flash. Flames engulfed my head with a blinding spiciness that made my eyes water like I was watching *Old Yeller.* Judging by the similar Kleenex moment the others were having, the habaneras had hit them too. We drained our beers, and then quickly ordered another round and some bread, all the while gasping for air.

"It's good, no?" the owner asked with a knowing smile, clearly proud of his wife's cooking.

"Excellent!" we replied in unison, conveying our sincere respect for the cultural authenticity as well as the spice.

Before I took up diving I thought of Cozumel, an island about 12 miles off the coast of Mexico's Yucatan peninsula, as a cheap place to party, like a lesser-known Cancun. So, I viewed our Cozumel cruise stop as a nice way to spend the day, but nothing special. Ted and Amy convinced me otherwise. They had rented a private dive boat for the day and invited us to join them. A private boat was a nice change from the larger boats that held a dozen divers or more, usually squeezed into a space meant for fewer bodies and gear. With four of us diving, the cost per person would be reasonable for a custom dive trip. Also, we could dive at a more relaxed pace and choose the dive sites we wanted to visit. I had no idea Cozumel had diving good enough to warrant an independent excursion, but I was glad they came up with the idea.

Mateo, the dive company owner, picked us up in a van at the cruise dock and whisked us to the dive shop located several blocks away. The shop was on a quiet side street off the main square, Plaza Del Sol. A Boston terrier puppy greeted us at the door and followed us through the process of filling out forms, picking out gear, and loading the van for the quick ride to the boat. Any dive shop with a dog is a good thing in my book, although this one had a cute, yet annoying, habit of biting my ankle when I stopped scratching him. Either he had fleas or he knew a sucker when he saw one. Probably both.

After a ten-minute drive we loaded our gear onto a thirty-foot boat. We had plenty of room for our equipment and for lounging between dives. The boat captain and our divemaster, Arturo, readied the boat for our trip. Arturo looked just like his name implied: tanned, muscled, festooned in a thick gold chain with an eagle pendant around his neck, and gifted with a thick Spanish accent. He wasn't attractive in an American frat boy sort of way, but he was rugged and manly; the person one wants as a protective and able divemaster.

We sped to our first dive site, Santa Rosa Wall. We anchored to a buoy over the reef and entered the water together by doing a back roll off the sides of the boat. I disliked this acrobatic water entry, but since a swift current moved along the side of the boat, it was the only way to ensure we stayed together. Arturo led us down over the side of the reef to explore the wall, which started at thirty feet and dropped down to more than 100 feet. The current pulled us along, enabling a comprehensive tour of the area without exerting much effort. Large coral mounds covered with swaying sea fans dotted the wall while bright purple tube sponges stuck their fingers at us accusingly. The visibility was excellent, perhaps 100 feet or more. We passed several car-sized overhangs that hid a wealth of sweet-lipped grouper, coral-banded shrimp, and neon orange elephant-ear sponges.

After fifteen minutes we ascended to the reef above to ride out the current with the rest of the air in our tanks. The tanks were constructed with high pressure steel, rather than the usual aluminum that most dive shops used. The stronger, heavier steel allowed more air to be compressed in the tank, which meant more time underwater and less stress about using up all of my air before the other divers in my party, a habit that can quickly make a diver very unpopular. I enjoyed the reef below me and the crystal clear water magnifying the view, enabling me to see even the smallest sea life, like hermit crabs and brittle sea starfish. A grey angelfish as big as a dinner plate followed me like a loyal puppy as I inspected the nooks and crannies of the ledge. I wondered if he expected a scratch behind his gills as well.

Back up on the boat we spent an hour doing our surface interval, which is a necessary rest between dives that allows the body to expel the nitrogen it absorbed under water. I sat on the bow, munching on a granola bar and soaking up the sun. Arturo handed me a Cozumel sea life identification guide to pass the time. All manner of fish, crustaceans, and coral appeared in the book and ignited my imagination. It would take years to find examples of all of these creatures under the waves. I immediately fell in love with the fish on the cover, the egotistically named 'Splendid Toadfish.' I suppose it isn't bragging if one could back it up, and this fish could. With a bright purple body, neon-yellow fins, and a burst of goatee whiskers, it practically shouted "I am one *good* looking fish." Toadfish are endemic only to Mexican coastal waters, so I made finding one my goal for the next dive.

The hour went quickly as we all laughed and compared dive stories. Ted and Amy had been diving for longer than us, but not by much. Their skills paired up nicely with ours, which made for a more relaxing dive experience. Soon we were back in the water hunting the toadfish. This time we dove at a site named Palancar Garden, a healthy reef that ranged from 20 to 70 feet deep, with plenty of mysterious fissures and mini caves to explore. The visibility was a little less there, only 80 feet or so, but was still phenomenal compared to some dives we experienced in French Polynesia. The current pulled us gently along, caressing us with warm water. I was so comfortable that, if not for the amazing scenery, I could have fallen asleep.

There is a direct correlation between the depth and the amount of air a diver consumes. The deeper one goes, the more air they use up in their tank and, thus, the less time they can spend underwater. We stayed at about forty feet for most of the dive, so we had an extended dive; in "dive speak" we had almost an hour of "bottom time." It was relaxing and serene; pure bliss for the mind and body. Bright yellow vase sponges flourished, some with juvenile fish inside and one with an orange arrow crab that saluted me with its little blue claws. A tropical array of fish such as butterfly, angel, parrot, and damsel joined us on the reef.

Before we ascended, I finally spotted the goal: a giant purple splendid toadfish peeking out from a short overhang. I waved my arms and legs like a break dancing octopus to attract my fellow divers' attentions. They swam over to see me make a spectacle of myself as well as to see the fish in question. The shy fish retreated deeper into its hole, horrified by the four of us. I drifted back to let the others have a closer look, floating slightly down the reef to give them space. To my dismay I came face to face with a sea snake, which was as unhappy to see me as I was to see it. Many sea snakes are poisonous, although fortunately, most are also interested in parting from divers as fast as possible. I made my break dancing octopus movements again to obtain the other divers' attention as the snake swam away, most likely because it was embarrassed to be associated with me. With the rest of our air expended from the excitement of spotting the exotic critters, we rose to the surface.

Back at the dive shop, Mateo and Arturo invited us to stick around for some late afternoon appetizers, or *mezes*, and beer. I had never encountered this sort of full-service dive experience, but boy I could get used to it. We stowed our gear, showered off, and pulled up some chairs in the back of the shop. I cracked open a local Modelo beer and appreciated the thirst-quenching feel of my first sip. The Boston terrier and his band of Mexican fleas were back, nipping at me until I gave him a nice scratch. The conversation naturally turned to the evolution of diving in Cozumel.

"Serious divers have been coming here for a long time," Mateo said. "After Cancun became popular, people then started looking for other places along the coast to go. Somebody in the government decided to call this the 'Mexican Riviera,' Nice, huh?" he laughed. "It isn't fancy, but more and more people come to Cozumel to vacation. Not just the cruises, either, but people who stay for a week or more."

"I opened my dive shop about ten years ago. Many people who come here want to dive. They are more serious than the tourists in Cancun. They just want to drink there."

"Has the reef changed a lot?" I asked. "I would think too many people would eventually ruin it."

"We try to be really careful," volunteered Arturo, who had been quiet until now. "We use the mooring balls instead of anchors, we don't let the divers touch the reef, and we won't let them wear gloves when they dive. Some sites are starting to look worn, but there are lots of sites all along the coast. We can spread out our diving so the same sites don't keep getting used."

"I bet the hurricanes do more damage than the tourists," offered Ted.

"That last one wasn't too bad, but some of them have been awful. They can really break up the reef. The sand can kill the coral if it coats it too thick," said Mateo. "It can be bad on the fish, too. A turtle that's lived on a certain reef for years may move to another reef or disappear altogether. One time after a storm we thought we lost a whole nurse shark family. They showed up several weeks later at a dive site a half mile down the coast."

Mateo's wife brought out plates and paper napkins. My mouth started to water as I smelled aromatic meats and fried dough coming from the kitchen somewhere in the building. I offered to help, but she smiled and shook her head kindly, disappearing back into the kitchen to serve the food. She quickly reappeared with two plates in hand. My intestinal distress-o-meter went off as I saw a sliced raw avocado and tomato on one of the plates. Happily, toasted empanadas were on the other. She left to bring out more: a basket of warm tortillas and a plate of roast chicken. If this was afternoon appetizers, I couldn't imagine what she served for dinner.

"Is any of this spicy?" I asked when she returned, remembering our encounter with the conch chowder. It had taken me two hours to regain full feeling in my tongue.

"No, but I have some hot sauce," she replied thinking I wanted more spice as she disappeared again to find a bottle. I didn't have the heart to let the gracious woman know that I would not be killing any more taste buds with it.

We all ate with gusto, Mateo and Arturo included, savoring every bite. I hadn't realized how hungry I was as juice from the chicken dripped down my chin and onto my dive shorts. All conversation stopped as we ate. I dunked my empanada in a chocolaty mole sauce and even embraced the raw vegetables. Somehow I had a feeling they would not make us sick. The terrier ran around enraptured by the smell, picking up tasty morsels dropped under our chairs. The diving had been superb, and the genuine meal with new friends made the day complete.

Back on the cruise ship we showered and changed. After all, it was New Year's Eve and we would still be in the Cozumel port until eleven o'clock at night. There was plenty of time to enjoy the town before we rang in the New Year on the high seas. We headed up to the outside bar on the Lido Deck

> "The proper behavior all through the holiday season is to be drunk. This drunkenness culminates on New Year's Eve, when you get so drunk you kiss the person you're married to."
> -P.J. O'Rourke

where we had a great view of Cozumel in the setting sun. Ted and Amy, along with our three other dinner couples, met us at the bar. I was getting accustomed to living on the cruise ship. "Meet us at the Lido Deck" almost rolled off my tongue. Almost. It still felt a little like we belonged in a sit com or a soap opera. But, we had eaten well on the ship, enjoyed the different lounge acts, spent way too much money in the casino, and had several relaxing days at sea with enjoyable books. It was a pretty nice way to travel, and I knew we would consider a cruise again in the future.

After finishing our fruity drinks we disembarked to explore the Cozumel nightlife. We headed back to the Plaza del Sol, which was lit with festive lanterns and filled with tourists and locals alike celebrating the coming year. A mariachi band attracted a large crowd on one side of the square, playing lively music in a way that displayed a serious amount of talent, the polar opposite of those found in fake Mexican restaurants at home. Here, mariachi music was a cultural art, not a stereotypical imitation. We laughed and clapped along with the music and gladly contributed pesos to their collection box when it was time for us to continue our exploration.

Our group walked on, eventually winding up in front of a famous bar, a Cozumel institution for visitors. I'll call it "Senior Amphibian's." It was touristy, loud, and obnoxious bordering on offensive, but everyone, even the bartender, looked like they were having a very enjoyable time. In we went. There wasn't a cover charge, but we did each get handed a tequila shot upon entering. No wonder everyone was having such fun. We pulled up a table and sat down to watch the action. Blaring out of the speakers was 1980's rock, not something one would want to listen to every day, but great when heard through tequila-handicapped ears. Someone in our party ordered alcoholic Jell-O shots and the night began in earnest.

The women in our group, myself included, made our way to the crowded dance floor and joined in the throng. We hadn't been up there for more than a few minutes when a group of guys came up and started dancing with our pal Irena, The Gyrator, who held her liquor surprisingly poorly considering she was Russian. From the little I knew of her husband, Vlad, he would not take too kindly to other men manhandling his new bride. Irena was not in any shape to even notice the guys around her, never mind get them to leave her alone. In an effort to stave off an international incident, I approached the new guys.

"Hey, we're an all girl band," I said pointing to Irena and my other girlfriends. *Where did I get that from?* Apparently the tequila had freed my mind, too. "We're an all *girl* band," I emphasized when the guys looked confused. "Irena here is *mine*," I stated, quite convincingly. Though they looked intrigued, the boy band backed off. Suddenly a bell over the bar rang.

"The S.S. Minnow is leaving," yelled the bartender. "Anyone who's here from the docked cruise please close out your tab. You've got thirty minutes to get back on board before it sails." His announcement triggered a mass exodus that included voluminous credit card charges and an unsteady mob weaving their way back to the boat.

"Um, why does Irena keep pinching your butt?" Michael asked as we staggered up the street back to the ship. I explained the finer points of the All Girl Band to our group. Even Vlad found my creativity amusing.

The ship was close now. There was just a vacant lot and some sand dunes separating us from our floating home. Most other people streaming back to the boat used the sidewalk that lined the field, but our group was still buzzing from all the excitement and plowed forward without even noticing the cacti scattered across the lot. The petite girl who had popped out of her shirt at our inaugural dinner was the first to brush against one of the spiny plants. Yelping, she grabbed her foot. It was a minor incident; she quickly pulled the one or two large stickers out. In a burst of chivalry her boyfriend offered to carry her, but then unceremoniously threw her over his shoulder like a bag of rice.

We continued along watching carefully for cacti, with the boyfriend and rice bag, her body bent over his shoulder so that her head dangled behind him, leading the way. About half way, the boyfriend turned to say something. Our group froze: there, for the entire world to see, were the poor girl's lower feminine charms on full display. What was wrong with her? Didn't she own *any* undergarments? There was a slight chill in the air. Surely she felt at least a little breeze.

By the time we reached the ship we were in hysterics. Fortunately the boyfriend had put her down. I'm sure we would not have been allowed on the ship with that particular emblem at the helm of our group. Once up the gangway we went directly to the observation deck to ring in the New Year with a clear view of the moon and stars over the Cozumel port. Ted managed to find a few champagne bottles for an appropriate salute. We raised our glasses and toasted to good friends, good diving, and good travel as the ship's horn thunderously indicated another great year had arrived.

CHAPTER 4

Australia: Down Under the Waves, Down Under the World

The people on the ground looked like ants from my perch on the top of the bridge that spans Sydney Harbor. Although I was strapped to a safety line, the climb up had been harrowing. A steady rain soaked me to the core and made the steel girder steps slippery. After an invigorating, twenty-minute climb to the top I had a soaring view of the city, once I unlocked my knees, remembered to breathe, and opened my eyes. From under my rain gear I could see the harbor spreading out before me, the Sydney Opera house to the right and the North Shore to the left. Even in the rain, Sydney was a visually striking metropolis.

Michael and I planned to visit the city for three days before continuing on to the north of the country to visit the Great Barrier Reef. We were but two of the 2.5 million plus visitors that visited the city in a year. Sydney was a place of superlatives, one of the most expensive cities in the world and also one of the most livable. We visited the sites in the mornings, and then spent each afternoon at dockside cafés watching the boats go by and talking to the Aussies. We fantasized about moving to the city, but found out the locals knew they had it good; work visas were harder to come by than a sober Aussie on a Friday night.

There was a great deal of sightseeing to fit into three days. In addition to the bridge, the Royal Botanical Gardens, and Luna Park, myriad art and history museums appealed to us. We took a day trip out to the famous Bondi Beach, one kilometer of golden sand, with tanned locals, white tourists, and sometimes monstrous waves. Unfortunately, its shark population shows a keen interest in eating those who enter the water, with several attacks a year. The threat of sharks didn't deter the surfers, though, who took to their boards with a ferocious intensity at the southern end of the beach.

A trip to Sydney isn't complete without a visit to the iconic landmark, the Sydney Opera House, located on Bennelong Point in the harbor. Danish architect Jørn Utzon designed it so ingeniously that no one could figure out how to build it once the government selected his design. Eventually, building started in 1959 and completed in 1973, a long time for a big clam shell. I was surprised to learn there were actually seven different performance venues within the giant shells, rather that the one big venue I had always pictured in my mind. Along with performances by Opera Australia, the Opera House is host to the Sydney Symphony, the Australian Ballet, the Sydney Theatre Company, and a variety of touring arts companies.

We were able to catch *The Magic Flute*, a light, humorous opera in two acts composed in 1791 by Wolfgang Amadeus Mozart. The performance overflowed with typical operatic themes of love, misunderstanding, intrigue, misunderstanding, deities, and more misunderstanding. Richly colored, larger-than-life costumes that exaggerated the characters' features and dramatic deliveries of verse stole the show, which was performed in English. Translation to English is, in some operatic circles, frowned upon as being "dumbed down" opera for the masses. Perhaps I'm dumb, but I enjoyed focusing on the show rather than squinting at the subtitles for three hours. Score one for the big clam shell.

Our three days in Sydney passed quickly. Soon we were on a jet to Cairns in Queensland to pay homage to the plus-sized goddess of underwater ecosystems, the Great Barrier Reef. As the plane descended I could barely contain my excitement.

Upon our arrival, we took a shuttle to Port Douglas, approximately thirty minutes west along the coast. I chose Port Douglas as our base because it was more quiet, and more authentic than its bigger and more trafficked brother, Cairns. If I wanted a touristy shore, I could have stayed on Bondi Beach. After a quick shower and a change of clothes we walked into town to find a local meal and nightlife. The town was small, just one main street lined with shops and restaurants bisected by a median of enormous Jurassic Park-like leafy trees and plants. A few of the stores were national chains, but the majority were local places with tin roofs, wooden walls, and friendly Aussies hawking goods, real estate, beer, and sometimes all three.

One open-air bar in particular drew us in with a promise of "Mighty Cane Toad Races." Well, that was new. I pictured the Warner Brother's frog riding a horse. That couldn't be right. We ordered a beer, pulled up a seat, and waited for the show to begin. The Foster's flowed freely with a minimum of food to balance it out. By the time the toads made their debut we were sufficiently inebriated and sufficiently impressed, as the other patrons seemed to have an astounding ability to consume large amounts of beer and still remain upright. For every one glass we consumed, others had three. Hourly deliveries of beer through the back door must have been necessary to keep the the bar stocked.

The National Trust of Queensland named the cane toad a state icon in 2006. The Aussies are so enamored with these warty ones that "cane toad" is actually a slang term for someone who lives in Queensland. This strange affinity aside, I still did not understand why the Aussies raced them. I really like dogs, but I don't stick them in Indy cars and take them

Australia introduced a few hundred cane toads to the Queensland region in the early 1930's as a way to control the cane beetle population. Unfortunately, the Cane Toads thought the beetles "tasted funny" and therefore didn't eat a single one. Now numbering more than 200 million, the toad has few predators. In a strange twist of Darwinism, some cane toads have recently been found eating the Australian creatures that once preyed upon them. Experts estimate that in another 10-15 years the toads will simply overthrow the Australian government and turn the entire state into a bog.

to Daytona. Perhaps they tried racing crocodiles, another amphibian in plentiful supply, but decided the toads were easier to keep as pets in the off-season.

Onlookers could "buy" a toad for the night, and then collect the proceeds if that toad won the race, like owning a racehorse, but infinitely less glamorous. The toads had an earthy, compost-y smell that made me retreat when I caught a whiff. I decided I did not need to actually own one of the little beauties, but perhaps just bet on my favorite. I eyed them each up, looking for…what? A "hoppy" look? A gleam in their eye that told me they were really a prince deep, down inside? I finally chose an olive colored, jolly looking fellow I felt resembled Frogger from the 80's video game. Since I wasn't controlling the joystick, this one might actually have a chance.

Across several tables, the bartender set up a long lane with wooden sides to stop any escapees. Each frog had a different colored tag on one leg in order for the crowd to definitively tell them apart. The owners lined their noble steeds up along the starting line. The bartender rang a bell to start the race. None of the toads moved, but rather looked around quizzically as if they thought we slipped them some Spanish Fly. Suddenly the toad owners went to work, slapping the bar and shouting at their great green hopes to move. But, these were seasoned race toads, inclined to ignore the encouragement. Still, they sat motionless.

The owners became more emphatic, yelling "Yah!" at the top of their lungs and pounding the bar, like crazed jockeys with beers instead of whips. The increased energy got the toads to move, but not all in the right direction. One cleared the guardrail altogether, landing on the floor and scuttling under the ice chest. Another directionally challenged toad actually turned around and leapt behind the starting line, thus cementing his place as the frog that came in last.

My frog lagged behind until the very end of the race, and then surprisingly flew over the finish line first after a final, vehement "Yah!" from its owner. I won $15 Australian dollars, just enough to buy Michael and me each another Foster's. I could see why the locals found this event appealing if it kept the beer flowing. I'm not into horse racing. I certainly don't support dog racing. But, I can say that I race amphibians with the best of them.

The Great Barrier Reef is enormous, covering over 300,000 square kilometers with approximately 2900 individual reefs and more than 600 islands. All of that space means plenty of room for fish, whales, dolphins, turtles, birds, mollusks, and hundreds of kinds of hard and soft corals. Fishing is allowed on some parts of the reef, but the majority of it is designated as the Great Barrier Reef Marine Park, which is intended to limit the impact of fishing and tourism. Humans have used the reef for thousands of years for food, cultural activities, and recreation, practices that continue to this day.

I expected the reef to be offshore, of course, but not a two-hour boat ride offshore. Our boat was a large, twin hull with enormous engines. It could hold up to fifty people, or so said the "Max Persons" sign in the main cabin. Fortunately the passengers numbered only thirty or so, which gave us a bit more room to move around and set up our gear. Half the people on the boat were Asian, the other half a mix of Europeans and Americans. The Asian contingent was an interesting mix of three families from China, two sisters from Singapore, and a group of bizarre-looking guys from Japan with long hair, strands of which were dyed blue and green. I was convinced that they were a rock band. They didn't speak English so I wasn't able to ask, and my Japanese was limited to "My name is Karen. Another beer, please." I waited for them at any moment to confirm my suspicions and break into song, like modern-day Japanese Beatles.

At least we could converse with the other English speakers. Somehow a family of four from Ohio had made it all the way to the reef. I remembered my own trips to the New Jersey shore as a kid, and hoped their two children knew how very lucky they were. Their fussing and pouting gave me an inkling they did not. We steered clear of them, instead striking up a conversation with an older, burly Brit who turned out to be a retired Navy captain. He was spending several months touring Australia on his own, which sounded like a lonely prospect to me. But, judging by his gregarious nature, I was sure he made friends wherever he went.

"I've been diving for twenty years," he said, clearly proud of his history with the sport. "The water here is beautiful, not at all like Britain where you can't see a darn thing. I figured if I was down here in Australia I had to come to the Reef to see it for myself."

"I hope we see some sharks," Michael said enthusiastically. He had been going on and on all week about seeing the "man eaters." The shark feed in Moorea had been a real highlight for him.

The Brit suddenly looked nervous. "Oh I don't like the fish, just the scenery," he said. "I once got bit by a barracuda in the South China Sea," he said, showing us a scar on his right arm, just below the elbow. "I don't want any more of that!" Strange that - a beefy Naval captain afraid of fish. I made a mental note to avoid him at all costs underwater lest his escape plans included feeding me to the sea creatures.

We made it to the dive site and geared up. My mask, fins, tank, scuba vest, and various other tubes, valves, and bits were in place, giving the overall impression of a medical supply warehouse, rather than a diver. Now came the most awkward part of any diving experience on a large boat: the Scuba Shuffle to the back.

The Scuba Shuffle is an aquatic conga of sorts, but without the maracas. The divers, who had plenty of time to suit up, all stood up at once due to some lemming-like intuition that drives divers' behavior. Invariably the wind picked up at that moment and the boat began to sway. Queue the tin-pan music and the bongos. While invaluable underwater, fins are the least graceful piece of sports equipment one can possess on land. A diver can't simply walk to the back of the boat and jump off, he or she must do a duck-like shuffle and flap, complete with the corresponding *shrrrr-whup shurrr-whup* sound. Like me, the others in the conga line were leaning forward to avoid falling backwards from the gear weight, but appearing as if we all found something fascinating on the rear of the person in front of us. Shuffle flap, *shrrr-whup*.

The boat continued to roll in the waves, picking up momentum as I shuffled past the more challenging boat features like the swinging wetsuit locker and the oblivious snorkelers with arms shooting in all directions at once. Snorkelers are generally not welcome on dive boats because they always seem to be in the right place to create the maximum hindrance to divers transporting and preparing gear. Much to our dismay, almost half of the tourists on the boat were snorkelers. We would consider using a different company the rest of trip.

Rather than jumping in, a logjam of divers formed at the back of the boat due to various forgotten pieces of equipment and irrational fish phobias. Like salmon in a swift current, the divers creating the jam could not get back upstream until the rest of the conga line passed. Shuffle flap, *shrrr-whup*. Finally, it was my turn at the back of the boat. I put my air regulator (the lifeline to my air tank) in my mouth, held my mask, and took a giant stride into the sapphire blue ocean. Unfortunately, my over-excitement caused an extra spring in my big step, thus loosening my right fin, which went swirling into the depths unattended. I can only imagine the fish thoughts below as they watched it sink to the bottom: "Oh look! Decorations for the calypso party!" One of the staff on the boat handed me down an extra fin and off I went into the blue.

Michael and I drifted towards the back of the dive pack. Being last in line made it much easier to get a good look at things and much harder to get kicked by someone else's fin. Each turn in the reef yielded a new and interesting site to see. A chameleon cuttlefish, a sort of iridescent squid, hovered before us debating which color would make him the least noticeable. He tried on several blues and greens before settling on a mottled brown to match the reef behind him. Christmas Tree Worms, their spiraled, bristly fingers sticking out in red, green, blue, and yellow, grew in clumps like multi-colored tree farms. It was a lovely dive at fifty feet that lasted almost an hour. But, to my surprise, we saw no sharks.

This was the Great Barrier Reef, otherwise known as the "Home of the Fat Sharks" to most people. Though I wasn't expecting to encounter Jaws on my first dive, I at least expected to see something toothy and menacing besides our invoice for our day of diving. While back on the boat for our surface interval, I inquired of the divemaster as to where the sharks were hiding.

"Oh, they're here," he said emphatically, like he had been asked that question many times before. "It rained last night, so they may have moved out to deeper water. I'm sure we'll see one on the next dive." His explanation sounded fishy, but who was I to argue? We did have one dive left, so I was optimistic.

Back in the water on our second dive we came across a garden of starfish. Fat blue starfish, skinny red starfish, long-legged green starfish, and squat yellow starfish were everywhere. Some appeared stiff and poker straight, while others drooped their arms over the reef like drunken starlets. The variety and volume were amazing, like looking into the Milky Way on the sea floor. Unfortunately, the predatory Crown of Thorns starfish also made an appearance. This unique animal can quickly devastate a reef by eating the coral, and have few natural enemies to control their numbers. The ones I saw didn't look too menacing, more like angry, leggy pincushions, but their mere existence did not bode well for that section of the reef.

Suddenly the divemaster clunked his dive knife on his air tank, a common way to call the attention of divers in a group because the clanging sound travels far and fast through the water. He had found something interesting to show us. He pointed to a rock and a small grey tail that stuck out from under it. He poked the tail with his finger, and out swam a foot-long grey fish. It swam in a circle, and then tucked itself back under the rock, most likely struck with stage fright in front of the group of ogling divers. I looked to the divemaster for guidance, as I had no idea why this shy, grey, unexciting fish had caused such commotion. The divemaster made the underwater sign for shark. Ahh. The Great White we had come to see was actually The Tiny White. I could have eaten it for dinner and still needed a hamburger afterwards. Mollified, the divers dispersed back along the reef to finish the dive.

The divemaster is always the last one on the boat at the end of the dive, making sure all the other divers get back in the boat safely. As he climbed on board, he couldn't contain his excitement, telling the other staff on the boat and the divers that it was a baby jagged tooth shark, a merciless hunter and a voracious eater. If that shark had merciless, voracious jagged teeth, it excelled in hiding them in its itty-bitty mouth. The best Tiny could have done was stick its tongue out at us.

A black spider the size of my hand decorated the outdoor archway leading to our section of the hotel. Day after day I saw it hang there, usually motionless, waiting for a snack. If a bug was unobservant enough not to see this giant predator, then it deserved to be eaten. At home, spiders are unpleasant. In Australia, especially Queensland, they are big enough to cart you off, wrap you up, and send a ransom note to your family. The Aussies seem to just ignore them, hence the continued habitation of our hallway adornment.

Queensland is host to all sorts of interesting creatures, many of whom live in the Daintree Rainforest, the 1200 square kilometer World Heritage Site located just down the road from Port Douglas. Not only is the jungle filled with creatures that want to eat the visitor, it also contains all sorts of confusing trails, swimming holes, and climbs that would require an emergency search party to find us if my husband and I tried to visit it alone. There were certainly people who ventured into the Daintree without the help of a guide, but they were probably the same people who thought the giant spider at our hotel was charming. We were just not that hearty.

I chose a tour that included a short paddle down the Daintree River. A 4x4 picked us up at our hotel along with four other folks who would join us for the day. Our guide looked like an Australian cowboy, with a worn hat, leather vest and boots, and an enormous silver belt buckle. I was sure that when he went home at night he put on a Nike t-shirt and sneakers. But, for his day job, his outfit instilled confidence in us that he would be able to lead us into, and more importantly out of, the rainforest. As we drove to the park, our John Wayne of Daintree told us a little bit about the area.

"The Daintree Rainforest is over 135 million years old. It is one of the only places in the world where the rainforest goes directly to the ocean," he said. "It has an amazing variety of plants, fish, and animals, some of which can only be found here. If we are lucky we'll see some today."

We stopped at a dock and boarded a small, flat-bottomed boat moored on a tributary of the Daintree River. The boat had a long pole the guide would use to push us along when we needed to shut off the motor and stealthily approach the local wildlife.

"Our goal today is to find one of the elusive Estuarine Saltwater Crocodiles. We'll also see a variety of birds and other wildlife while we float," he said. We motored down the muddy river. The shores were filled with aquatic grasses, fallen tree limbs, and mangrove plants. Abundant nutrients and hiding places provided a good habitat for plants and animals alike. We saw herons and other types of waterfowl. Orchids clung to the trees and flowering bushes popped up in every nook and cranny. Turtles and crabs scurried along the banks as we drew close. Palm fronds waved overhead. The experience relaxed me, that is, until I saw a pair of gleaming eyes piercing the surface of the water.

The eyes, of course, belonged to something submerged. I pointed out Sneaky Pete to the guide, who immediately turned off the motor. He used the pole to push us closer to the animal without scaring it. Only ten minutes in the boat and already we had found the perhaps not-so-elusive saltwater crocodile. As our boat inched closer I could clearly make out the outline of its snout right below the waterline. The guide informed us it was about ten feet long, which was about nine feet too long for my taste. Then, with a graceful thrash of its tail and a splash of water, it was gone.

The proof of its existence unnerved me; something that big could be hiding right under the surface and I would never know. To my relief, the boat glided back to the dock soon after our encounter.

We loaded back up into the 4x4 to begin the next part of our adventure. The truck bounded over unpaved roads and forded small streams. The guide knew a great deal about the plants that grew in the rainforest; to me most all of them looked like palms. There are 19 primitive plant families on earth, meaning that only 19 types of plants have remained the same over the millennia. Twelve are found in the Daintree area, many of which our guide pointed out to us. Several times we got out of the truck and tramped through the brush to see a species he was eager to show us, like the ribbonwood plant, otherwise unfortunately known as the "idiot fruit." Over the past 50 years researchers discovered this tropical wonder, lost it, and then discovered it again. Perhaps it was named after the people who misplaced it.

As we drove on, I saw periodic signs warning of crossing animals. At home these are usually "Deer Crossing" or "Goose Crossing" signs. In the Daintree forest, however, the signs had a silhouette of a fat bird with a long neck and a bumpy head, like the chicken that crossed the road, but uglier. I had to ask the guide about the signs alerting us to the presence of the unattractive creature.

> Cassowaries are anti-social creatures, preferring a solitary life except when Barry White music is playing. Reclusive by nature, they do not like being approached by people. Their key defense mechanism, in addition to their startlingly bad looks, is to kick and employ the one large talon at the end of each foot. There are documented cases of humans being killed by these kung-fu maneuvers and deadly toe nails.

"Those are to warn motorists about the cassowaries," he responded. "They're large, flightless birds native to this area. They can run very fast and even swim, but they don't fare well when they meet up with cars head to head. They are an endangered species so we try to be very careful of them. Over half of cassowary deaths are because they get hit by motor vehicles." Although I scanned the forest throughout our tour, I never caught sight of one of these rare, car-dodging beauties. Strangely enough, I heard they have one at the Atlanta zoo. I guess I didn't need to leave home after all.

We stopped for lunch at a small restaurant outside the modest town of Daintree. The menu presented no surprises, the main meal was grilled barramundi. This fish appeared on every menu we saw in Australia. The Aussies were sure proud of their native fish, though it tasted like any basic white fish to me, similar to flounder or tilapia. I suppose if one is used to eating cane toad or crocodile, mild white fish is a real treat.

I enjoyed the platter at the end of the meal the most. It overflowed with a variety of exotic fruit, some that I had never seen before. There was a sour sop, which had a hard brown outside concealing a slightly sour, gelatinous yellow center. The stunning, neon pink, softball-sized dragon fruit seemed to have put all of its effort into looking good since the inside was tasteless. I also sampled passion fruit, pineapple, sugar cane, and two different types of bananas. But, my absolute favorite was the rambutan, a cherry red fruit with bright green flexible fingers sticking out of its skin in all directions. It was similar to a lychee nut: I peeled off the Halloween costume that was its outer layer to reveal the white flesh that surrounded the pit. Thought it looked bizarre, it tasted great. I wanted to fill my suitcase and take them all home with me.

After lunch we piled back into the 4x4. The next destination was Hidden Falls, a secluded spot in the forest with a small waterfall culminating in a cool pool at the base. After driving for only 20 minutes, the guide stopped the truck by the side of the dirt road.

"We walk from here," he said. "Take your swimming gear and water with you."

At first the ground was level and packed from many hikers' feet, making it easily traversable. Then the going got tougher, with steep inclines and descents to get over mounds of earth, fallen trees, and petrified forest bits. We crossed a small river with perfectly shaped stepping stones to keep the hiker dry. I, of course, found the sole wobbly stepping stone, and thus continued the rest of the hike with one wet shoe.

From the ground the trees looked enormous. Strangler fig vines embraced large ancient trees and fan palms waved at us in the breeze. Before long I could hear the rush of water that could only mean a waterfall or that my old washing machine was overflowing again. I was betting it was the waterfall. As I came around the last bend in the trail, the waterfall appeared, glistening in the sunshine. At 50 feet tall it wasn't the largest one I had seen, but time had carved a beautiful set of undulations in the rock at the ridge of the falls, causing the water to rain down seductively, rather than just fly over the edge and fall to the bottom.

We had to climb down a muddy, ten-foot embankment to reach the graveled area around the pool at the bottom of the falls. The guide made it look easy: just "hold on to this root, then put one foot here, then one foot there." No problem. I made it look hard by dangling perilously from the root, completely overshooting the foothold and eventually just sliding down on my stomach. Ten seconds and a very muddy shirt later I reached the bottom. We put down our packs on the graveled area where Mother Nature had kindly strewn a few small boulders to act as comfortable stools.

"Anyone who wants to swim in the pool can do so. If you don't have on your bathing suits, boys can change in the forest on that bank," he said gesturing to the right. "And girls can change over there," pointing to the left bank. How Biblical. Just like the Garden of Eden: one can hang out naked, just avoid the snakes and ....oops we already ate the fruit. The process gave new meaning to "fig-leafing it." I opted to stay in my shorts and only go into the water up to my knees.

Two of the couples changed into their bathing suits and slipped into the water. Michael and I, along with the other couple, waded in the rocky shallows and soaked in the moment. The setting conveyed a sense of peace, with the water dropping down to the pool, the ancient trees around us and the occasional song of a tropical bird. I was beginning to drift off into my own little Zen state when a sudden scream pierced the air.

"That is sooooo cold!" shouted one of the guys who had gone swimming. The cold water rendered the other swimmers speechless. My feet in the shallows started to get frosty; I could not imagine how unpleasant it would be to submerge my whole body. Swimming in a waterfall pool may be romantic, but it is also cold and rocky, with a healthy crop of squishy aquatic plant life underfoot.

I sat on one of the boulders at the edge of the pool and rested my feet on a smaller rock that was partly submerged. It was such an inspiring scene that I was rethinking a swim despite the cold. I put my weight against the smaller rock underfoot, and it wobbled, nearly causing me to tumble onto the bank. I righted myself on the bigger rock just in time to see an enormous, four-foot eel uncoil from underneath the smaller rock and glide soundlessly into the pool. I could ignore the outdoor changing rooms. I could brave the ice water. I could even overcome the slippery rocks and seaweed salad bottom. But, I drew the line at Jurassic eels. A girl's got to have her standards. Some romantic notions are best left unfulfilled.

With rippled golden dunes containing sparkling mother of pearl pieces, our hotel's beach resembled an ideal destination, the kind featured on a cable travel channel. The fine grains stretched as far as the eye could see, their warm-hued glow offset by the lush green foliage of the surrounding tropics. Not quite so striking were the signs posted every hundred feet that sported a danger-indicating orange background with a black silhouette of a bulbous jellyfish sporting long tentacles. The sign's wording warned of the onset of box jellyfish season, suggesting serious skin protection or complete ocean abstinence.

Box jellyfish spawn at river mouths, and then get washed downstream and into the coastal ocean during the rainy season where they hang out for about half the year. The sting of the jellyfish is exceedingly painful and can induce cardiac arrest within minutes. The Aussies set up nets along some coastal areas to prevent the creatures from approaching the shore, but this does not keep all of the wily creatures away from humans. These cube-shaped jell-o mounds have rudimentary eyes and can swim fast, attributes that make them unusual in the jellyfish world and highly lethal. Worse yet, these gelatinous predators ruined my beach fantasy; I had to settle for cooling off in the hotel pool.

A keen awareness and appreciation for the jellyfish presence was apparent on the dive boat the following day. The divemaster required that all the divers had to either wear a wetsuit or a skin suit, a thin membrane of material meant to keep the jellyfish tentacles from coming into direct contact with the skin. I never go into the water without my wetsuit, knowing how cold I get underwater. However, several divers on our boat did not like to use insulating wetsuits; their alternative was to look like aliens, with thin, neon pink and green spandex skin coverings provided by the dive company. Certain parts of the body were just not meant to be highlighted in glow-in-the-dark material.

Although the large number of snorkelers on the boat disappointed us, we decided to continue to dive with the company we used the day before. They had our gear all ready to go, we were comfortable on the large boat, and they already had our credit card number. Sometimes simplicity is the best policy on vacation. A new divemaster replaced the one from the day before, giving us a refreshingly new perspective and more knowledge about the reef.

"The box jellies are usually only found near the coast. They don't frequently make the trip all the way out to the reef. But, I'm glad to see everyone is prepared," he said, raising his eyebrows at the alien divers in the bunch.

"If anyone does get stung, please do not pee on them." Was this a concern? Did this occur often enough that he had to instruct us not to do so? Everyone knew the old wives' tale that urine stopped jellyfish stings, but I had no expectation that anyone would put the information to use. It was bad enough to get stung in the water. Getting peed on by a fellow diver was just adding insult to injury.

"Only vinegar works to disable the stingers. We have a bottle in the first aid kit at the front of the boat." How versatile these Aussies were. They were prepared for jellyfish *or* a salad.

"Our first dive site today will be Charlie's Reef," he continued.

"Who's Charlie?" I asked.

"Charlie was a very old sea turtle that lived on the reef. We won't see him, though. About a year ago he disappeared. Most people think he died, but some of us just think he swam away." I loved that idyllic explanation. Nothing dies in the sea, it just swims away.

We geared up and jumped into the ocean, which was a flat blue plane. The lack of waves meant less granules suspended in the water, and, thus, better visibility. The sun streaked through the sky and pierced the water, its rays dancing around us as we swam slowly enjoying the view. This patch of reef was healthy, with lots of living coral and darting fish. The divemaster stopped the group when he located his goal, a field of giant clams. The clams measured all sizes, some up to four feet across. Their green and blue mantles vibrated as the mollusks filtered water in and out, searching for suspended food. The clams didn't snap closed, like in the movies where the aggressive bivalves grab the legs of passing swimmers. Rather, they gently shut to protect themselves when threatened, such as when my nosy shadow passed overhead.

We circled the clam bed for quite some time, studying the features of the creatures, their mesmerizing combination of colors, iridescence, and shapes making each one a unique piece of art. I realized I had not played with my gear once the whole dive, not even to adjust my mouthpiece. I had become comfortable with the sport and was able to enjoy what the sea had to offer. My novice status swam away, just like the turtle.

CHAPTER 5

Bahamas: The Art of the Chicken Bag

When the trainer opened the gate between the pen and the ocean I thought: *That dolphin is not coming back.* It shot out of its enclosure like a bullet, heading straight out from shore, a dark, sleek shadow racing through the waves, disappearing in the distance. We boarded the boat and began the short, ten minute trip to our designated dive site. The trainer scanned the horizon for signs of the dolphin, the corners of his eyes pinched with the beginnings of worry. We spent the travel time gearing up so that we would be ready to jump into the water as soon as we arrived at the site.

The captain cut the motor and a mate lassoed a mooring ball cemented to the sea floor so that the anchor would not damage the reef. We shuffled to the back of the boat with the rest of the divers, prepared for entry into the ocean. Our eyes were focused on the surface, looking for the dolphin, our designated dive buddy for the day. Its disappearance surprised crew and passengers alike, causing us all some concern. Suddenly, it leapt from the water at the stern of the boat, its silver-grey sides glistening in the sun. Its face held intelligent eyes and a smile that said "Hi! It took you long enough to get here!"

Our group of six divers and one divemaster eased into the water and descended to the ocean bottom, about thirty feet down. We knelt in a large circle on the sandy floor. The dolphin trainer swam in the water with, of course, the dolphin. The trainer had taught the mammal well; it kept an eye on its teacher, watching for queues. Flipper swam to each of us, allowing us to pet his back and interact. The dolphin was surprisingly strong, able to push even the largest diver around with ease.

Amazingly, we swam in open water with no barriers around us. At any point the dolphin could have simply left our group and never returned. At certain points the dolphin did disappear from sight, dashing out into the blue and then back again, perhaps resting or refocusing its efforts. The trainer patiently waited until the dolphin appeared ready to move onto the next person or activity. The dolphin seemed to enjoy the experience, having a purpose and freedom at the same time.

Sometimes humans come upon dolphins that have been injured or neglected from birth. Across the globe groups work to rehabilitate these animals, but not all can be returned safely to the open ocean because of the lasting effects of their injuries or their acquired dependence on humans. The company we dove with had rehabilitated many dolphins, some of which needed to remain in captivity, destined to live out their lives with beings that walk instead of swim. Our dolphin was born in captivity, its parents rehabilitated from injuries, but too weak to survive in the wild.

I was excited to swim with him, but hoped it would be an educational experience, not just a circus act. I found a beautiful creature that had a job it clearly enjoyed with significance that far exceeded swimming around a pen. And, it could have simply swam away, but didn't. As the dolphin came close to me and inspected my mask, I almost forgot to breathe. It turned to make eye contact with me and I thought: *The Bahamas are a great place to be.*

The Commonwealth of the Bahamas is a Caribbean archipelago of more than 700 islands. The islands' reasonable cost and proximity to the US made it our "Got to Get Away" weekend dive destination. In addition to fantastic experiences with dolphins, sharks, and a host of other aquatic life, it also offered topside enjoyment filled with a nice mix of island relaxation and vacation fun. Over the years we made numerous trips to the islands, each time finding new and exciting things to do and see both under the waves and above.

As a process improvement consultant, I traveled all the time. Unfortunately in my world, a direct correlation existed between the amount of help a company needed and the remoteness of their location. I had been to every city that no one had ever heard of, and had memorized the Cracker Barrel menu. But, every once in awhile, I got lucky. The Bahamas has two main pillars of their economy, tourism and financial services. One of my banking industry customers established a high-risk branch in Freeport, Bahamas and I needed to perform a site visit. Michael planned to meet me at the end of the week so we could enjoy a long weekend in the sun and surf.

I did actually work that week, albeit in a building that overlooked the bay and with people who all went home at 4pm. Although the U.S. headquarters considered the branch high-risk because of its location and size, I found it to be well run. The staff were knowledgeable and well intentioned, and the business processes sound. The co-workers also fostered a feeling of "family" among themselves. The familial feel did not negatively affect the way the business ran, but rather made the staff more intent on running the business properly, almost like they took it personally. The office manager did have trouble finding qualified staff to fill vacant roles, but once she located the right person, the business appeared to run smoothly.

Each day I went to lunch with members of the company, as there were no restaurants within walking distance of the office. Most people brought lunch from home, but I lived in a hotel. The lunch options in town were limited; Subway, the sandwich place, was a popular stop. Subs were not quite the tropical meal for which I hoped, though the staff insisted we go there each day and I obliged without complaint. I understood that the change from their normal, home cooked diet presented an infrequent and welcome occasion for them. Also, they were demonstrating their hospitality by taking me to a place they thought I would find to my liking. On my last day at the office I asked if we could have lunch at someplace less "American" than Subway. I could not eat another "foot-long" sub. As we were driving to the restaurant, we stopped at a red light and a group of Rastafarians approached our car.

"What are they selling?" I asked the office manager, who drove the car.

"Boiled peanuts. They sell them to make money to buy their drugs," she said angrily, as she waved them away without opening her window. "I never buy any from them because I don't agree with their religion. You don't need to smoke the herb to find God." I hadn't known that Rastafari was a religion. I learned that the Rastafari movement believes in one God, Jah, who was reincarnated as the former Emperor of Ethiopia. The movement originated from Jamaicans of African descent that believed they were being persecuted by Western society, though now world peace and racial harmony are commonly espoused. With this peaceful feeling comes the ganja, used in a variety of settings including social gatherings and religious activities. Rastafari believe that marijuana use is sanctioned by the Bible.

"I wouldn't encourage them if you run into them while you're here," she said. "If they think you are interested they can be very fanatical." I found this strange since I thought smoking marijuana made people mellow, not assertive. I thought on this for a bit as we drove, and came up with a few lines I could use to be discouraging but polite if they approached me.

Things To Say to Discourage Peanut Sales from a Rastafarian
1. Were those boiled in a commercial grade kitchen?
2. I bought at the last corner. You might want to relocate.
3. I'm more of a cashew girl, really.
4. Bob's dead. Sorry.
5. I'm on an all meat diet.

I wasn't sure these statements would work, but I was prepared nevertheless.

Another day, another shark feed. In scuba diving circles, the Bahamas are pretty well known for their sharks. Divers commonly see black tips, white tips, grey reef, and nurse sharks on dives. The only way to pack more of them into a dive is to feed them, which is what several companies have started offering in the Bahamas. While no shark feed is 100% safe, we chose one with an environmentally conscious reputation and an impeccable safety record. Better to stack the deck in our favor from the start.

When the dive boat tied up to the mooring ball I was surprised to see how close we were to shore. Specifically, how close we were to several large hotels. If the guests only knew what lay in the nearby waves, they would spend their time in the pool.

We donned our dive gear and waited for instructions. Funny how the dive briefing before a shark feed is similar no matter what part of the world the dive takes place.

"No sudden movements. Don't stick your hands out. Do not reach for any sharks. Do not leave the group for any reason," said the divemaster. The speech sounded so canned, it must have come from the world-wide, super-secret, divemaster-only manual that no tourist ever got to see.

This dive would be different than Moorea, however, as we would be kneeling on the sandy bottom, all lined up and facing forward. The sea floor was forty feet deep, which eliminated that pesky wave surge that plagued us on our last shark feed. It sounded like an easy dive: go to the bottom, line up, watch in awe. I could accomplish that. The other divers appeared confident as well.

Sir Fish Head slipped into his chain mail suit. Clearly the shark-feeding Round Table claimed the membership of knights scattered throughout the globe. As before, this knight carried a lance for feeding. His fish bag functioned better than last time, however. It looked like a giant thermos, designed to keep a maximum of fish bits and blood in the container until the user wanted to access the contents. This ingenious device would avoid driving the sharks to a feeding frenzy until the divers were ready. I began to truly appreciate my choice in dive companies for this event.

All six divers and the divemaster entered the water at the same time via a back roll off the sides of the boat. This maneuver causes the diver to enter the water head first, tucked in a ball, then bob to the surface. This roll is an effective way of entering the water, but requires a huge leap of faith on the part of the divers. One hopes that the water will not instantaneously evaporate when the diver rolls blindly backwards. One hopes that the other divers all go at the same time (hence the 3-2-1 countdown by the divemaster) so that the person upstream does not infringe upon the personal space and good will of the next diver. One also hopes something big, nasty, and hungry does not appear behind the diver when they turn to face the center of the boat before rolling back. As I said, its effective, but it brings pleas for a merciful higher power from every diver.

Once in the water, we quickly descended to the bottom. I could already see a shark cruising the perimeter of my vision, curious about the splashing and hungry for food. The divemaster lined us up as discussed. We were tightly packed; any closer and I would have to sit on Michael, who fidgeting next to me in excited anticipation. More sharks joined the circling one, keeping an eye out for the food they knew was on the way. The downside to feeding fish and sharks in particular is that they come to expect it and may become quite aggressive if their expectations are not met.

Sir Fish Head entered the water and plummeted to the bottom from the weight of his suit. He walked along the sea floor towards us in slow motion, like a knight in shining armor walking on the moon. I expected him to stop about thirty feet away from us, similar to our shark feed experience in Moorea, but he kept approaching us, closer and closer. He finally stopped six feet from our diver line. Any closer and he could have sat on Michael's lap too.

Sir Fish Head pulled the first piece of fish out of the thermos and five sharks swooped in to grab it. They swam so fast I did not see them approach. They just appeared, grabbed the food, and disappeared. The fish feeder continued to pull bits of fish out, sometimes dangling it on the end of the lance to feed the sharks, sometimes handing larger pieces directly to their waiting jaws. The sharks began circling closer to us, their shyness replaced by their growing excitement over the fishy snack.

One shark glided between Michael and me, bumping me in the head with its tail as it passed. I was glad the divemaster had briefed us on shark etiquette, but absent that education no one could have paid me to move or raise my hand an inch. The sharks were so numerous and so close that I would have come into contact with one had I shifted any body part too much. The closeness of the sharks unnerved me, but also enthralled. I could see the detail of their black marble eyes and the electrical sensors on their snouts that looked like enlarged pores. One shark had a large hook in the side of its mouth, the result of a fisherman's bait theft gone badly. Their faces grinned with rows of large teeth, exuding menace even when the sharks' mouths were closed.

When the food disappeared from the water the sharks disappeared from sight. The divemaster ushered us back to the boat. Sir Fish Head stayed behind to distract any remaining sharks in the area, keeping them away from us as we ascended. I took many photos of the event with my underwater camera, though I had not paid too much attention to the viewfinder in favor of focusing on the real thing in front of me. When I developed the pictures they were all of parts of sharks: a tail, a head, some fins. The sharks had been so close that the lens had not captured a single one in its entirety.

When I was a kid I owned a big, floppy sombrero-type hat made with woven palm fronds that had "Nassau" stitched on the front in pink lettering. My Mom had a similarly styled woven bag that she would use to carry our towels when we went to the community pool. A family member had visited the Bahamas and brought us back these treasures. For many years I envisioned the Caribbean as a place where people sat around all day weaving random items out of palm leaves. With my adulthood came the understanding that the islands had much more to offer, though my fond childhood straw memories remained. On our first visit to Nassau I insisted we tour the Straw Market.

I approached the front desk of our hotel to find out where the market was located. The clerk told me that the straw market had declined over time as the worldwide demand for woven palm goods had diminished. Where once thrived a market that spanned several city blocks a modest one-block event now existed. The conversation left me marveling that there actually had been a crest of worldwide demand for palm goods in the first place.

A five minute cab ride dropped us off in front of an open-air alley between two three-story buildings. The space occupied an area 50 feet wide by a city block deep and contained so much straw product that I doubted we could actually fit down the narrow walkway in the center. Apparently they had taken all of the straw products from the multi-block market and stuffed them into this one-block space. We entered, wondering if we would ever find the light of day at the other end.

It is apparently possible to craft a reasonable representation of almost any item on this earth using palm fronds and a bit of imagination. I saw palm frond tables, palm frond toy horses, palm frond candlestick holders, and even palm fronds woven to look like different types of fruit. Some appeared useful, like placemats and drink coasters. Others posed user challenges such as lamp-shades that were bound to burst into flames when employed and flimsy fencing that could not have held back a sleeping conch. All manner of clothing, including hats, capes, jackets, and even bra tops promised to be a scratchy alternative to the real thing. Honestly, if I required feminine support from a palm tree, I would opt for stringing two coconut halves together.

At least purses and hand bags provided some practical use. There were many from which to choose. I particularly liked the ones with the neon-colored, raffia flowers tied onto the sides right next to the "Nassau" hand-sewn logos. Some things didn't change over the years. Stall after stall sold similar items, much to my disappointment. I began to lose hope that I would find anything unique.

Then I saw it, the hand bag of all hand bags. It was shaped like a highly dignified bird, not a peacock or a swan, but rather a fat chicken; its wings pinched at the top to serve as handles. The chicken face glowed with neon raffia detail, its beak made of pleated palm fronds so sharp it drew blood when I accidentally bumped it into my arm. It was an awkward size; too small to carry a load of practical items, but too big to just be for a lipstick and tissues. Best of all were the words "cluck, cluck" stitched lovingly onto the side of the body in uneven, green letters. It was wonderful. I had to have it.

Michael appeared somewhat hesitant about the purchase.

"I don't want to be seen with you if you carry it around," he said.

"This is museum quality," I claimed, patting the bag gently. "It should be displayed as a true cultural item. Maybe in our living room?"

"It should be in a closet somewhere. Under a blanket and some old t-shirts. On a high shelf that most people can't reach."

"I'll give you five dollars for this bag," I told the vendor, hoping to startle him into a bargain.

"I'll take it. Do you want a plastic bag to put it in?" he asked, just as quickly. I began to think that my opening bid was too high. Then again, five dollars was a fair price. The materials were not expensive, but someone had spent a significant amount of time creating a product with such barnyard character. I had to free the avian goddess. I paid the money, declined the plastic bag and tucked the chicken, cluck-cluck side facing out, under my arm. Michael walked about fifteen steps behind me all the way back to the hotel, refusing to acknowledge me until the bird bag nested in my suitcase, safely out of sight.

Underwater, many things look the same. Sure, reef looks different than sand patch, which looks different than never-ending blue abyss. But, most divers could not differentiate when pressed to identify one piece of reef from another or one sand patch vs. a different sand patch. When one is diving with a divemaster who is intimately familiar with an area, a diver does not need to pay attention to such things. However, when one is trying to navigate back to the boat without a guide, as Michael and I tried to accomplish on one Bahamian trip, topography takes on an unsurpassed importance.

Our divemaster gave us divers a choice. We could follow him or venture out on our own to practice our navigation skills. Most of the other divers chose to go it alone. Not wanting to appear like helpless tadpoles, we also opted to dive independently. The water ran only 40-feet deep, no current existed, and the shore could be easily seen from the surface. These factors, as well as the lack of man-eating sharks in the area, made us bold. Armed with our compass and what we perceived as our keen sense of direction, we jumped in and began our dive.

The divemaster suggested heading straight off the back of the boat, swimming for 20 minutes in a straight line, then turning around and swimming back. The sandy bottom had large boulders of coral strewn about, so this dive plan would enable a maximum tour of the area with a minimum of navigation. Easy enough, it seemed. We oriented ourselves with the boat on the surface, and then headed in a direction that looked like north by northwest, according to our compasses.

I immediately fell in love with going at our own pace. Without a group to follow, we could spend as much or as little time as we wanted looking for sea life. I found nudibranch sea slugs that looked like bunched up ribbons of yellow, white, and pink hidden in the cracks of the reef. Under the edge of one boulder hid a yellow stingray with blue and green spots, a type I had not seen anywhere else. I loved looking for the small, unique creatures, which I now could do at my leisure.

Michael indicated I had begun to drift off course. I started swimming in the north by northwest direction again. I found it hard to keep perfect to the course because of the swings my compass made anytime I turned even the slightest bit. On land a compass can be held steady, but underwater it is like trying to grab a full cup of hot tea offered by a blind man: unsteady, unpredictable, and potentially harmful if guessed incorrectly. I decided to let Michael handle the compass directions and I would memorize the topography.

When things look so similar, differentiation becomes challenging. In order to memorize the seascape, I began to assign characteristics to the coral boulders based on what they looked like to me. The first few were round, square, triangular. The next few looked like a dog, a nose, and a chair. I was about to christen the next boulder Elvis-shaped when I spied an attention-grabbing item covered in coral and fish. A large, old piece of abandoned machinery, perhaps a generator, lay on its side covered in corals. Small fish swam in and out of the openings, using it as a safe place to hide. In the machinery cavity I spied an adult drum, a rare fish decorated in dizzying designs of black and white. Although it provided a nice artificial reef, I wondered how the machine wound up on the sea floor. It loomed large enough to pose a challenge to bring out there to dump. Leaving it onshore at the side of the road or in an abandoned lot would have been easier. Also, there were no shipping lanes or major docks nearby. The enterprising Bahamians discovered something new: underwater storage, a cheap and efficient way to keep one's goods as long as they did not mind a little rust and coral encrusting.

We continued on our journey past coral mounds of Sinatra and one I swore resembled the Chrysler Building. Another machine appeared, this one looking like a cross between a large lawn mower and a chicken coop. It was equally encrusted in coral and equally as mysterious as the generator. Several other manmade items revealed themselves on our journey, such as a car door, an iron gate, and some large pieces of tin roofing. The folks living on the island must be missing a lot of stuff. *Now where did I put the roof of my house?* Either the islanders were litter addicts or they desperately needed a local dump.

Our 20 minutes were up; time to turn around and head back to the boat. Immediately we became confused and could not agree on the direction. I thought we needed to head towards the boulder that looked like a Toyota. Michael insisted his compass pointed us in a different direction. We followed the compass and, lo and behold, there sat the tin roofing. We continued on, only to then see the gate. We were making progress! Abandoning the compass and the celebrity heads of coral, we navigated by the line of manmade junk all the way back to the boat.

We congratulated each other when we saw the boat in the distance at the surface. Our celebration ended quickly, however, when I saw the tail of something big sticking out from behind another coral boulder. We swam around carefully, not wanting to disturb the creature. There lay an enormous nurse shark sleeping on the bottom, perhaps the largest one we had ever seen. All eight feet of it rested while we gawked, using up the remainder of our air in our tanks as we floated around the shark in awe.

We ascended to the boat making excited hand gestures to each other about the great finish to our long, successful dive. I even pointed to Michael's compass and gave him the thumbs up sign indicating my appreciation of his basic navigation skills. Not bad for our first time alone. We climbed up the ladder at the back of our dive boat, only to realize we did not recognize any other divers onboard. A crew member approached us, a gleam in his eye.

"I don't think this is your boat. That dive boat over there is yours," Captain Obvious said, pointing to another, more familiar boat, parked at the next mooring ball along the reef 200 feet away. On the swim over to our boat we agreed that in the future we would follow the divemaster to the ends of the earth, or at least back to the correct boat.

Although the ocean plays a large part in many Bahamian activities, not all are done under the waves. Sport fishing, for example, is quite popular. The Great Bahama Canyon, an enormous submarine trench, runs right by the islands enabling all sorts of sizable game fish to visit the shores. A marina backed up to our hotel, providing ample fishing vessels for hire right at our doorstep. After a little negotiation and a flash of cash, we were headed out to sea.

Deep sea fishing teaches lessons in patience and quick response. The boat may troll the water dragging its enticing lures for an hour or more without any fish exhibiting an interest. Then suddenly, something will take the bait and the fisherman will be required to spring to life from his tropical daze, grab the fishing pole, and expertly reel the unlucky fish into the boat. I have never been able to excel at this abrupt transition from half dead state to fish battle royale.

After a twenty minute boat ride to a "secret" fishing spot, the captain slowed the boat and the mate prepared four separate fishing lines for the water. Ballyhoo, an unfortunate fish with an extremely pointy nose and streamlined body that makes it a favorite of deep sea fishing outfits across the Caribbean, headlined as the bait of the day. The mate tied a frozen ballyhoo to each hook ("The frozen ones last longer in the water," he assured us) and dropped the lines in the ocean. Now came the painful part: the wait.

The captain drove the boat in a long oval over the area, dragging the bait behind us. Back and forth we went until I finally lost count of the number of times and the direction of the boat. The captain sat at the flying bridge, the perch on top of the main cabin, so he could look for schools of fish while steering. The mate leaned against the side of the boat, staring off into space, saying little. After taking people out on the boat day after day he probably had run out of topics to cover, lost faith in humanity, or both. We trolled in silence.

Michael and I sat at the back of the boat, facing each other. I drifted off, lulled into a semi-conscious state by the rocking of the waves and the heat of the sun. For 30 minutes the boat trolled while I napped.

"Zzzzing!" one of the reels sang as a fish grabbed the bait and headed out as far away from the boat as it could get. Michael and I looked at each other blankly, awaking from our siestas. The mate grabbed the pole and gave it a hearty yank, attempting to set the hook in the mouth of the fish. If the hook isn't set, the fish can spit it out and escape at any point.

The mate handed me the pole and told me to reel. The fish pulled line out as quickly as I could collect it. I began the cadence of landing a fish on a pole; pull the tip up with all my might, then point the pole back down and quickly reel in the loose line. Up, down, reel in, over and over. My arm began to cramp, my brow to sweat. Then, I demonstrated the third lesson of deep sea fishing: know when to duck. The fish decided the snack did not warrant the effort and managed to free itself from the hook. My energetic reeling snapped the now-empty hook clear out of the water and set it on a course for my head. I felt it pop out of the water before I could see it coming so I dropped to the deck like a frozen ballyhoo to avoid being hit by the razor-sharp barb. It passed by Michael's nose with only inches to spare, flashing a bit of bait guts and his life right before his eyes.

> "Somebody just back of you while you are fishing is as bad as someone looking over your shoulder while you write a letter to your girl."
> -Ernest Hemingway

The mate shook his head sadly, re-baited the hook, and dropped it back in the water. I really wasn't to blame for losing the fish, but I could see the disappointment in his face. Protocol dictates that the tips for the captain and the mate increase with the number and quality of fish caught, so each one lost equates to dollars lost from their pockets. And, of course, it's more fun to take pictures posing with the monstrous fish caught rather than the frozen bait. I vowed to perform better next time.

We drifted back into our respective happy places, waiting the next fish strike. Another 20 minutes passed by without activity. I should have brought a deck of cards or *War and Peace*.

"Zzzzing!" went another reel, driving the mate to frenzied activity. He set the hook, and then handed the pole to Michael. Michael willed all his effort into the catch, but the fish put forth a valiant effort. Reel in, swim out. Reel in, swim out. The fight continued for more than ten minutes.

"It's got to be huge!" Michael said. "It feels like the big one!" he promised.

After a long, hard fight, Michael brought the fish to the side of boat. The mate grabbed the gaffing hook, and then replaced it in favor of a large net. A gaffing hook is used if a fish is particularly large or if it has mean teeth or pointy fins. A net is used if the fish is tiny or toothless. Michael had not landed Jaws. The mate scooped up Michael's fish and brought it into the boat. It was a perfectly tasty, but perfectly small wahoo. The mate removed the hook and held it up in front of Michael so I could take a picture

"You guys are cute together" I proclaimed, much to Michael's dismay. "It's like your little buddy! We could bring him home and put him in our fish tank." Michael's gestures indicated he did not agree with my assessment.

The rest of the afternoon passed as before, with long lulls punctuated by bursts of fish catching excitement. Several fish grabbed the bait, but spit it out before we could land them in the boat. I did manage to bring one all the way to the side, but it wasn't an edible kind so we set it free. After four hours we headed back to shore. I felt surprisingly tired despite the minimum of activity I had encountered. Somehow the rocking of the boat combined with bursts of adrenaline had wiped me out.

The mate filleted Michael's fish at the dock and gave it to us for dinner. A restaurant at the end of the dock had an excellent reputation for cooking up the catches of the day. We were famished, so we went directly to its door.

"We've got some wahoo from our trip today," I said to the woman seating us. "Can you grill it up for us?"

"Sure thing, I'll bring it back to the kitchen," she said.

A few minutes later our waiter approached with drinks and a confused look.

"Which one of you is having the wahoo?" he asked.

"I caught it, but we thought we would share it," said Michael generously, sounding like the prehistoric caveman who has hunted food and killed it for his family. *Ugg found fish to eat, now woman his forever.*

"Well...it's a petite portion. Maybe you want another meal to go with it?" he asked.

"We'll be okay with the fish. How about some veggies on the side?" Michael asked.

The waiter took our order and went back to the kitchen. The restaurant began to fill up as the charter boats returned to the dock. The establishment knew its target market well; the visiting fishermen were not going to take their catch back to their hotel room and cook it over an open fire on their balconies. As we waited for our fish to arrive, we plotted how we could open a similar place near another dock on the island and throw our current day jobs permanently into the ocean.

Ten minutes later the waiter reappeared with our plates and a basket full of bread. My plate swelled with sautéed vegetables. Almost unnoticeable next to the veggie hill, a silver dollar-sized piece of fish sat grilled to perfection. Apparently the cooking process had reduced Michael's meager catch down to children's menu proportions. The meal gave new meaning to masculine "shrinkage factor." Michael kept poking under his similar hill of veggies, looking for the rest of his fish.

"I brought some bread also, just in case you're still hungry after..." the waiter trailed off, not wanting to acknowledge the obvious, and quickly walked off to another table.

The fish took four hours of trolling to catch and four minutes to eat. But, it tasted delicious, and belonged completely to us. We toasted our exciting day with our beers and ate the entire basket of bread.

At the tail end of long vacations I always yearn for the basics. I enjoy fancy food and drink, but when I've had it for a week straight I start to want something...less complicated. On our last day in Freeport we found ourselves at a makeshift table at a small outdoor bar drinking local beer and contemplating the high points of our near-gone vacation. It was close to dinner and our stomachs rumbled.

On the wind blew a tasty smell, a pleasant combination of grill smoke and briny foods from the sea. A local vendor had set up shop across the street with a makeshift push cart that contained a small grill, space for a fry pan, a cooler, and a workspace with a cutting board. He was prepared for any meal a patron could request. *Could you please braise this reindeer?* No problem.

> Conch is a healthy food, both high in protein and low in fat. But preparing conch is not so easy. In order to get the meat out of the shell there are two options. The more violent way to access the tasties is to break the shell with a hammer, then wiggle a knife inside until the meat detaches from its home. Alternatively, pacifists can boil the whole shebang for 45 minutes then pull with all their might until the meat comes loose. True Caribbean cooks use the former method, which is a lot faster and retains the quality of the meat.

Then I spied a large bucket and the vendor's specialty became apparent. The bucket overflowed with the shells of tasty marine gastropod mollusks: he was the Conch Cook. With a quick blow to the top of the shell to break the snail's hold, he quickly wriggled the meat out, dispatched the animal to its maker, and then prepared it per the patron's tastes. Conch can be eaten raw, marinated in lime, or cooked a variety of ways such as fritters, stews, and even burgers. This particular vendor's specialty appeared to be grilled conch, the meat flattened and tenderized with a mallet, painted with some sort of sauce, and then thrown on the hot coals to roast to perfection.

We immediately agreed that the Conch Cook would be the source of our dinner, but the desired preparation was still up for negotiation. Michael favored conch ceviche, the body sliced thin and marinated in lime, salt, onions, and cilantro. I favored gastric wellness and thus preferred something well cooked. To me, the grill appeared the only way to go. We watched the patrons to see their orders and responses to their meals.

Tourists and locals alike visited the vendor. I noticed that the tourists always picked the largest conchs from the bin, keeping with the "bigger is better" theory. But, the locals chose the medium and small conchs exclusively. It cost the same, so I theorized there must be a superior taste or texture to the smaller ones that tourists just didn't know. Armed with our conch knowledge and ravenous appetites we finished our beers and walked over to the vendor.

"We'll take two," I said. "One ceviche and one grilled." The vendor reached for two of the largest conch sitting on top of the pile.

"No, I'd prefer those two," I said, pointing to two smaller ones further down in the pile.

"But these are larger," he said.

"But those taste better," I replied.

"Ah, you know the way of the conch," he said with a smile and a sincere glint in his eye, like I had been inducted into a special mollusk club. I waited for him to try the secret club handshake on me, but he went back to preparing our dinner. In a flash he had hammered mine, dispatched it, pounded it, painted it, and threw it on the grill. He moved so fast it was almost a blur. Just as quick he sliced up Michael's snail and set it in a bowl with the appropriate ingredients to marinate while mine cooked.

We paid the vendor, collected our dinner, then sat down at the nearby dock to watch the boats come in and the sun go down. Garlic butter, my snail's special sauce, dripped down my chin as I indulged. Michael's ceviche tasted excellent too. We were sad to see our vacation end, but we knew we would be back to the Conch Republic soon. After all, we were now members of the club.

CHAPTER 6

Mexico: Parasites in Paradise

The view from the top of the Temple of Kukulkan made it seem like the ancient building was taller than it looked from the ground. The step pyramid sides contained steep stairways that led to the formal temple at the top. Climbing the 91 tall and uneven steps left me breathless. I sat down and rested in the temple wall shade, laughing at Michael as he collapsed dramatically next to me from the same exertion. Breathlessness seemed to be a common ruin affliction, though, as I looked out over the vista and the captivating Mayan city of Chich'en Itza took my breath away.

The ancient Mayan were an impressive bunch. They successfully used a calendar, measured time, and performed astronomy. Without beasts of burden, machinery, or access to aliens they built monumental structures that long outlasted their empires. Even today, pockets of indigenous Mayan still live in Mexico and Central America, despite the Spanish Conquistadors' best attempts to wipe the tribe off the planet 300 years ago. They painted and sculpted, they communicated in verbal and written forms, and they traded with the outside world while maintaining their own individuality. In short, they existed brilliantly until their civilization eventually declined, leaving archeological sites that provide small but fascinating insights into this great culture.

The drive from Cancun to the Chich'en Itza ruins took three and a half hours over potholed, bumpy roads. Many tour companies make their living by shuttling tourists back and forth while educating them a little along the way. Our tour guide repeatedly referred to the site as "Chicken Pizza," clearly having grown jaded in his profession over the years. But when we arrived, his attitude changed for the better. He gave us an informed, educated site overview, demonstrating that while the tourism had become mundane, the ancient city's history and magic would never grow old.

In addition to many other marvels the Ancient Mayan accomplished, they apparently also overcame vertigo. Looking back down the steep stairs I wondered how I could climb down, envisioning a tumbling scenario that would rack

> **The Mayan Long Count calendar is reset to day 0 every 1,872,000 days, a period known as The Great Circle. The day of the reset is considered either the day the world will end, or alternatively, the day the world will be aligned and reborn (Is your glass half empty, or half full?) The next date to reset the calendar is December 21, 2012, the winter solstice.**

me up an impressive bowling score by knocking down other climbing tourists like pins. The site caretakers considerately strung a large chain down the center of the stairs so that modern day Indiana Joneses, like me, could escape the mortal peril in which they had placed themselves. I went down the stairs one at a time on my behind, clutching the chain in my right hand all the way back down.

The Mexican jungle and the elements had not been kind to the buildings' aesthetics. The basic structures were there, but the decoration and the more delicate architectural touches have eroded over time. Over the years several groups, including the Mexican government, restored many of the buildings in order to learn more about the Mayan civilization and also to drive tourism. From the temple top I had a commanding view of the sprawling building complex, which looked to me like a large city. From my reading, however, I knew the surrounding jungle concealed and consumed many more of the ancient city's buildings than I could see, hiding them from view. In its heyday, the city was positively enormous.

The site boasted a variety of buildings for different purposes. I loved the collection of temples, many dedicated to animals and warriors. I found the creative stone carving reliefs on the buildings both fascinating and disturbing. Graceful carved faces of deities, animals, and glyphs mingled with unsettling human sacrifice and mutilation scenes. Like any big city, some buildings were functional, like the bath house, and some were meant for a higher, unintelligible purpose, such as the "House of Mysterious Writing." Even the buildings meant for education were aesthetic, such as El Caracol, a snail shell-shaped structure built to enable astronomical event observation.

"So what happens to your Red Sox when they win?" the guide asked Michael, who could not go a day without his favorite team's hat on his head.

"I collect my gambling winnings and the Yankees cry," he said, hopefully. We stood at one end of a huge, sunken sports field, about 500 feet long, by 300 feet wide. The ancient architects built long walls on either side to contain the sports activity. Two stone rings carved with snakes jutted out from the opposing walls.

"The Mayan played the game *pitz* here in the ball court. Two teams would try to hit a rubber ball through the rings using their hips. As the losers, the Yankees would be killed. Look here," he said, pointing to a pitz team carving in the side of the wall. One carving was particularly gruesome: a man with his head cut off, spurting blood that became serpents. The Mayan were not a subtle people.

"We think that the winners were also killed, sacrificed to the gods to honor their victory," he added. Michael thought through that idea with a frown on his face. Today, when the Red Sox win they are thrown a ticker tape parade to appease the fans. When the Mayan teams won they were thrown into the nearby Sagrado sinkhole to appease the gods. Fans could be brutal, but I think I know which era of teams got the better end of that deal.

The Chich'en Itza complex sprawled, with more to see than could be accomplished in one day. After four hours of visiting the site, we piled back into the tour van for the bumpy ride back to the hotel. The trip, though long, provided one of the few truly cultural and educational activities a visitor to Cancun could do. From then on I would think about the Mayan every time the Red Sox beat the Yankees.

The ocean has its share of things that go "bump" in the night (though underwater they sound more like a "swish"). My fear of the unknown swish drove my aversion to night diving. Anything swimming around in the dark in the ocean must have better eyesight than I do and worse eating habits, making me the perfect snack. Not to mention that when the sun goes down, the water feels cold, even if the actual temperature doesn't change much. Nope, I harbor no love for diving in the dark.

Many people, however, are fans. They argue that some sea life can only be seen at night. This argument does not sway me, since I know on what end of the hunt I would land. Many divers also like the thrill of the unknown, preferring to be surprised when something bumps them or swims unexpectedly into the light of their underwater flashlights. These are the same people who like really scary horror movies and roller coasters. I am not one of these people.

Our diving friends from our Caribbean cruise, Tim and Amy, joined us in Cozumel for a long diving weekend. They are the scary movie and frightening roller coaster sort, and tried to convince us to do a night dive with them. Michael looked so excited when they invited us that I could not say no. Maybe it would be a good dive. Maybe the ax murderer would not kill the whole family before the movie's end. Who knows?

We four divers, the divemaster, and the captain filled the boat. As we sped out to the dive site, I piled on wetsuit layers to keep me warm. The dive company lent me an extra black neoprene vest and a thick hood. I looked like an evil Michelin Man.

Before I knew it, the boat stopped and the captain anchored to a mooring ball. This dive would be a drift dive like most in Cozumel. The current would gently pull us along, taking us on a nighttime, underwater world tour. Or, alternatively, the current would rage, smashing us into the coral heads and damage us beyond repair. It would just depend on the current strength, which we would determine only after we entered the water. *Fun.* After a brief dive overview, the divemaster handed us each underwater flashlights and we entered the water together via a backroll.

The hood disoriented me underwater. The neoprene over my ears caused sounds to echo and muffle. An air pocket lodged itself in the top of the hood, making me look like a conehead. I focused on slowing down my breathing, cognizant that I would use up my air quickly if I did not relax.

We descended to 35 feet, and then turned on the flashlights. The illuminated burst of reef activity surprised me; no one had told the fish it was bedtime. Some sea life I recognized, but others were completely new to me, having hidden themselves in the reef cracks during the day. Lobsters walked along the sandy bottom completely exposed. The crustaceans looked huge with their whole bodies on display, rather than just their antennae they extend during the sunshine hours. The epicurean sight made my stomach rumble.

Several fish were encased in what looked like a whitish bubble. These were parrot fish sleeping, covered in protective mucus to ward off hungry predators. Basket stars, starfish that spread their arms to filter feed at night, lined the coral, making the most of the passing current cafeteria line. Before long, I realized my fear had been replaced by curiosity.

The divemaster led us into a shallow cave, a place in which I would have felt very uncomfortable during the day. Normally I would have avoided its dark, monster-hiding recesses and claustrophobic size. But, at night, our flashlights reflected off the walls illuminating every nook and cranny, revealing a tie-dyed riot of colorful coral growing on every inch of exposed rock. I could see why divers appreciated night diving. If one could overcome the fear factor, it was...a whole different world.

We swam out of the cave and drifted over the shallower reef. The current pulled us along gently as our flashlights enabled a voyeuristic fish peep show. Suddenly, my flashlight went out. The divemaster warned me this might happen, as the enormous light bulbs easily overheat. One by one the other flashlights also extinguished. I clung to Michael's hand, not wanting to lose him in the blackness. My nighttime fears returned.

Michael shook my hand gently. I could see an outline of his other arm making a sweeping gesture to the reef below. As I looked out over the reef I realized I could see without the artificial light as my eyes became accustomed to the darkness. The reef and my fellow divers bathed in an eerie illuminating glow from the moonlight and its reflection against the sandy bottom. We floated effortlessly along taking in the picture of the reef as a whole, rather than pinpointing any one item living there. For me, dives had always been about finding specific examples of sea life, but this put it all into perspective; the fish and reef all existed together. It was beautiful.

We finally ascended and climbed into the boat. The excitement and the exertion had exhausted me. I handed my flashlight back to the captain, remarking that all five flashlights had all burnt out and would need new bulbs.

"You think?" he asked with a smile in his eyes.

"Um, Karen..." said Tim hesitantly "We all turned ours off when yours burnt out. We knew it would be a better experience without them, but we didn't want to freak you out at first."

I just smiled, not able to be mad after the transcendent dive we just enjoyed. Some things must be learned through experience to be believed.

Sometimes car rental is a necessary evil. We wanted the flexibility to drive to some of the towns near Cozumel, but all that stop and go would not work with a taxi. After taking the ferry to the mainland, we planned to visit some local places such as Playa del Carmen. The rental agent first tried to give us a rusty old Ford. When I opened the passenger side door, a cockroach leapt to its freedom. We requested a different car minus the rust and critters. The agent offered a tiny, emerald green Honda that appeared fine, though a strong wind could have knocked it off the road. We waved as we sped away, promising to return the car later that day.

The countryside appeared peaceful, though desolate between towns. It looked like tourism brought money to the hot spots and forgot the rest. Playa del Carmen was colorful, but definitely meant for visitors. I didn't get the sense anyone actually lived in the city, but rather in its more authentic environs. We had a nice lunch and stopped at a roadside market for some handicrafts on the way home. It wasn't the truly Mexican experience that we had wanted, but we enjoyed the day anyway.

We headed back to the ferry dock, approaching it down a road with farmland on either side. Suddenly, a large pig stepped out into the road from behind some machinery and rocks at the road side. Michael swerved the car and sped up, narrowly managing to miss it. As the beast oinked angrily, we let out a relieved sigh. The pig looked sturdy, the car not so much.

Suddenly, sirens and red flashing lights appeared behind us, the international symbol for police. Michael pulled over to the road side to let them pass, but instead they pulled up behind us and got out of their car. *Not good*, I thought. Michael turned off the car and rolled down the window to talk with the approaching officer. I could almost hear the pig laughing as it ambled off down the road, unscathed.

"Hola. What are you doing out here today?" the officer asked.

"We were just going back to our hotel," Michael said. "We visited some towns on the coast."

The officer chewed gum, looking at us with a sneer that expanded with each chomp. I noticed my hands had gotten sweaty, like moist guilt indicators. Except, we hadn't done anything wrong. Funny how mere police presence makes me feel guilty, even when I'm not.

"You were speeding, amigo. We don't allow that around here."

"I didn't think I was speeding. I had to swerve around that pig, I didn't want to hit it," said Michael, nervously.

"Yes, but you were speeding around the pig. You will have to go to court to be fined. Give me your license."

"Will I get it back?"

"Yes, after the court hears your case."

"Do we go there now?"

"No, it will take the court a week or two to get to it," the office said with a smile.

Michael looked at me hesitantly. I nodded with a "go ahead" gesture. I knew what he intended to do. I really didn't think we were speeding. I also did not think that the officer wanted to go to court. I did think that the police were looking for a small "donation" to their cause, presumably called Save the Pigs. Clearly Michael thought the same thing.

"Perhaps we could just pay the fine to you, sir," said Michael innocently. He excelled at "tipping" compared to me. I fumbled and stuttered with crumpled bills while he could smoothly shake hands with people while transferring a bit of cash to the other palm. It was a gift in which my honest face could never excel.

"Yes, I think that is okay," the officer said with a smile, probably pleased that he did not even have to suggest it first. "The fine is 100 pesos."

One hundred pesos? All of this drama for $20? Michael eagerly handed over the money and started up the car.

"And give me the bottle of tequila," the officer said, pointing to an expensive bottle in the back seat that we bought as a souvenir. "You must not drink and drive in Mexico. It could be very dangerous."

Not as dangerous as wandering pigs, however.

Divers are always looking for the next big adventure. Somewhere in history a diver decided that scuba diving in the Mexican oceans lost its luster. He packed up his gear, hiked through the jungle, and jumped into a cenote to up the adrenaline factor. Some people are just never satisfied.

A cenote is an open sinkhole that contains groundwater. It connects via tunnels to subterranean water bodies. The water in a cenote is crystal clear because it is filled with rain water that has filtered through the ground. Cenotes are not known for fish sightings. Instead, it's the amazing rock formations and the thrill of cavern diving that call to divers time and time again.

The Yucatan Peninsula, the part of Mexico where Cancun is located, abounds with cenotes. Several famous cave systems are there, including Ox Bel Ha, the longest underground river and cave system in the world. Many cave explorers believe the cave systems are actually all linked, though only a few connection points have been found. Year after year cave divers find new pathways and pieces to this mysterious underwater world.

Normally cave diving requires a specialized scuba diving certification due to the increased skill needed to navigate in a closed environment and the heightened danger level. It is possible, however, to explore some cenote parts without this certification because of their size, shape, and availability of large breathable air pockets throughout the caverns. The thought of diving inside a cave scared the heck out of me, but we could not leave Mexico without trying this location-specific extreme sport.

The dive company we hired took us to Dos Ojos, or two eyes, named for two openings in the cavern wall that appear as if they are watching the divers inside the cave. Ronnie, our divemaster for the day, picked us up in a 4x4 and drove out to the cenote site in the middle of the jungle. We arrived early in the morning, which enabled us to avoid the crowds. Later in the day snorkeler groups would show up to float on the top of the open cenote, blocking the light and stirring up sediment.

The cenote appeared as an open slash of water on the jungle floor. The water clarity reflected the sunlight, making the pool glow an unearthly turquoise that disappeared under a large cave overhang at one end. We carried our gear the short way from the dirt parking lot to the pool edge. Fortunately the water line was near the rim, requiring only a giant stride to enter the deep hole. Some cenotes have high, steep sides that necessitate the use of rope lines and rappelling to reach the water surface. My lack of coordination would have prevented me from successfully executing that Spider Man maneuver.

Standing in my 30-plus pounds of gear at the lip of a flooded under-water cavern made my heart pump fast. I wanted to jump in, and at the same time, run back to the jeep and drive away. I was excited yet terrified of the unknown before me. I took a giant step into the pool, and the tur-quoise swallowed me.

I could see over 200 feet in every direction, an almost unheard of dis-tance in the open ocean. Boulders lined the cenote bottom, with an occa-sional stalagmite sticking straight up, created from years of limestone depos-its dripped from the ceiling before the cavern roof collapsed and filled with water. The grey and black rock shadows stood in stark relief to the glowing turquoise water around them. The sight conveyed a sense of eerie calm.

After ensuring our group successfully made it to the bottom, Ronnie led us to a large, dark opening. My heart beat, which I had fought to calm after entering the water, raced again at the thought of entering the black hole. As anyone who has ever watched a *Star Trek* episode can attest, nothing good ever happens to a person who enters a black hole. There is usually an intergalactic funeral service before the next commercial runs.

With great trepidation and determination, I followed Ronnie through the hole. I knew I would sorely regret it later if I did not complete the dive. After just a few moments my eyes adjusted to the ambient light shining from the cavern we left and from a few small holes in the ceiling in the new cavern we entered. An almost completely intact roof overhead indicated that we swam in a true cave. Stalactites hung down from the ceiling, the result of more limestone deposits dripping over the years before the cave flooded. It was *Jurassic Park* meets *Finding Nemo*.

Parts of the cave ceiling resembled flat mirrors, like liquid mercury floating at the surface. After getting Ronnie's attention I pointed to the phenomenon and made a clear sign: "What in the world is that?" He led us slowly upwards to the reflection and indicated we should put one hand above our heads as we ascended in order to avoid bumping into anything sharp.

Like magic, my hand pierced the liquid metal reflection and entered... air. I continued to ascend with our group and surfaced above the water line but still inside the cave. Surprisingly, five feet or more of room stretched between the water and the ceiling. Ronnie took out his regulator and motioned for us to do the same.

"Here is the reason so many divers can enjoy the cenotes," he said. "Air pockets like this exist throughout the cave system. And, the water is so clear that the light from the skylights reflects off of every surface, lighting our way without the use of torches."

We descended back into the water to tour the room, exploring the unique geological collage that decorated the cavern. The strange underwater world attracted my attention so much that I forgot my camera in my pocket. I pulled it out towards the end of the dive and captured a few rock and diver silhouettes against the blue. The impressive panorama provided opportunities for pictures that made even my meager photography skills look good.

We returned to the main cavern back through the opening in the wall, once menacing, now enchanting since I knew what lay beyond. The turquoise glow grew brighter as the sun rose overhead, hitting the pool directly. I looked up towards the surface and saw...a rear end. The end had dangling feet, a neon orange inflation vest and several other similar ends bobbing around it.

A snorkeler group had entered the water, providing us with an underbelly view of natural wonders we did not care to see. We returned to the surface and loaded up the jeep before too many more people arrived. The solitary quiet had added to the formation's beauty, and I preferred to remember it that way.

"The road has too many holes, I can't drive down it," the cab driver said. "Number 571 is there on the right," he added, pointing down a dark street to a series of nondescript, shadowy doorways that could have been the entrances to anything: homes, brothels, pet shops, prisons. We paid him the small fare and exited the cab, hesitating to leave the only sign of congenial life around.

Cabo San Lucas is a sea side resort town with money flowing through its veins. Tourists come in from all over the world for the area's notorious big-game fishing and irrigation-fed, sprawling golf courses. Michael, my father, and I came to Cabo to celebrate my father's birthday. Our hotel concierge had provided the name of a unique, local restaurant where we could celebrate the big day.

As I exited the cab, however, I started to have doubts. The dark street appeared deserted except for a small group of men standing at the far corner, staring at us. I'd watched enough low-budget horror movies to know it is always the innocent woman who gets carted off first by the monster, mobster, or man-eating lizard. We walked down the street and I awaited my fate.

The door marked "571" functioned only as a portal and not as a decorative item. Its matte black paint flanked by dark windows stated "ignore this door" rather than "restaurant inside." I hesitated. Did I knock or do I just open the door? It looked too much like someone's home to just barge in, unannounced. I knocked.

A well-dressed man answered the door and ushered us into a small vestibule containing a few uncomfortable-looking chairs and little else. In the corner stood a woman at a podium with a reservation book, the first sign that this place provided food and not funeral services. She verified our reservation by asking me a long list of questions including hotel, arrival date, and origin country. If she asked my bra size we were leaving, I decided. Fortunately, my powers of persuasion convinced her we really were the Begelfer party of three. How many could there be?

The man who greeted us at the door led us down a narrow dark corridor that would have been creepy except for the faint but luscious scent of food wafting our way. We turned a corner to face another doorway. Unlike the first one, however, skilled hands had carved this door from warm brown wood, polished to perfection by many years of tender care and frequent use. Golden light and a sweet, warm breeze blew through the door, as we stepped into an enchanted world.

Stairs led down to a lush green lawn. Linen-covered tables were sprinkled around the grass, partially hidden by various bushes and shrubs covered with blooming flowers. Ancient trees grew at the lawn fringes, their top limbs soaring one hundred feet or more into the sky. The contrast between the stark public street and the captivating yard made the scene even more startling. It was truly a fairy garden.

The lighting caught my eye the most. Large baskets made with loosely woven tree branches were hung in the trees at all heights like natural chandeliers. The baskets contained twinkling bulbs that gave off a warm glow, giving me the impression of cages of fireflies. Candles appeared on every table, and on several small holders in between for extra light. The overall effect radiated an ethereal and elegant presence.

The man showed us to our table, leaving us in quiet amazement. While we soaked in the beauty, the waiter brought us Spanish-language menus. When our attention finally turned to the meal at hand, we realized we were clueless as to what to order. The questioning hostess we met up front came to our table to kindly translate some of the main ingredients into English. I have a weakness for shrimp, no matter the preparation, and so my decision was easy. Michael ordered chicken while my father chose the "mild white fish," its exact name lost in translation. We sat back with glasses of cool white wine and enjoyed our surroundings.

Just as soon as my stomach began to protest from hunger, our dinners arrived. Calling my meal shrimp insulted this sea life. These were surely king prawns, almost as large as softballs. They were artfully presented on the plate, staring cheerily at me with their heads still attached. My father's fish tasted light and tender, and Michael's chicken was bathed in a rich butter and mushroom sauce. No fancy hotel restaurant could have compared to this local wonder that excelled in food and ambiance alike. We toasted my father's birthday, a night we would not soon forget.

Although it is unfair to address an entire country's highlights with a list of superficial "best of" thoughts, I'd like to try. Below are some Mexico traveling insights I have compiled from my experiences.

<u>Eat something very spicy for the taste, not the heat.</u> At a small restaurant in San Jose de Cabo I ate one of the spiciest and tastiest dinners I have ever had. The chef grilled the firm-fleshed fish with a local pepper and onion sauce that had a spicy heat, but incredible flavor. I believe the local, most popular dish is usually the best one to pick, especially if I'm not familiar with the cooking style but I want something authentic.

There are two kinds of spicy: spicy flavorful and spicy hot. Americans tend to think of spicy as a blinding pain on the tongue, rather than the epicurean experience it can be in other cultures. Mexican cooks use a variety of hot peppers in many dishes, which adds not just spice but also loads of flavor. Avoiding anything considered "spicy" might very well mean missing some of the most flavorful dishes on the menu.

<u>Be prepared for the trip, but don't pack like the voyage is to Mars.</u> Before a business trip to Monterrey, one of the administrators at my office handed out "health packets" that included every known pill, ointment, and bandage that could be purchased legally in the U.S. One Band-Aid extended to a good six inches, though I think if any of us had a reason to use it there would be some larger issues at hand. The Mexicans in our group were offended, as the packet seemed to indicate their society had not progressed beyond the Prehistoric age.

Be prepared. Be comfortable. Be mindful of things that could be detrimental (for example, do not consume anything that came from a rusty spigot, rusty machete, or rusty restaurant.) But, don't be limited by ten suitcases and a weighty amount of concern that some great necessity will be unavailable. Mexico has drug stores, grocery stores, and even gracious people who are willing to help if the traveler just asks nicely.

<u>Drink tequila that is meant to be sipped</u>. Many people, including myself, have learned the hard way that tequila can be a vile mistress. But, I also now know that sipping tequila is not an oxymoron. At a small, classy bar in a not-so-small, not-so-classy Mexican town a bartender introduced me to top shelf tequila, a whole shelf of them to be exact, that were never meant to be mixed with syrupy juice and crushed ice. The alcohol resonated with an earthy greenness and a quality to rival a good scotch or bourbon.

Embrace tequila, the local drink of the gods. Pour it into a fruity drink if necessary, but at least try sipping a high quality one while in Mexico. Top shelf tequila by the glass is easier to find in Mexico than in other countries. Many people who seek out the best wind up going home with a new favorite beverage.

<u>Get absorbed into the culture</u>. While working in Monterrey I learned that some of my co-workers were going to spend a few hours on the weekend volunteering with the surrounding community. I volunteered with them, painting a local school building inside and out. The two-story, cinder-block structure held barred windows with no glass. One electric light bulb hung in the middle of each classroom for light. I met some of the children who were playing ball in the courtyard out front; their rudimentary facilities not affecting their enthusiasm and joy. They were happy and thankful, and I could not help but fall in love with them all.

The closer one can get to a place's people, the better one can understand a country and a culture. Vacations can be all about rest, relaxation and decadence, but to truly experience a place, the visitor has to eschew the glitz and glamour for a bit and search out the true essence of a place.

This usually means leaving the beaten path and taking advantage of good opportunities when they come along. Hanging on my office wall I still have a thank you card, drawn in crayon, from one of the students.

<u>Swim with the sea lions.</u> In Cabo San Lucas I swam with sea lions. I snorkeled, actually, but spent just as much time with my head above water watching them on the surface as I did with my head in the water watching them dive. The lions stayed a reasonable distance from me, but also did not seem concerned by my presence. Serious restrictions about how a person interacts with the creatures have preserved the activity's quality as well as the lions' respect for the swimmers.

Sure, swimming with lions sounds a bit dangerous. And it can be, if one is not careful. But, there are many things a visitor can embrace in the Mexican seas that are not to be missed and wonderful to experience. Sea lions, dolphins, migrating whales, even whale sharks all enjoy the country's nutrient-rich waters. All of these amazing aquatic animals will impress, and most likely none can be found in the visitor's home town.

<u>Stay in a local hotel.</u> The hotel I stay in when visiting Cozumel has a lot of charm and few Americans. It is affordable and clean, with a decent breakfast and warm, welcoming service. Once, we checked in wearing dripping wetsuits while a friendly maid stood behind us with a mop and a smile during the whole process. On another occasion we helped the staff capture a snake that had slithered into the pool. There are a lot fancier hotels in Cozumel, but now this one feels like home. I would not stay anywhere else.

Sometimes a local hotel just won't do, like when high-end luxury is a must or to see and be seen is the goal. But sometimes a local hotel can give the traveler just what they need: a quality place, at a good price, with friendly, personal service. And best of all, a local hotel enables the traveler to get closer to the country they are visiting, as opposed to a generic hotel room that could be located anywhere in the world.

Dance on a table. I'm not that person. Really. My idea of a good time on a Friday night is reading an interesting book accompanied by a full bag of Oreo cookies. But there I was, shaking my groove thing while standing on a table in a cool bar on a hot night in Mexico. The bouncer had to encourage me to stand on the chair only, as someone might want to use the table for its intended purpose later in the evening. It was out of character for me, it was silly, and it was fun.

Mexico is a great place to let loose, as many people do it, and therefore any one individual will probably go unnoticed. Whole cities, like Cancun, are dedicated to the hedonistic and the inebriated. Make no mistake about it, there is nothing cultural about this pursuit, as tourists surrounded the table dancer in question. However, life without any fun is, well…no fun. Mexico is great for enabling the traveler to party with abandon, even if for just one night.

Get lost in ancient ruins. People have inhabited Mexico for tens of thousands of years. Many civilizations, including the Aztecs, the Mayan, and even the early Spanish left a wealth of ruins and artifacts behind, countless of which can be seen today with ease. For example, Chich'en Itza, the great Mayan city, is only four hours outside Cancun. Modern day Mexico City sits atop the ruins of the Aztec capital city of Tenochtitlan, parts of which still can be seen today.

Visiting the ruins is a great way to learn about a country's past by seeing the relics that still exist today. The Mexican government and other philanthropic foundations have worked hard to preserve many sites, making them simple to access, safe to view, and easy to interpret.

Leave Cancun. My first three trips to Mexico I went to Cancun, possibly the most famous Mexican destination for U.S. tourists. The hotels were nice, the food tasty, and the nightlife entertaining. I spent most of my outdoor time at the pool. I realize now that if I only went there for the hotel, American food, bars, and pool, I could have stayed at home (or at least went to Florida instead) and saved my money.

Cancun is easy to get to and certainly a fun town, but has little true Mexican culture to it (Senor Frog's Bar definitely does not count). It is a great place to vacation if one wants to simply get away vs. get away *to* somewhere for the purpose of experiencing that destination. There are plenty of other Mexican towns that combine creature comforts with a more authentic Mexican experience. If Cancun is a must, then at least consider leaving for a day trip to see some of the surrounding towns and cultural destinations like ruins or local beaches. The true traveler will be glad they did.

CHAPTER 7

U.S. Virgin Islands:
Duty Free Rum, Lack of Rhythm, and
Other Indications You Might Be a Tourist

St. Thomas

The U.S. bought St. Thomas, St. John, and St. Croix from the Dutch for $25 million in gold during World War I. They've been reselling it to cruise ship visitors ever since. From our mega ship's deck, St. Thomas' capital, Charlotte Amalie, looked sprawling. People swarmed the main street and alleys, like ants on a seaside mound. As we pulled into port, passengers crowded the Lido deck, chomping at the bit to get into the downtown shopping haven. Michael and I decided to take in the view from the top deck and give the antsy steeds an opportunity to get out of the gate first.

As a general rule I don't purchase souvenirs in the places I visit. Michael and I are known to bring home pieces of artwork or indigenous, quality handicrafts to decorate our home and remind us of our travels. But, T-shirts, carved coconuts, maracas, goods with a 'Made in China' sticker on them, and other tourist kitsch never make it into my suitcase. The St. Thomas vendors, however, tested my resolve.

From the moment we disembarked, vendors bombarded us with goods of all shapes and sizes. We strolled down a tree-lined and vendor-ladened road, our eyes wide with amazement. Each T-shirt vendor sold clothing in hundreds of different designs. The woven palm frond vendors had a palm hat haberdashery and a zoo's worth of palm animals. Need a personalized key chain for that special man in your life? Find his name in the pile that included Tom, Dick, and Harry as well as Francois, Fernando, Sven, and Vlad. This place was an international shop-a-holic's dream.

As we approached the downtown area, the tourist crowd thickened. Five ships docked in port that day, practically doubling the St. Thomas population. The collective anticipation of a bargain hung thick in the air. Despite the heady mix of tourists, sun, and a lack of deodorant, we pressed on, wanting to see the city before escaping back to our ship.

> **"We are rapidly approaching a world comprised entirely of jail and shopping."**
> **-Doug Coupland**

We arrived downtown, where the vending delivery system evolved from goods on tarps to goods offered in brick and mortar stores. The nature of the goods changed too; I realized the initial vendors were small-time, like shopping appetizers. Before us lay the main course: stores overflowing with jewelry and alcohol. Tourists streamed into the stores like they were giving away product for free.

The scene provided a case study in selling techniques. Signs advertised irresistible opportunities like "Duty Free" and "Going Out of Business." Attractive men stood at the store fronts hawking good deals and free samples. Air conditioners blew cold gusts out the store doors towards hot tourists. We had to give them credit. They knew their market well. Intrigued by all the excitement, we entered a liquor store to see what all the fuss was about.

"How can I help you today?" asked a smooth-talking gentleman with a gold front tooth.

"I'd like to price some rum," Michael said. He did? This was news to me.

Mr. Gold Tooth showed us his impressive selection. The familiar brands sported economical deals and the lesser known kinds were priced to really move. How good could a five-dollar gallon of rum be? It would be a shrewd purchase because it could double as paint thinner.

"These are all nice, but I can see you are connoisseurs," the salesman said. "This is the one you really want," he promised, as he caressed a rainbow-colored bottle shaped like a marauding sailing ship. "Captain's Rum" proclaimed the label, complete with a winking pink parrot. The bottle's design made an alcoholic political statement for gay pirates.

"This is the finest rum we carry, captured in a hand crafted, souvenir bottle that will be the envy of your friends." *Sure.* The bottle could decorate our mantle with pirate chic. I could not imagine my friends envying this find. Perhaps I had the wrong friends.

I turned to Michael, ready to deliver my "let's think about it" line in order to escape the salesman before he really turned on the charm. A glimmer in Michael's eyes surprised me, indicating that this pirate ship of rum would be sailing home with us.

"You have *got* to be kidding me," I said, with genuine disbelief. Items like this fueled the yard sale trade across America.

"You don't even know if it is any good. We can get a bottle of Cutty Sark when we get home. It has a nice picture of a ship on the bottle."

"But this is handcrafted. We'll be the envy of our friends." Michael had lost all rational thought; I was not going to win this one.

We left the shop, the gay pirate rum tucked neatly in a bag under Michael's arm. The salesman's gold tooth gleamed in the sunlight as he walked us to the door and wished us safe travels. I could only picture the high fives and back slapping that would occur between the salesmen after we left, celebrating the superlatively hideous bottle sale. Michael strutted down the road as we continued the tour of conspicuous consumption, clearly pleased with his special find.

We walked down the road, window shopping. The jewelry stores, in particular, provided a great deal of visual entertainment. All manner of ropes, chains, and gold and silver strands shared the spotlight with unicorn charms, horseshoe-shaped earrings, and bracelets spelling out "Yankees Rule" in semi-precious stones. One store's window highlighted their crown jewel: a gaudy gold headdress that would have made King Tut jealous. I had to enter the store and see what other treasures lay inside.

"How can I help you?" asked a salesman with another gold tooth. I sensed a trend.

"We just wanted to look around," I said, trying to discourage rabid sales tactics.

"You need sapphires. Everyone is buying sapphires. It is the hot item right now, mon."

Did I need sapphires? I wasn't sure. I certainly did not feel a burning need. I did have a sapphire engagement ring, however. Perhaps I needed something to match it? I shook my head, trying to clear my mind that was clouded by retail temptation. I struggled. *Must...escape the call of the... tacky...jewelry.*

"Do you have any pendants?" I asked dreamily.

Out flew three trays of sapphire pendants, almost as if by magic. Each sparkled prettier than the last. One with sapphires set in a square, geometrical pattern in white gold called to me, appealing to my Type A need for balance and symmetry.

"How much?" I asked.

"Do you really need that?" asked Michael. "You have lots of necklaces at home." Logic possessed him, but jewelry fever possessed me.

Before I knew it, the pendant hung on a thin white gold chain around my neck. By the time my wits returned, we were on our way back to the ship. We walked in silence, both proud and horrified by the purchases we never intended to make and surely did not need. We hurried back up the gangway before the vendors could work any more island shopping mojo on us. As I closed in on the last few feet of land, I practically ran onto the ship; my desire for a "Sven" keychain could not be contained for much longer.

"Move a little to your left," I said, waving my arms towards Michael, trying to get a mental picture of how our wedding would look if it took place on the cliff on which we stood at the mouth of the St. Thomas harbor. For this visit we flew to the island to stay for a long weekend, rather than stop there for a few hours while on a cruise. Our visit's purpose was unique: to determine if St. Thomas would be the site of our ceremony.

The rich blue Caribbean ocean stretched out behind him as far as the eye could see. The hotel built the manmade platform, balanced precariously on the cliffside, to host breathtaking events amid the breathtaking view. I had to admit it was a spectacular place to get hitched.

"If the sun sets over there our pictures would be fabulous," I said, as our nuptials continued to unfold in my mind.

"And if it sets over there we will be blind during the ceremony," Michael said, stating the obvious and practical, with a hint of impatience. I had dragged him all over the hotel that morning, looking at the function rooms, evaluating the catering, and discussing the room options for our guests. I saved the best for last, the actual ceremony location, because I knew it was the hotel's best feature. I did not want it to cloud my judgment about the rest of the facility.

I never thought I would say it, but thank God for Cindy Crawford. One Sunday morning my mother called to inform me that Cindy had gotten married in the Bahamas. The *People* magazine photos were amazing, she assured me. What did I think about getting married in the Caribbean? Based on our mutual love of the ocean, Michael and I had already embraced the tropical wedding idea. However, we had not figured out how to broach the beach wedding subject with my parents without suffering the nuclear war fallout affects. Thanks to Cindy, our problem was solved.

We spent a long, enjoyable weekend on St. Thomas. Being based on the island, we were able to avoid the cruise ship crowds and embrace the more subtle appeal of the place. The island offered a lot to do once a visitor got past the duty free frenzy that engulfed the downtown area.

With only three days to spare, we didn't have the usual time to dedicate to scuba diving. We wanted to experience some of the island's pastimes our wedding guests might try. We booked a short snorkel cruise with a middle-aged couple that had realized their dream of selling their home, buying a sailboat, and moving to the islands. We snorkeled the local reefs, which were surprisingly alive despite Charlotte Amalie's large port nearby. Colorful tropical fish exploded around each bend, while large green sea turtles accompanied us on our aquatic tour. So far, so good.

We booked a tour on a World Cup sailboat, learning about the race, the ship's history, and how to sail. Our visit to the MountainTop complex provided breathtaking views of St. Thomas and the British Virgin Islands. The fishing charters we saw returning from their day at sea held piles of mackerel, bonefish, grouper, and snappers. Even the restaurants were a positive experience, simple local eateries with fantastic fresh food, like diamonds in the rough. Since we avoided the most crowded places, like the rum factory and the shopping districts, our opinion of the island increased dramatically from our last trip.

Late in the afternoon on our last day in St. Thomas we purchased two fruity, tropical drinks from the bar and headed back out to the cliffside platform to overlook the harbor and the open ocean. Several empty lounge chairs sitting in the shade of a large palm indicated we were not the only hotel guests that appreciated the spot. We relaxed in the chairs and soaked in the view.

"What do you think?" I asked Michael.

"It certainly is pretty. I think that people would have plenty to do here. I can't really see a downside."

"I could easily see us getting married here," I said. The process of finding a good location for the wedding had been long, but St. Thomas seemed like it was worth the wait.

I saw something move out of the corner of my eye. A lizard, a really large one, walked towards us lazily. Judging by his size, the hotel guests fed this monster frequently. I tossed him the orange slice from my glass, hoping he would take it and return to the bushes. Big mistake. Another lizard friend emerged from the bushes, wanting to share in the daiquiri bounty. The second loomed even bigger than the first, over three feet from head to tail.

"Look! We could have extra guests at our wedding!" Michael exclaimed. I didn't find it odd to see the creatures stalking about the palms, but I could imagine the panic from the guests if one followed me up the aisle. Would it agree to wear a little lizard tux? Maybe I could ride it.

Suddenly a green blur flew from the palm tree above, bounced on Michael's lounge chair, and landed on the ground between us. We, in turn, levitated out of our chairs and wound up standing several yards away, with shared looks of surprise and horror. A third lizard now sat on the ground between our chairs looking out of sorts and a bit pissed, as if we had something to do with its plummeting descent. With a hiss and a sassy tail swish, he turned around and headed back to the bushes. Honestly, what kind of lizard falls out of a tree? I swear I could hear the other two lizards laugh as they followed the sky diver back into the foliage. If party crashers like this came with the location, we might have to find a new venue.

St. Croix

Certain times of the year the only way to get from St. Thomas to St. Croix is by sea plane. This was one of those times. We stood on the floating airport patio, ducking as our ride arrived, buzzed overhead, and executed its planned landing with an unceremonious splash in the harbor. Our pursuit of scuba diving had introduced us to some unique means of transport over the years, none the least of which was this great Caribbean duck.

St. Croix is the largest, but least talked about destination in the U.S. Virgin Islands. Columbus landed on the island in 1493. It changed hands many times over the years until the U.S. purchased it from the Dutch in 1917. The island's combination of European and American influences make it a modern, sophisticated vacation destination. But its legendary fish-filled reefs and menagerie of super-small sea creatures were what really spurred Michael and I to make the trip.

Michael and I were joined by six other passengers on our flight to St. Croix. Our bodies and our luggage had to be arranged to keep the weight balanced for the flight. The crew used a rusty scale to weigh the luggage and then placed each piece strategically in the various cargo holds. A crew member then turned his attention to the passengers, quizzing them on their weight and placing us accordingly throughout the seats.

I have accused the scale at the doctor's office of being "a few pounds off, no?" At the weigh-in at Weight Watchers meetings I have taken off my shoes, socks, jacket, jewelry, and other clothing pieces not meant to be discarded in public in order to keep the scale from tipping too far in the wrong direction. My self-declared weight listed on my driver's license is... optimistic. Surely I am not the only person in the world with this weight-driven, self-conscious character flaw. If plane balance proved an issue, was the honor system truly the best way to determine our weights and ensure our safety? I would have preferred that they loaded us each onto the rusty scale for verification, just to be sure.

Before I knew it, we loaded up, shut the door, the lone pilot climbed in, and the twin engines roared to life. After a quick taxi to a clearing in the harbor, the engines throttled to full force, and we lifted gracefully off the water into the air. After the jarring landing I witnessed before, the smooth takeoff surprised me.

The plane droned loudly, drowning out any attempt at conversation. The view, though, was expansive enough to keep my interest the whole flight. From the sky, the harbor looked busy, but attractive in its own tropical way. The plane flew low the entire 20-minute flight, enabling me to keep the mesmerizing waves in sight the entire time. We also got a brief glimpse of the Christiansted harbor as the captain maneuvered the plane to land.

We touched down, the plane's pontoons dragging along the water, slowing the sea plane to a stop. The landing was not as gentle as the take-off, but also not as harsh as it appeared from the ground. The benefits of traveling by sea plane were apparent as we moved from our seats to luggage collection and finally to a cab, all within five minutes. In a blink of an eye, we were speeding through the warm morning sunshine to our hotel. St. Croix had a delightful collection of small, independent places to stay, each one more appealing than the next.

We had no time to luxuriate by the pool, however. We were staying on the island for only a night in order to squeeze one last diving day into our USVI itinerary before going back home. We dropped off our bags at the hotel, and then went straight into town to the dive shop. Many dive companies made a living on the island, but this one had serious credibility and a long history. With only one day to get it right, I did not want to chance our diving on an unknown company. Bill, the owner and boat captain, waited for us at the shop. The shop's massive Sheepdog mascot, Tank, waited patiently as well. He stunk like wet, salty dog and particularly appreciated rubs about his ears. The shop had won us over already.

After a quick sign in and a certification card review to prove we were legal, we made our way to the dock a block away. The boat was huge, at least 45 feet long. Michael and I exchanged glances and grimaced. We both hated diving in large groups, which a boat this size practically guaranteed. Fortunately we were the first ones on, enabling us to grab a desirable spot near the rear of the boat to set up our gear. Once ready, we climbed onto the bow to bask in the sun and await the rest of the divers.

Three people approached with their gear. They were tanned and relaxed, and seemed to know the boat and each other very well. The two women introduced themselves as dive shop staff who were squeezing in some free diving on their day off. The third guy introduced himself as Christian, our Dutch divemaster for the day.

"Are you guys ready to go?" he asked.

"Yes, I guess we're just waiting for the rest of the divers," Michael said.

"Nope. You're it today. A whole boat to ourselves!" Christian said with genuine happiness. It had not occurred to me before, but divemasters must hate a full boat as much as we did.

We pulled away from shore, Tank staying behind, wagging his tail and barking his farewells as we left. We already set up our gear, so there was not much to do until we reached the dive site. I decided to avail myself of our divemaster's knowledge, asking a question that had bugged me for some time.

"I go through air pretty fast. Michael usually has more air left at the end of a dive, if I have any at all. Why does that happen? What am I doing to burn through all that air?"

"You're an air hog!" Christian said with a smile. I did not like the barnyard reference. I preferred to think of myself as an air-consuming goddess.

"Lots of extra movement underwater or rough conditions can get you out of breath, just like on land. Nerves can do the same thing. If you take quick, shallow breaths, you burn more air."

"But how can I make my air last longer?" I asked.

"Think of breathing underwater like drinking a cup of coffee. A long, slow drink is a lot more satisfying than a series of quick sips. You breathe more efficiently when you inhale deeply and slowly. Your body has a chance to process more of the oxygen that you intake. So, you'll actually need less air and your tank will last longer."

"Try taking a breath in slowly, breaking it into three parts with a short pause in between. Hold it for a beat, then exhale slowly again in three parts with a quick pause in between."

The advice gave me something to think about. I had never considered my breathing technique before. I vowed to practice it underwater.

St. Croix has an enormous living reef that almost completely surrounds the island. Most diving on St. Croix occurs on the north and west shores, where there are 52 different sites with mooring balls that dive boats can use. Less than 20 minutes after we left the dock, we arrived at our first site, Cane Bay Wall, at the north shore's western end.

When I booked our dives, I requested this site, one of the most famous and rumored to be one of the most rewarding in the Caribbean. As the motor stopped and the captain prepared to attach the boat to the mooring ball, Christian approached us to deliver the dive briefing.

"So, we're at Cane Bay now. There's a coral garden behind us at about 30 feet. We'll descend to the bottom, then swim straight out from shore to get to the wall. It starts at 40 feet and goes to about 3,200 feet, so don't drop anything, okay?" he said with a smile.

"We'll swim along the wall against the current for awhile. There is some great stuff to see, including some old anchors. Don't forget to look behind you into the blue from time to time. We've seen a lot of large sharks patrolling this area lately." I wished I had eyes on the back of my head.

We geared up and entered the water from the large swim platform at the back of the boat. The other dive staff waited until we entered the water before gearing up. Immediately after jumping in I could see the underwater visibility was great, at least 80 feet or more. The tops of many underwater walls have what are called "spur and groove" formations. These formations, caused by current and wave movement, undulated along the wall's rim, the high points covered in coral with sand drifting down the valleys in between. Christian led us down a sand chute towards the deep blue.

There is always a moment right when I get to the edge of an underwater wall when I feel like I am flying. The coral under me fades away and I go sailing over the edge into the endless blue, like a bird floating effortlessly on air currents. No matter how many times I have done it, I always get the urge to extend my arms and experience the feeling of graceful flight. I'm sure I look like a crazed Big Bird to other divers, but that moment always fills me with a strange cocktail of zen-like peace mixed with adrenaline rush that compares to little else on land.

Christian let me glide a bit, and then turned us west to swim along the wall. Large stands of round plate corals extended from the sand chute bottoms. Wire corals poked out into the depths, while vase sponges reached upwards. I spotted miniature coral banded shrimp defying gravity by clinging upside down under coral overhangs, and even a red Caribbean lobster in a deep coral crevice. Swimming at eye level to the wall, rather than looking down on a reef, gives the diver a unique perspective and a great opportunity to see a variety of things normally obscured from view.

Christian provided a comprehensive tour, pointing out all sorts of interesting items. He showed us two anchors wedged into the wall, ditched by boats in a hurry to leave. He also called my attention to a sea fan with what looked like an algae lump growing on it. Closer inspection revealed a tiny crustacean, a decorator crab, which attached plant life to its back in order to blend in with its surroundings. As I gestured wildly to Michael to show him the crafty crab, a large reef shark swam behind us, causing me to gesture wildly in the other direction as well.

All too soon our dive computers indicated the need to retire to shallower water for the remainder of our dive. Bad things happen to the nitrogen levels in a body if it stays in deep water for too long. We chose another sand groove and swam back to the coral flats on top of the wall, passing big-eyed, spiky porcupine fish and triangular trunk fish along the way. Although we had to leave the depths, the shallow coral garden up top offered warm, sunny, and fish-filled water that promised a dazzling finish to an already spectacular dive.

All sorts of soft and hard corals filled the garden. A rainbow of tiny tropical fish swam in every direction, making it hard to choose just one to watch. Michael found a small green moray eel smiling at us from a small cave. A pair of curious grey angelfish the size of large dinner plates followed us as we wove between the coral heads. Without needing to worry about other divers' interests or remaining air, we poked around as we pleased until I used most of the air in my tank and the time to ascend arrived.

"What a dive!" I shouted, surfacing with glee. Michael and Christian agreed heartily. The reef was incredibly healthy and the sea life had been amazing. No wonder that location had such a good reputation.

"How did your breathing go?" Christian asked me. *Oops.* I completely forgot to practice the techniques he suggested. I also forgot about my camera tucked in my scuba vest. The ocean does that to me sometimes.

The captain moved the boat to our second and final dive site, Gentle Winds. This location, named for a condo complex nearby, boasted more spur and groove formations, but bottomed out at 60 feet. Generally, a scuba diver's second dive will be shallower than the first, again a precaution for minimizing nitrogen levels in the blood. A maximum depth of 60 feet would be safe, while also allowing for plenty of bottom time to explore the reef's nooks and crannies.

As soon as we reached the bottom, Christian reminded me to practice my breathing. I had already forgotten again as the underwater scene pulled my attention in a thousand directions at once. I inhaled in three separate parts, and then exhaled slowly in three separate parts. The cadence felt awkward. Several times I caught

Shark attacks are on the decline, according to the International Shark Attack File, which is part of the Florida Museum of Natural History. In 2008, there were 59 recorded attacks worldwide, but only 7% of those were related to scuba diving and snorkeling, with the rest made up of slow swimmers and surfers with tasty boards. The odds from dying of a beach-related activity such as swimming or stepping on a rusty pop-top, is 1 in 2 million, far greater than the odds of getting attacked by a shark at 1 in 11.5 million. If one does find themselves in that great minority of shark attack victims, the *International Shark Attack File* has these suggestions:

"If a shark attacks, the best strategy is to hit it on the tip of its nose...If you do not have anything to poke with, use your hand, but remember that the mouth is close to the nose, so be accurate."

myself lapsing back into my old breathing routine as soon as my focus turned to the reef. Slowly, though, the process became more natural.

Again, the variety and colors of the hard and soft corals were incredible. Instead of going down the side of the wall, we hovered at the edge in search of pelagic fish like sharks and tuna. From his wetsuit, Christian pulled out a partially flattened water bottle. As he squeezed it repeatedly I could hear its telltale plastic crinkly noise, though I had no idea why Christian was playing with it. He motioned us to wait and look into the blue.

The wait stretched on for several minutes. Our aquatic rest stop gave me an opportunity to get my breathing in order, but I was starting to wonder why we were still parked on the edge of the abyss. Just as I was about to protest the long standstill, an enormous grey reef shark, maybe ten feet in length, rocketed toward us. He veered off at the last minute swimming south along the wall and leaving us with beating hearts and soiled wetsuits. The shark did not return, but one monster sighting was enough for me. Christian later explained that the scrunching water bottle noise sounded like a wounded fish to predators, drawing them from the depths for a closer look.

After our close encounter we moved back up to the top of the reef to scout for sea life unique to St. Croix. Christian pointed out a scorpion fish, a highly poisonous fish seriously adept at camouflage, with a face only its mother could love. A school of flying gurnards, fish with huge, colorful pectoral fins that walk along the bottom looking for snacks, meandered about the shallows. As promised, macro critters, such as stinging bristle worms and lettuce sea slugs littered the reef, tricking me into feeling like I was actually good at spotting the usually hard-to-find guys. I spent time hovering over anemones looking for the small and shy shrimp and crabs that called the creatures home. Not every anemone had a resident, however, so I had to wait for a few minutes to see if something interesting peeked out from between the purple and pink fingers. The sea life was rich and prolific, and as enjoyable as advertised.

Tank greeted us vigorously as we returned to the dock. We grabbed a quick dinner at a local restaurant with a tasty menu and an excessively large wine list. We ate and drank with gusto and then retired to our hotel to enjoy the last few hours of our St. Croix trip, sound asleep. The day exhausted me, but the diving was superb. We were glad we made the extra effort to discover the waters of St. Croix.

St. John

The rhythmic parade undulated down the road. Skilled performers combined flashy costumes and colorful masks with orgasmic dance moves. Men in festival attire walked with ease on giant stilts over the uneven road. Bands marched in time, their drums pounding out the cadence. The parade even involved school kids proudly displaying their uniforms and flags as they walked in formation. All that coordination impressed me; I am known to fall down when I chew gum. But the revelers on St. John really knew how to pull it all together.

Europeans brought many traditions when they colonized the Caribbean, including Carnival, the festival of excess before the religious Lent holiday. Over time this celebration evolved to be one of cultural, rather than religious, significance, incorporating African dance, music, and party customs. Now, Carnival festivities take place on all of the Caribbean islands at different times of the year. St. John celebrates it in late June, culminating in early July, which coincided perfectly with our visit.

By some accounts, the St. John's Carnival celebration lasts up to a month long, bringing crowds and frenetic activity to the otherwise sleepy island. I imagined that even the most die-hard partiers eventually lost steam after 28 days of merriment. But, no sense of flagging energy appeared as a female parade dancer wearing nothing but strategically placed feathers enthusiastically tried to pull Michael out into the street. Judging by the happy look on his face, I would be purchasing some plumes for home use.

We had spent a long morning hiking past 18th-century Danish plantation ruins, mysterious petroglyhphs, and panoramic views in Virgin Islands National Park, which covers more than half the land on St. John. Tired and hungry, we went to Cruz Bay to find some food and watch the show. With all the scrumptious aromas from the food stalls lining the road, I knew a formal sit-down meal would not be in the cards.

"I got the Johnny cake, lady. You want some?" a woman called to me from one stall. I honestly did not know how to answer. Would Johnny mind? I approached her table to learn more.

Althea, the Johnny cake vendor, informed me in no uncertain terms that she made the best cakes on St. John. She then educated me on the ingredients (mainly cornmeal, milk, and salt) and the process for making the cakes. "It got to be fried in lard. Other ways no good, lady."

I could not argue with her; the cakes smelled really good. I handed over my dollar and walked away with two thin cakes scorchingly hot from their lard bath, wrapped in grease paper. Althea backed up her claim with results. The snacks were delicious.

On we walked to ogle the other food vendors' fare. Two types of vendors ruled the street: the salty food vendors and the sweet food vendors. Interestingly, no vendors combined the two, preferring, I guess, to specialize. The salty food vendors offered up tasty bites like meat and seafood kabobs, fried fish chunks, kalaloo soup, stewed Caribbean lobster, and the regional food requiring the most acquired taste, salt fish.

The sweet vendors drew Michael to their stalls like flies on, well... sweet vendor stalls. Bakers tucked various fruits into pies and tarts, their juicy tropical goodness leaking from the pastry seams. Some vendors offered raw fruit, like pineapple slices on sticks, whole mangoes, and papaya halves complete with a spoon. Stalls offered fruit juices too, squeezed from nature with manual contraptions; no juicer machines were in sight. Michael trailed behind me, a banana in one hand, a fruit tart in the other hand, and a big smile on his face.

After consuming our weight in island food, we made our way further down the street towards the sounds of steel drums. At the road's end lay the Carnival Village, filled with craft stalls, more food and drink vendors, and a performance area with a stage on one end. The performers vary throughout the celebration, but that night a calypso band rapped out their beat on tin pans.

I always thought of calypso music as a cheesy art form from the islands, complete with band members in neon-colored clown outfits and Carmen Miranda with her head-fruit dancing on the side for added flair. Boy, was I wrong. This calypso band was as far from goofy as possible.

Four band members dressed in T-shirts and black jeans pounded away with a sincere ferocity. Calypso is a music form sometimes used as a vehicle for somber commentary. Although it sounds lighthearted and upbeat, it frequently accompanies a political or social message. The scene was a stark contrast to my vision of the merry men of the cruise ship entertainment set that usually played calypso.

From what I could hear, the band sang about local kids and their opportunity for education; the sound system crackled so much I couldn't catch all the words. The music, however, did not require a mic, their melodic tin pangs ringing out over the crowd. Visitors and locals alike danced around us to the music. We joined in, demonstrating our serious case of left feet.

Soon it grew dark, and our next day of diving loomed closer. We grabbed a ride back to our hotel in the island version of a taxi, a pickup truck outfitted with bench seats in the bed and a makeshift top to keep out the sun and rain. The truck drivers slowed down to ask where the traveler headed. If the destination was on their route, they quoted the traveler a price. If the destination was inconvenient, they'd leave the traveler by the roadside with a sad head shake and a dust cloud as they pull away.

Several vehicles passed by before we found one of these taxis to take us back to our hotel a few miles down the road. The driver must have been on his way home to take our fare as not many people would be heading back into town from our hotel at that time of night. We agreed to the four buck price tag. A regular, roofed taxi, if we could even find one, would have been a lot more expensive and a lot less fun.

Our truck driver either had a flair for the dramatic, or a penchant for mismatched, tacky fabrics. Multicolored pom-poms hung from the roof sides, while sewn neon material bits were stretched over the bench seats. The owner painted the vehicle body in an animal print pattern using pink and green contrasts. It almost hurt to look at it directly. When he parked it in his yard, I bet his neighbors begged him to cover it up with a tarp so as to avoid being awakened in the middle of the night from the radiance.

We climbed into the back using a small step fastened to the bumper, joining several folks, all locals, on their way home. The taxi stopped numerous times as it wound through the town streets and then the environs. Our fellow passengers thinned out as the number of people climbing off outnumbered the people climbing on.

We stopped on one particularly dark street and had to wait while the passenger got change for the fare from her house. A clean-looking, non-rental car approached from the opposite direction. From the drivers side window leaned a middle-aged American man with a Midwestern accent.

"You guys alright?" he asked, aiming the question at Michael and I specifically. "Are you broken down? Do you need a ride somewhere?"

The questions floored me. First, at the kindness and concern from the American stranger who did not know us, but clearly knew the island. And, second, at my naïveté that crime could not occur on the idyllic island.

We thanked him profusely and declined his offer, opting to stay on our chosen course. We rode the rest of the way in silence, arriving at our destination safe and sound, if not more than a little introspective at mankind's nature and the fine line between strangers and kin. It had been a long, interesting day. I fell asleep before my head hit the pillow.

The next day dawned clear and bright. We booked a dive trip with our hotel's dive company. The process could not be easier: roll out of bed, roll onto the dock, roll into the dive boat, and then roll towards the ocean.

Though expensive, the full service operation gave us our money's worth. The crew set up our gear, filled a cooler with water and soda, and had a freshwater rinse tank ready for my underwater camera.

Since we last dove, I upgraded my underwater camera equipment courtesy of birthday, Christmas, and anniversary gifts. In underwater camera equipment, an upgrade in quality also equals an upgrade in suitcase volume. I now toted a land camera in an underwater housing along with an external flash that sat on a long arm protruding from the main camera housing. My chance to get good pictures and a great hernia increased substantially. The captain provided a large freshwater camera bucket on the boat. The tank was huge, but rig pieces still protruded out the top like a giant electronic crab.

We planned to dive four days in a row on St. John, a reasonable amount of time to get to know the underwater landscape and the diving routine. We relaxed under the canopy as the dive boat sped around a cay to our first location. We chatted with the two other divers on board, but eventually lapsed into comfortable silence. The island looked like a box of Crayolas, light blue sky, cerulean blue water, canary yellow sun, and kelly green hills punctuated by pastel houses and buildings.

In 1956 Laurence Rockefeller donated most of the land he owned on St. John (which is to say most of *the* land on St. John) to the national park service. This land became the Virgin Islands National Park, which we hiked the day before. From inside the park getting a perspective on the island proved difficult; green and healthy growth continually blocked my view. But, from the boat, I could see that having the park added something special to St. John, a natural peace and quiet that the other U.S. Virgin Islands lacked. There were more trees than tourism, more bark than brick; humans lived amongst nature, rather than trying to conquer it. The more I saw of the island, the more I liked it.

"We're almost at the dive site. You'll want to start suiting up," said the divemaster, who introduced himself as Ray at the beginning of the trip. Ray practically shouted white bread, sourced from the corn fields,

American. He exuded calm and friendliness while still managing to appear professional. He seemed to have a respectful rapport with the other boat staff, even the two young local boys who served as mates and general handymen. I couldn't help but think it would be a good dive.

The motor's drone slowed, a mate dropped the anchor, and the captain cut the engine. Ray gathered us in the shade for the dive briefing.

"This site is called Champagne Cork. It is your basic reef dive. We'll drop down to the bottom under the boat at about 50 feet, then swim south down the reef until it reaches 80 feet. We'll do a little tour down there for a few minutes looking for interesting things. This site is known for turtles and some small sharks, so keep an eye out for them. In the shallows there are tons of angelfish and other colorful tropical fish," he said.

"On our way back from the deeper part of the reef to the shallower part, there are several swim throughs. You don't have to go through any if you don't want, just swim over top of them. You can follow our bubbles."

"There is one really cool one. It's the source of the site's name. You swim through this narrow tube - be careful of the sharp rock and coral - and then wait at the end of the tube until the surge pops you out the hole at the end into the calm waters over the reef. I'll help you if you get stuck."

Okay. Although I became accustomed to the whole scuba diving thing, sharp rocks and "popping" surf still made my heart beat faster than normal. I'm a bit of a control freak, so losing control of my underwater movements ranked high on my "Not So Good" list. As usual with diving, however, I had this "must try it" mentality, so off we went. Having Captain American as our divemaster helped as well. I supposed he could extract me from the hole like an escargot if the surge didn't do its job.

Into the ocean we went, ass over tea kettle. Divemasters seemed to really like that backroll maneuver. It was much easier to start the dive with everyone in the water, rather than one diver still on the swim platform counting down from 100 to 1 before jumping. Ray gave the "descend" hand signal, and down we went.

The cloudless sky that enabled the bright sun to penetrate the water contributed to the good visibility, about 80 feet. The reef teemed with vibrantly colorful coral gardens, sea fans, and sponges. Almost immediately Ray made the hand signal for a sea turtle, and then pointed out to the right. The green gem swam toward us, looping lazily among the coral boulders, hunting for a snack. He barely noticed me as I snapped picture after picture with my giant crab rig.

Down the reef we went, the reds and oranges fading as we drifted deeper and deeper. Water gradually filters out color as a diver descends through the water column. The sea life may still contain the vivid hues of the rainbow, but only a strong light source can bring out the shades at significant depths. Time after time my strobe surprised me by revealing outrageous colors on fish and coral that only seconds before looked grey.

On some parts of the reef, the coral formed a maze. Certain corals grow together creating bridges and tunnels called swim throughs. We ducked in and out, playing follow the divemaster, careful not to damage any of the living structures around us. Then, our conga line slowed up. I was at the back of the line, so I couldn't see what caused the holdup. While waiting, I poked around the reef, finding an interesting nudibranch, a blue and yellow sea slug, to photograph.

I got carried away with my photography. Not that the sea slug was that interesting, but its lack of speedy locomotion enabled me to practice changing my camera and strobe settings. When I looked up from my slug lesson, I saw the rear end of the diver in front of me squeezing through a small opening in the reef. I quickly followed, not wanting to get lost in all the cracks and crevasses. This swim through was striking; the walls encrusted with corals that looked like someone had taken spray paint cans and graffitied the wall: "Nemo was here," or perhaps "I Love Clams!"

A little further into the swim through, I could feel the surge start to pull me forward, then push me back. I checked my depth gauge and, sure enough, we were a lot shallower now. I could see bright sunlight up ahead as the tunnel ended. As I reached the end of the tunnel, the surge grabbed me and thrust me through the opening into the shallow warm water over the reef. A stingray eyed me warily from the sandy bottom, watching me execute the champagne cork maneuver.

The remainder of our dives in St. John brought the same: sunny days, clear water, friendly divemasters, interesting fish, and fascinating underwater topography. Surprisingly, I even managed to capture a few good pictures with the fish centered and the camera lens focused. We ended our week tired, but content. Diving should always be that way.

CHAPTER 8

Hawaii: The Gods of Sun, Sand, and Retail

Hawaii, The Big Island

Hawaii, The Big Island
Through the clear, plexiglas helicopter door I could see lava dripping over the cliff into the ocean. Each molten dribble produced an explosion when the unimaginably hot rock met the cool Pacific Ocean, sending steam clouds billowing into the sky. The clouds provided a stark white contrast to the pinks and purples of the atmosphere as the sun slowly set in the distance. Hawaii has a knack for doing the most memorable things with Mother Nature's basic tools.

In another 250,000 years visitors will be able to see a ninth island in Hawaii, courtesy of a currently submerged, hopping mad volcano south of the existing chain. Until then, the youngest of the eight existing islands is the "Big Island" of Hawaii, the first stop on our tour of the state. The Hawaiian alphabet contains only thirteen letters. This lack of phonetic options was the reason, I believed, that native Hawaiians confused us all by sharing the same name with the entire state as well as one of the islands. In order to reduce the confusion, Hawaii the island went by the "Big Island" nickname, an unfortunate situation that, in my mind, set unrealistic expectations that everything there was supersized.

My headset muffled the helicopter drone while also piping in the pilot's guided tour. We opted to take in the view of Hawaii Volcanoes National Park by helicopter, rather than hike its 377 square miles. Hiking enabled the visitors to get the full sensory effect: as the ground grows hot underfoot and the sun grows hot overhead, one begins to feel like they are *in* the Kilauea volcano. But, the helicopter route provided a sweeping view and a front row seat to see the lava meet explosively with the water on the cliff's edge, something no sane person on foot would attempt.

The arid fields of cooled lava that covered part of the island were very different than the Hawaii I pictured, one of green rainforests, colorful wildlife and birds, and virile, native men clad in strategically placed leaves. The Big Island's two volcanoes are actually "shield" volcanoes, meaning that lava oozes from them down gently sloping mountains rather than exploding violently like Hollywood volcanoes and my soufflés. As we drove to the small town of Hilo for dinner after Mr. Toad's wild helicopter ride we passed rock fields that looked like chocolate fudge had undulated voluptuously down the slopes, then froze in place soon after. The fields sat dark and stark, with little plant growth or living creatures. It would take a long time for nature to visibly return to the lava fields. My shoulders relaxed from tension I didn't even realize I held as we left the barren fields and entered more verdant Hawaiian surroundings that continued all the way to Hilo.

The wooden storefronts are remnants of the town's historical heyday, when sugar plantations covered its rich coastal land and ocean voyagers from all over the world visited its harbor. At some point in the mid 1900's, the town changed from being on the forefront of Hawaiian political, economic, and social efforts to being a "preserved" township representing historical plantation living. We walked through its quaint streets filled with art galleries, open air markets, and restaurants. Due to its prior run-ins with tsunamis, Hilo housed an outstanding oceanfront museum dedicated to the oceanic phenomenon (at least until the building gets washed away by the next one).

We chose a small restaurant and settled into a wooden plank table and a welcoming atmosphere. One glance at the menu told me we were out of Kansas and solidly in Hawaii. I never saw a more abundant use of macadamia nuts with such a variety of foods. The list included spinach salad sprinkled with nuts, meat with a nut chutney, fish encrusted with the chopped nuts, a nut desert tart, and even a macadamia nut ice cream. Anyone with a nut allergy and a desire for travel should visit Alaska instead.

There are copious macadamia farms on the Big Island. Flying into Hawaii I could see rows and rows of trees growing some of the highest priced nuts in the world. Though the nut was native to Australia, enterprising entrepreneurs imported the seeds to Hawaii in the late 1800s. About 700 farms produce today's Hawaiian nuts, and while some operations are partially automated, harvesting and preparing the nuts for sale are still mostly manual, hence the high cost.

I ordered mahi mahi encrusted with, of course, macadamias. The dish was incredibly flavorful if not a bit too rich, bringing to mind the other key fact about macadamias: they have the highest monosaturated fat content of any nut. What starts out as a tasty treat quickly begins to coat the tongue with oil and turns that five-mile jog you've been putting off into a necessity. The little fat balls are crazy nutritious, but also ridiculously high in calories.

I ended the night with a big cup of black coffee to cut down on the meal's heaviness. The waiter brought out a French press and ceremoniously placed it in the table's center.

"Please let the press rest for five more minutes before plunging the top and releasing the essence," he said, dramatically. What could be in the pot? I expected a cup with some warm brew in it, not floating grinds and fanfare. Michael and I watched the press expecting it, I guess, to do something exciting. But alas, it just sat patiently, which was better than I could say for us.

The five minutes finally passed. Eagerly I fondled the press, a toy I did not have at home. Before I could mess up the process the waiter returned to our table and pushed the plunger down, compacting the grinds at the bottom and leaving the inviting liquid to be poured out unfettered by bits. The waiter poured me a cup with a flourish. Based on the built-up anticipation, Michael and I stared at the cup, waiting for it to tap dance or recite the Constitution.

"Do you think I need to say some sort of incantation before I drink it? Maybe there is some super special club-members-only way of holding the cup?"

"You can probably skip the pre-sip prayer service, but I wouldn't try to add milk or sugar to it," Michael said. "They may take it away from you and kick us off the island."

I raised the cup to my mouth and let the strong, bitter brew roll across my tongue. It tasted smooth, with a tinge of butter and nuttiness. One sip later and I believed all other coffees paled in comparison. After watching my reaction with approval, the waiter let the caffeinated cat out of the bag; my drink was Kona Coffee, grown and roasted right there on the island. Since the late 1800's, farmers grew the orgasmic beans in Hawaii's perfect climate and soil mix, producing outrageously expensive but completely awesome coffee. Families owned many of the hundreds of Kona coffee plantations, passing them down along with valuable crop knowledge from generation to generation. If every day started out with a cup of this nectar of the gods, I might actually change into an optimist.

In the interest of keeping the optimism going, the next morning I found a coffee shop that sold brewed 100% Kona coffee. I needed it; we woke at 6am to catch our charter to go deep sea fishing for half a day. The Big Island provides a great opportunity for fishing, as the volcanic island's steep slopes extend into the sea, making the sea floor over 6,000 feet deep just three miles off the coast. Before my coffee could cool we boarded the boat, left the dock, and reached the trolling grounds. Spearfish, marlin, swordfish, tuna, mahi mahi, wahoo, and amberjack all patrolled the Kona coast, waiting for a tasty lure to pass by.

Well, usually they waited off the coast. That day, however, they visited friends in Acapulco. Nothing bit our lines for hours. On the upside, John, the captain, filled the time with interesting stories. Michael and I munched snacks and listened to John's tales as we trolled.

John was divorced and retired when he decided to move from California to Hawaii. A friend needed an extra mate for his Kona-based fishing charter company that took out tourists and serious anglers alike. He liked to fish and needed a job, so off he moved to Hawaii. John earned decent tips as a mate and enjoyed the work. He found a nice apartment, met a like-minded lady friend, and settled into Hawaiian ways. The story sounded idyllic.

We joked with John that we wanted to do the same thing, except instead of fishing we wanted to own a Kona coffee farm. The brew's quality and price impressed us; we were ready to go native. John laughed and agreed, but then turned serious as he relayed the rest of his story, a cautionary tale of chasing a tropical dream.

"I got tired of working for other people. I had a little money saved up, so I decided to buy a boat and start my own charter company. There was plenty of fishing business to go around," he said with a wistful smile.

"I really could have used help from others on the island. You know, guidance on how to get things done like permits and advertising and things. No one actually refused to help me, but they didn't make it easy. The community here is pretty closed. They don't take too kindly to strangers trying to set up shop. I've heard some of the other islands, like Maui, are better. They're more used to outsiders, so new people don't faze them."

Just then a reel zinged, indicating a fish had grabbed the bait and ran. The mate handed the pole to Michael who proceeded into the traditional fishing dance of "reel the fish in a bit, fish runs out with the line a bit" until the reeling in overcame the running out. Ten minutes later Michael landed the fish, a small but respectable tuna. The mate threw the fish into the cooler for keeps. Sadly, it was the only fish we caught all day.

It was interesting that an island which seemed so welcoming and offered so much opportunity held undercurrents of "Keep Out." I assumed that all the Hawaiian islands would have similar social perspectives when it came to outsiders, but that did not sound like the case. I wondered if having tourism as the primary revenue source affected the inhabitants' perspective on visitors. The Big Island had a healthy macadamia nut and coffee farming industry in addition to tourism. But, tourism provided

Maui's main income source. When each visitor represents your livelihood, does one encourage them any way they can to keep the cash flowing? With my black thumb, growing anything would be a hefty challenge on its own, never mind throwing in protectionist neighbors. Perhaps our dreams of a coffee oasis would have to wait.

Although Hawaii offered so many things to do above the waves, we couldn't visit without dipping into the vast, dark blue Pacific Ocean. Several years back a hotel on the Big Island noticed that the underwater running lights on their dock attracted plankton at night. In turn, the plankton party attracted fish that liked to eat plankton, most notably manta rays. Someone figured out that they sat on a gold mine, as the opportunity to see manta rays up close and personal is not a common occurrence, though many people would jump at the chance. And jump we did, right into a taxi that dropped us off at the doorstep of Hotel Ray.

The program and process for attracting the rays evolved over the years. The hotel replaced the dock running lights with powerful lights placed on the sea floor in 15 to 20 feet of water. The lights shone upwards towards the surface, creating illuminated water columns. The columns' contrast to the dark surrounding water was in itself a sight to see, from the water as well as from the land.

Two types of people comprised the manta watcher group: snorkelers and divers. Snorkelers would float at the surface, looking down on the manta action. Divers would descend to the bottom, sitting on the sea floor to watch the excitement above. The tour leader instructed both groups to stay still, a tough task in the surging shallow waters. Fortunately, the sky was clear and the sea was calm. To enter the water we would climb down the ladder at the dock's end. What thoughtful mantas; they could not be more convenient.

The purpose of the lights was to entice the plankton into a condensed and tasty group. But, the lights could not do the job until the sun went down. So, we sat on the beach and waited for an appropriate amount of darkness while our divemaster briefed us on the impending plankton palooza.

"Manta rays are notoriously shy creatures," he said. "Touching them could cause them to leave, so please look with your eyes, not with your hands. Although the moon is pretty bright tonight, it will be quite dark in the water if you are not near the lights. Stick to the group; no swimming off on your own. We would hate to have to feed you to the mantas for not following instructions," he said with a smile. Some of the other tour members looked stricken. Perhaps he should have explained that mantas don't eat people. Or, perhaps watching squirming tourists provided an enjoyable diversion for him. Surely some people would tip him well at the end of the night if they didn't get eaten.

As darkness approached we made our way down the dock and off the ladder into the water. The divers entered first so we could descend to the bottom without causing a traffic jam. A staff member turned on the lights as we descended. The lighted streams looked like Bat Signals. I wondered if the beam's middle held a black symbol in the shape of a manta.

The light attracted small fish in droves, perhaps out of curiosity. The water in the light columns began to look cloudy, a clear indicator that the plankton had arrived. Plankton, microscopic tasties that are the oceanic food chain's building blocks, can't be seen with the naked eye, but large volumes of the critters create a milky haze. We waited for the mantas just like we had waited for the tuna when we went deep sea fishing. The Hawaiians sure possessed patience.

Then, a shadow passed through the light, blocking it momentarily. The shadow moved so fast I could not even tell the animal's shape; it appeared and disappeared instantly. My adrenaline popped and my legs tensed as I strained to look all around from my kneeling position. I didn't need to be a contortionist; soon the mantas flew through the water from all directions, swooping in and out of sight. As my eyes adjusted to their speed, I could make out their aerodynamic, triangular shape. Their bellies were white and reflected the light. I imagined it would be tougher for the snorkelers on the surface to see the rays since their backs were a dark color, enabling them to blend in with the shadowy water. The mantas fed with abandon, funneling plankton rich water into their gaping mouths.

After 50 minutes that flew by like five, the divemaster indicated it was time to ascend. Many of the snorkelers already returned to the dock, tired from keeping afloat. The divers were ready for another 50, however, after enjoying their own version of theater in the round on the sandy bottom. The divemaster left the lights on to illuminate our way back to the dock. We followed him along the bottom the short distance to the ladder, ensuring we did not disturb the feeding mantas.

The entire group gushed about the experience once we surfaced and dried off. The mantas were beautiful and graceful and...sooo close. Hawaii offered a unique opportunity to easily see the animals. Last time they graced our presence Michael and I traveled thousands of miles to Bora Bora to see them. And as a bonus, the company that coordinated the Hawaiian event did a great job caring not only for the tourists, but also for the sea life. We recommended the experience highly to everyone we met on the remainder of our Big Island trip.

Maui

Legends say the ancient Gods of Sun and Surf inhabited Maui. Recently, a long lost cousin joined the ancient deities, the Demi-God of Retail (some call him a semi-precious deity, but I refer to him by his street name, 12-Carat).

"I just didn't think there were this many strip malls in paradise," said Michael as we drove from the airport to our hotel passing one retail oasis after the other.

All types of goods were sold in brick and mortar establishments by owners with a good eye for giving the masses what they wanted. Almost every store overflowed with visitors fondling the merchandise and handing over cold cash for tropical trinkets. After dinner one night, we wandered around the shopping mecca of Lahaina, a beautiful town on Maui's western shore that included many such retail establishments. Time after time I thought: *What exactly does one do with that item when they get home?* Instead of contributing to the economy through wanton spending, I compiled a list of the items available for purchase on Maui that I felt might produce buyer's remorse at a later time.

Hawaiian Print Undergarments – One store advertised Hawaiian print accessories in the front window. What started as an innocent opportunity to purchase a tropical tie quickly turned into an obscene effort to cover all of man's (and woman's) most intimate parts with palm trees, shells, waves, fish, and other vestiges of island life. Other than Robinson Caruso's wife, has any woman ever comfortably covered their breasts with coconut halves? Does having a palm tree emblazoned on one's boxer shorts enhance sexual appeal? Perhaps the print has an elongating effect on the eye. Best leave the fern-print tidy whities and banana hammocks at the store.

Jewelry that includes that popular new gem, Touristite- Man has thoroughly explored the earth's mineral deposits in search of useful or valuable stones. The chance of "discovering" a new gem is pretty slim. My theory is that any "new" gem advertised in a vacation destination jewelry store probably started life as shiny plastic pellets or the proprietor's driveway gravel. The chance that a previously inexpensive stone will suddenly grow in value is also unlikely, unless it cures cancer or produces winning lottery tickets. Popular new stones, such as PrazIolite and Tanzanite may shine and sparkle, but most likely their intrinsic value is closer to Lucite and Vegemite than their hefty price tag indicates.

Sacred items that bring the Gods' vengeance down upon the purchaser – The native Hawaiians should know better then to sell sacred objects to unsuspecting tourists. After living on the islands for so long, they have an idea of what makes the gods cranky. Pele, the Volcano Goddess, is known to bring her wrath of bad luck upon those unfortunate enough to return home with pieces of lava rock. Turtle shell items like combs and jewelry are immoral and illegal to purchase, as the "artisans" frequently take the shell before the turtle is done using it. Remember that Hawaiian *Brady Bunch* episode where bad things (including a rampant tarantula) begin to happen to the family because Greg took a tiki statue? Don't be a Brady. Leave these items in the store.

The moment we exited the minibus into the darkness, one of our fellow tour members tripped over a curb and landed head first on a sharp lava rock, splitting his forehead wide open causing projectile bleeding. I felt pretty bad for the guy, sacrificing his head to the Gods of the Dawn. The sky was so dark I was surprised I didn't fall myself.

The top of Haleakala Crater is possibly the best place in the world to watch the sunrise unless one can see out an east-facing window from Brad Pitt's bed. The active, but not currently erupting volcano rises over 10,000 feet above sea level, putting it even with the clouds. The bus ride to the top took an hour over curvy, uphill roads and started at 3am, so only insomniacs and those possessing an iron stomach fared well on the drive. The tour company lured terminal travelers with the promise of beautiful views and spiritual awakening, which was how Michael and I came to be at the summit, at 4am, in the pitch black, with a bleeding tourist at our feet. So far darkness obscured the views and the only thing awake was… well nothing was awake. It was freaking 4am.

We side-stepped the tour guide as he walked back to the bus with the injured tourist, mumbling about the "damn rocks" as he staggered. Inconsiderate volcano, it was, leaving rock scattered all over the place. Never cleans up after itself. Definitely off the Christmas card list.

"Do you think it will warm up?" Michael asked as our teeth starting chattered. Most people in Hawaii wear shorts, grass skirts, or loin cloths (okay, maybe that last one was just in a dream). This little known piece of Hawaii apparently required a different dress code, namely a down coat, ear muffs, and a portable fireplace with extra kindling. I estimated the thermometer did not top 40 degrees. The glacial temperatures having a direct correlation to the event's enjoyment, one would think our tour company would have mentioned the need for some bearskin products at some point during the booking process. Other people on the mountaintop wore long, wool-lined coats provided by their tour operators. Our company, known from that point on as Cheap Ass Economy Tours, did not.

We walked to the crater's rim as the sky grew light. From behind the volcano, the hidden sun sent pink and purple fingers of sky to let us know it was on its way. Everyone was whispering, perhaps afraid to wake the sun before its time. A park ranger, a native Hawaiian, began to chant a song to welcome the sun and thank the volcano. Later, our guide gave us the song translation, but even in Hawaiian we easily interpreted the worshipful nature of the words the ranger sang.

Then, the first edge of the sun peeked out from behind the rim of the volcano's distant side. The orb seared the sky, reminding me of the red lava piercing the ocean from the Kilauea volcano on the Big Island. But whereas the ocean changed little from the absorbing the lava, the sky changed dramatically with the rising sun, turning pink, then orange, before shimmering gold. The colors reflected off the misty clouds surrounding the crater rim, making the scene even more dramatic. Everything sat still and quiet, no tourist chatter, no camera clicks, no bird calls or animal rustles. At that moment it really was the most serene place on earth. Time stood still.

The crowd waited and watched in silence until the sun's entire glowing sphere cleared the opposing volcano edge and began its journey across the sky. Only then did murmurings pick back up and the groups start to make their way back down to their transportation. We asked a guy next to us to take our photo with the sun behind us. In the picture Michael and I huddled so close together from the cold that we looked conjoined. Our noses glowed a festive red usually reserved for times of serious alcohol consumption. The apparel of other people at our photo's edges looked like we superimposed our bodies on a picture of an Arctic expedition. But, we smiled from ear to ear and besides cold, one might say we looked... awakened.

One nice thing about Hawaii is that there is no volcano shortage. From Haleakela we moved onto Molokini, a submerged volcano crater two and a half miles south of Maui. Above water there is not much to see, only a crescent shaped hill emerging from the waves. Even if the mound did look interesting, the state prohibits visitors from climbing on it because the land houses a bird sanctuary. Molokini's appeal really picks up though when one looks below the waves. The crater houses a mind-blowing sea life variety. Even the underwater topography produces "ooo's" and "ahh's," with coral gardens on one side and steep drop offs on the other. The volcano's unique shape protects the underwater environment from the effects of strong currents and wind, making it a calm place to snorkel or dive with amazing underwater visibility, sometimes 150 feet or more.

Our Molokini dive began as usual: find a dive company, sign our life away in waivers, get gear, set up the gear on boat, and then relax on the bow while motoring to the dive site. Though the passengers were a mix of divers and snorkelers, the large boat provided ample space; snorkelers on the starboard side and divers to port. As long as the crew kept the boat well organized and roomy, I didn't care if Godzilla made the trip with us.

We left the dock at the unpleasant time of 7am in order to beat the crowds at Molokini. Many people visited the spot; companies shuttled sea enthusiasts out there all day long. Our boat arrived and anchored up first, giving us at least thirty minutes of peaceful diving with un-spooked sea creatures before the masses appeared. In the blink of an eye, we six divers squeezed into our wetsuits, threw on our gear, heard a short dive briefing, and eased off the swim platform.

We descended to the reef at the crater's center. Though divers could go to the deepest part of the reef at 80 feet, the shallowest part ended at 30 feet, making it perfect for snorkelers too. More than 250 types of fish can be found at Molokini. Thought I did not count them all myself, I think the statistic was realistic. Some fish I recognized, like tangs, trigger fish, and puffers. The boat's fish reference guide provided answers to those I didn't know, namely trumpet fish, pennent fish schools, and snowflake eels. White tip sharks of all sizes cruised the coral carpet, their beady black eyes accusing us of disturbing their peaceful reef. The sea life flourished around us, like we landed in someone's obsessively appointed aquarium.

After forty minutes our group made almost a full circle around the site, taking in the highlights as pointed out by the divemaster. Our tour's end crept closer. Michael and I had become good at regulating our breathing; we no longer consumed air like Hoovers. Since we had plenty of air left in our tanks, the divemaster let us poke around the reef for a bit longer.

Suddenly I noticed movement in my periphery. Something large moved with purpose, dipping in and out of view from between the coral. I tapped Michael and pointed in the general direction in hopes he could help me locate the find. From behind a boulder swam a rare monk seal, its chubby body swimming surprisingly athletically along

> "Will you walk a little faster?" said a whiting to a snail, "There's a porpoise close behind us, and he's treading on my tail! See how eagerly the lobsters and the turtles all advance: They are waiting on the shingle--will you come and join the dance?"
> - Lewis Carroll, *Alice's Adventures in Wonderland*

the reef. The creature sported that knowing smile, almost like a dolphin's, which humans always assume indicates intelligence, but probably just means the poor creature has gas from one too many clams.

I once read an article comparing seal behavior to that of a friendly, playful dog. This seal had not read the same article. It gave us some initial attention, but then hurried along on its journey like the delayed White Rabbit in *Alice's Adventures in Wonderland* once it realized we were neither food nor predator. Perhaps it intended to leave the crater before the tourist masses arrived, a scenario that would become a reality soon. As the pudgy pelagic swam off we watched in awe, wondering how far we had come down the rabbit hole.

Island of Kauai

The moment I stepped off the plane in Kauai, I felt like I was home. Not in that "put a pot roast in the oven and thank God I have access to a washing machine again" sort of way, but spiritually, like I felt more whole, more connected with my surroundings…more comfortable in my own skin. The feeling only intensified as we took the one main road north over the Waimea River, past the Kapa'a village, through the Coconut Coast, to our ultimate destination of the North Shore. Southern Kauai's lush, tropical shores housed beautiful hotels and elaborate tourist amenities. As we drove north, however, things got less touristy and the scenery became more primitive, with jagged peaks rising into the sky and sheer cliffs dropping into the sea.

By the time we hit our destination we ran out of superlatives to describe the view. Soaring green, jagged mountains with white waterfall ribbons appeared to our left while to our right Hanalei Bay lined the cobalt blue ocean with a strip of sandy eggshell beach. I fought the urge to shout "Stop the car!" so I could jump out and absorb the good juju directly. After many twists and turns in the road, we found our hotel. The accommodation's appearance made me think twice about checking in; the tropical tree overgrowth did nothing to soften the starkness of the barren, whitish-grey façade. I left Michael to discuss the bags with the porter, and walked inside.

Sometimes small but unique things about our travels really stick with me, like the scent of a local flower wafting past our dinner table or the feel of a dock's worn wood planks under my feet. This place, however, provided a whole new level of sensory overload. The three-story lobby encompassed the whole width and length of the hotel's first floor. Comfortable plantation-style couches were arranged under an enormous chandelier hanging in the center. The space managed to look lofty and open but also cozy and inviting all at the same time.

Of course, the decorations were secondary, just an afterthought that provided a place to sit. The architects seemed to have known that nothing they could create could compare to what lay outside the hotel. Two walls of the lobby were made of glass and framed the stunning Hanaelei Bay and the multi-hued mountains of the Napali Coast in the distance. I crossed the great room in a heartbeat to access the beauty directly from the terrace.

The brilliant sunset softened the edges of the cliff faces and mountain ridges, bathing them in oranges, pinks, and purples that faded into one another with each crest. Mist clung to the shore, rising off the water or perhaps from the tropical jungle that lined the land. Looking down I could see an explosion of healthy coral on our side of Hanalei Bay, the waves breaking half way out as their troughs met the reef. Other people also sat silently on the terrace, enrapt by the heartbreakingly beautiful view. Nature made it look so easy.

Michael joined me with two glasses of chilled white wine, possibly the only thing that could have made the moment even better. We stood in silence, as the sun's rays pulled our gaze out to sea and gave the ocean a mystical, almost beckoning quality. If the underwater panorama was half as good as above the waves, we had chosen our vacation well.

"We really need to find some scuba tanks," I said. Michael agreed wholeheartedly.

My grandmother had a creepy wind chime when I was a kid. It was a coconut head wearing a hat woven out of some sort of tree bark or palm part. The chime came in the form of long red sticks hanging by strings from the hat's brim. The stick's impact produced a ceramic-sounding clink. The bit of macabre kitsch fascinated me as a child, for what reason I have no idea.

Michael and I were diving off of Brennecke's Beach on Kauai's south side when I spotted the darn thing again. Not the shrunken head part, but the clink, the red sticks. Pencil sea urchins help to keep the coral reef from becoming overgrown and algae covered. Apparently, they also make great wind chimes. The finding made me wonder who initially thought "Those animals are really beautiful. Let's dry them out and then hang their spines from a hat."

This trip down memory lane would not have occurred without executing an ungainly diving ritual, a shore dive. Michael and I dove exclusively off of boats for our whole diving career and figured it was time to learn a different, and more self-sufficient, approach. Shore diving is common among more seasoned divers, especially in locations where the reef is so close it makes a boat obsolete. Brennecke's Beach presented a great opportunity to practice this new skill.

The word urchin is from Latin *ericius* meaning 'hedgehog.' Humans are the sea hedgehog's primary predator. In addition to using the shell as decoration, we eat the animal's roe and even use it in public aquariums as an indicator organism for water quality. But the seemingly benign sea hedgehog has a few tricks up its sleeve to keep humans at bay. It can maneuver into unbelievably tiny cracks in the reef and even cover itself with rocks to hide. If confronted, the urchin's spines can often penetrate even the thickest wetsuit and their pedicellariae, hook-shaped organs between the spines, can deliver a venomous punch when they come in contact with skin.

We carried our gear from the dive truck to the beach, a fairly straightforward task made difficult by forty pounds of gear and 90 degree heat. The divemaster demonstrated how to lay out gear on the sand without getting the grains in all sorts of unfortunate places. He then continued our education with some inspiring thoughts.

"You'll need to walk backwards to get into the water with your fins otherwise the flaps will prevent you from making any progress," said our divemaster, Mr. Positive Thinker. "Once in, you'll want to swim out past the breaking waves pretty quickly because you'll get tumbled easily by the surf with all that gear on." Why were we not jumping from the back of a boat, embracing instant gratification?

"Once you submerge, you'll notice that the water is hazy. That's due to the fresh water running out of the creek over there and mixing with the salt water. Swim out a little further and the visibility will increase as the water gets more saline," he said, his positive tone contrary to what seemed like a lot of bad news.

"Once you get off of the beach, follow the reef to the right for about 20 minutes, then turn around and come back. Don't go to the left. The rocks there are really sharp and if the wave surge throws you into them you can get cut up."

This dive master summed up what I loved about diving. Scuba divers don't partake in the sport accidentally. A diver has really got to *want* to dive to make it happen. Some monstrous creature always wants to eat you, waves to crush you, coral to cut you, dive company-provided lunch to sicken you, snorkeler to flash his unmentionables while underwater...in short, there is always something that will deter a person from diving unless they really, really desire it. But at the day's end when successful dives have been accomplished, all body parts are accounted for, and new dive buddies have been made through tackling the insurmountable together, it's a great feeling.

And so we put on our gear, now searingly hot from sitting out in the sun, and began walking towards the water backwards. We looked ridiculous, like a bunch of aquatic addicts trying to resist the ocean's pull, but failing as it sucked us back. In all fairness, the guy in our group who tried to walk towards the water facing forwards fared worse than us. He kicked his legs high in order to take steps, throwing his body off balance repeatedly, causing his arms to flail in all directions in a sort of epileptic can-can dance that attracted pity from onlookers and concern from the lifeguard who assumed a "rescue" was imminent.

We backed into the ocean, holding our own as the waves crashed against our legs. I turned to begin my paddle out past the breakers when I realized the waves broke *really* close to shore. The waves crashed where the water stood only three feet in depth. I attempted to swim, but found that the depth limited me to scuttling along the bottom on my knees. Then, in a moment of vindictive Darwinian evolution, a large wave knocked me over and washed me back onshore, taunting me with the fact that man left the ocean long ago and was no longer appropriately equipped for it.

I lay on my back and tank like a great upended sea turtle with arms and legs flailing helplessly until a kind observer came along and flipped me back over. I hoped they did not expect me to lay eggs in the sand. Instead, I bumbled back into the surf, backwards, making sure to get to deeper water before attempting to paddle. I made it out to the group who patiently waited for the little sea turtle to return to the pod. The divemaster made the thumbs-down descend sign, and off we went.

To say that the mixing of ocean water and fresh water has a disorienting effect is factually correct. To say is it like combining vertigo with car sickness and eating potato salad that's been sunbathing all day is a more accurate description. The dizzying blurriness combined with the chaotic motion of the waves brought a raging case of sea sickness to my head and stomach before I could even think of my Dramamine tucked nicely in a baggie at the bottom of my suitcase at the hotel. But, just as soon as the blurriness occurred, it disappeared as we entered the ocean's full salinity. Stomach on the mend, I followed the group swimming to the right to see the promised reef.

Though the visibility had cleared up, I noticed I could still not see very far into the distance. A haze hung in the water, looking like silt had been stirred up. Michael swam up next to me, pointing to my mask. The darn thing had fogged up like London in November. My body and my equipment grew so hot from sitting out in the sun before our dive that my mask turned practically opaque when it hit the cold water. I purposely flooded it with water, then cleared the water out with a whale spout of air from my nose, a useful trick that I had only recently mastered after many attempts that left me half-drowned at 50 feet under. I'm pretty sure the maneuver doesn't look dainty, probably like an enormous and aggressive underwater sneeze, but it worked. The mask cleared and we began our dive in earnest.

Urchins lined the coast, the prickly buggers squeezed into every fissure of the reef. As I hovered and watched, I could see the pincushions waving their spines in the air sensing food and danger. Next to the urchins hid tiny crabs, their carapaces rainbows of reds, yellows, greens, and browns. They had an amazing ability to press themselves into the tiniest cracks like crustaceous contortionists. Macro critters filled the dive. No sharks or turtles passed by, but miniature sea life thrived.

The strenuous water entry left us taxing our regulators to catch our breath. The dive ended at 40 minutes so that no one ran out of air before we hit the beach again. The idiosyncrasies of entering the ocean via the beach magnified during our exit because of exhaustion from the dive. At least walking backwards allowed me to see oncoming waves, so I could be prepared as the big ones rolled in. To my credit I didn't fall down this time. I did, however, give the beach onlookers some final laughs as I crab-walked out of the ocean, arms and legs extended wide in an ungainly marine display in order to keep my balance. We may not have been a pretty sight, huffing from exhaustion and coated in sand that intended to stay stuck, but we celebrated our newfound shore diving skills. I would never again take for granted the ease of stepping off the back of a boat.

Calling the Wailua a river is sort of an exaggeration. Sure, it's wide enough (in parts) to qualify, but its warm water, Zen-like scenery, and the absence of major traffic make it more like a bubbly soak rather than a true active waterway. Inland kayak tours are unique to Kauai because the island has the only navigable rivers in Hawaii. Though the promised "paddling adventure" we booked looked more like river relaxation, we climbed aboard our two-person kayak along with several other tourists and followed our guide upriver to do some exploring.

We paddled slowly upstream as the guide educated us on Wailua lore. The historical Hawaiian Kings all seemed to have a soft spot for the place. Over hundreds of years the inhabitants built many *heiaus*, or temples, along the river, pretty much cementing it as a sacred, favored location. The *huaka'i po*, or Ghost Warriors of the royalty, are said to walk ancient trails along the river, but unless they were masquerading as tourists in cheap flip flops, I didn't see any on our trip.

After floating along for over an hour, my arms ached from the repetitive paddling motion. I also suspected that Michael, seated behind me, took advantage of my disability, namely the lack of eyes in the back of my head. I was pretty sure that sightseeing was his only physical activity. Was his paddle actually dry? Using my paddle I splashed backwards to remind him that his need to paddle outranked his need to tan evenly. Before we disturbed the peace with an epic water fight, the guide pulled the group over to the river bank and announced the start of our waterfall hike and subsequent picnic.

Experience taught me that a "waterfall hike" sounded more romantic and exotic than it typically turned out to be. Bugs and gallons of sweat usually accompanied me as I made my way through the jungle towards the waterfall, as waterfalls don't usually occur in barren areas and arid regions. Once arriving at said Garden of Eden, the water usually ran mind-numbingly cold and the lack of bathroom facilities wore away at me until I finally went au natural behind a large jungle leaf. On our trip to Australia I learned that I could add creepy waterfall pool eels to the list of reasons why "waterfall hikes" did not always turn out great. Are waterfalls beautiful? Absolutely. Are they meant to be enjoyed by a city slicker such as myself? Not all the time.

From the kayak's interior, we grabbed the tour-provided dry bags that held our picnic lunch and towels to begin our hike. The early day sun sat low in the sky, keeping the temperature cool. Prior hikers wore down the path, but surprisingly we did not encounter any other people along the way. We did need to cross a stream, though with the help of a rope and the guide's strong hand I emerged from the other side relatively dry. After 40 minutes of comfortable walking complete with interesting commentary from our guide, we arrived at Uluwehi Falls, or "Secret Falls" as everyone kept calling it. I wasn't sure why. The trip was well advertised, the trail well marked, and the waterfall well labeled on all maps we saw. Not much secrecy there.

Water dropped over the lip, plunging down 100 feet to the pool below. The shore around the pool teemed with bodies... of lively Kauai chickens. Colorful and assertive, they reminded me of native dogs looking for a lunch handout. In a mass of feathers and excited clucks they rushed our hiking group. A few hand claps sent them scattering, but not before I noticed their iridescent feathers and brightly colored beaks and combs. Not like I am a chicken connoisseur, but they really were attractive birds, much more so than the usual collection of scraggly feathered, domesticated peckers we encountered on other tropical islands.

My McNugget thoughts aside, I went about the task of deciding whether or not to brave the waterfall pool. The body of water was small. I could wade in, paddle about and, at the first sign of trouble, escape out the other side in seconds. I let some of the other hikers venture into the pool first to offer instant food to the potential underwater carnivores. Then, I ventured in a toe. The water was refreshing, but comfortable, the rocks underfoot, slick, but not slimy. I retreated to the shore, stripped down to my bathing suit, and stepped in. After a short and alert, but pleasant swim, I climbed back out. I sported no leeches, no fang marks, not even a little sun-burn.

Our group sat along the pool bank eating cheese sandwiches and drinking lukewarm ice tea. After a few chocolate sandwich cookies, we prepared to return to the kayaks and make our way back to civilization. On the hike back we began to appreciate our tour's early starting time, as we passed three separate groups of people going to the falls. Indeed, the "secret" was truly out.

Shaved ice never tasted so good. Then again, top a gym shoe with macadamia nut ice cream (as this shaved ice was) and it would taste good too. I loved travel for the fine food and drink we consumed over the years. But Kauai offered something unique, a consistent stream of salt-of-the-earth food without pretenses, all insanely tasty and surprisingly cheap. Kauai has plenty of fancy places to eat too, but good-n-basic restaurants rule.

Day one on the North Shore we drove towards Hanalei for lunch. Perhpas our hotel's $20 salads tasted good, but surely we could find other, more interesting gastronomic options. We didn't get far down the road before we came across a small worn wood structure with a gift shop and a down-home bar/restaurant with a quaint view of a meandering river from the nearby taro fields. As our stomachs growled, Michael turned the car into the gravel parking lot joining several already parked there. If we didn't like the menu we could always drive onwards.

Snack bar food ruled. Hamburgers, hot dogs, club sandwiches, and other simple dishes filled the menu. I asked the waitress about the fish and chips, the only innovative item to be found.

"We get the fish locally," she said. "It's usually whatever is in season, right now I think it's ono – you guys from the mainland call it wahoo. We dunk it in a beer batter, and then fry it up. It's my favorite thing on the menu."

A few minutes later two large baskets of fish and chips arrived at our table, along with two Fire Rock Ales, a Hawaiian beer. The beer was cold, while the meal was straight from the fryer, too hot to touch. I'm pretty sure I never ordered fish and chips anywhere before, ever. But, add a beautiful day, a tasty beverage, and fresh local ingredients, and I swooned.

Our Hanalei area tours continued to produce incredible food. We screeched to a halt in front of a restaurant with a huge line snaking off the front porch. We weren't sure what food they were selling, but that many people couldn't be wrong. The line turned out to be a run on hamburgers, hand-formed, cook-while-you-wait beauties that were juicy and perfect, wrapped in their little grease papers of happiness. We waited on line, ordered at one window, paid at another window, and then waited for our name to be called. We got our burgers and our frings (fries and onion rings mixed, a weakness of mine that invariably leads to happiness and heartburn) and sat down at the well-used picnic tables on the restaurant's front lawn. Fending off aggressive birds intent on stealing our fries, we savored every bite.

On another afternoon, during that strange time when lunch service ends but dinner service was hours away, we couldn't find a thing to eat. We were starving from a long hiking trip to Waimea Canyon, an enormous fissure on Kauai's west side with breathtaking scenery. We needed sustenance. We stopped at several places in Kapa'a, but none were open. Finally, one off-duty hostess took pity on us and recommended a local place. The diner sat on a side street in a strip mall that looked dilapidated and infrequently maintained. Faded gingham curtains hung in the windows and dust gathered in the cracks of the crumbling brick façade.

Locals filled the place's well-worn, wooden tables and benches. But, no person shot us dirty looks as the hostess squeezed us into the corner. One glance at the menu and we realized we had found the Hawaiian version of IHOP. We could get meatloaf or a sandwich, but the bulk of the dishes were breakfast items.

After burning a months' worth of calories hiking the canyon, I welcomed any carbohydrates that had the misfortune of coming near my mouth. Just a few minutes later, a monumental stack of roasted macadamia nut and banana pancakes sat in front of me, butter dripping down the side lazily. A cup of black coffee in a chipped white mug balanced the sugary goodness. In a feeding frenzy I completely finished the pile, leaving barely a crumb. Amazing food in genuine places does that to me.

CHAPTER 9

Aruba: The Goats of Wrath

G oats have a distinctive aroma when one is standing downwind. The
fragrance combines gaminess with thoughts of "Did I step in something?" Though they run wild throughout the island of Aruba, the goats
are used to humans, almost assertive with them, expecting the usual handout from sympathetic people with snacks. As Michael and I toured the
famous California Lighthouse grounds on the island's northwestern tip, the
herd followed us en masse like a stinky shadow.

We were at the lighthouse at just the right time of day, when the sky
hung in purple and pink wisps over land that started as rock-strewn desert
near our feet, then turned to scrub, then to beach and blue ocean beyond.
A light breeze blew in from the ocean then changed direction, bringing a
stinking reminder of our hooved stalkers, still close at hand. The scene was
serene, with only an occasional, impatient "Baaah!" breaking the silence.

After spending our first full day in Aruba baking on the beach we
decided to get motivated and explore the island. A glance through the tour
guides and brochures at the concierge's desk indicated our interests did not
match many of the sightseeing opportunities. Only two options, the lighthouse and the natural blowhole, sounded unique to Aruba. Undeterred,
we packed up the rental car and drove off, armed only with our misguided
sense of adventure and a cheap hotel map.

We located the lighthouse easily, the whitewashed sentry standing
100 feet in the air at the end of the main road. In addition, had the map
and the height not helped, we could have rolled down our windows and
followed the furry welcoming party's perfume to our destination. The

restaurant next to the lighthouse had a patio for sunset viewing, its lounge lizards gaining a rising inebriation level as the sun went down. We vowed to return to the spot for just that activity later in our island stay. In the meantime we said goodbye to the goats and continued on to the natural blowhole on the northeast coast.

The western and southern coasts of the island have sandy beaches while the northern and eastern coasts contain a more rugged environment and fewer tourists. Our drive to the blowhole led us through arid desert terrain punctuated by divi-divi trees that grew in bizarre right angles because of the ever present tradewind. But, what the desert lacked in upright plant life it more than made up for in iguanas. The four-legged future handbags seemed to stare out from underneath every cacti and rock, watching us like we provided the most interesting thing to see all day...which we probably did. Not a lot of tourists drove out that desolate way.

We pulled into the makeshift gravel parking lot in front of the blowhole, making the most of the fading light. The empty lot indicated the place's raving popularity. We walked up to the viewing platform, a flat piece of concrete with a fence in front to prevent hapless tourists from plummeting to their untimely demise on the sharp rocks below. From the slab, we could see a flat section of rock with a cliff on one side facing the sea. A few waves washed in and out, but nothing much happened.

Technically a blowhole is a just an opening in the top of a rock cave that has contact with the sea. Theoretically, a wave rushes in, enters the cave and, with a burst of fanfare, spouts water out the hole and into the air, the whole shebang accompanied by thunderous noise from the pressurized rushing water. Either no one told this particular blowhole about the fanfare requirement, or it had stage fright. Whatever the cause, the blowhole did nothing interesting but gurgle from time to time when hit by a heartier wave.

We stood in silence, expecting the blowhole to dazzle us. *Any moment now.* After ten minutes we gave up and started walking back to the car. Just as we reached the parking lot, a roar erupted from the hole and soaked our backs in a fine, salty mist. I swirled around, expecting to see the geyser, but gravity had already reclaimed the water. Michael and I agreed to go back to the platform and wait it out a bit longer in order to see the phenomenon. It took us 15 minutes to reach the darn thing by car, so five more minutes of standing around was not asking too much.

We stood. We waited. We willed the magic hole to do its thing.

"Maybe its low tide," I guessed, trying to make sense of the deficient natural wonder. "What if it needs two waves in rapid succession in order to build enough pressure?" Maybe it was broken.

"I don't know. I'm not a sea cave expert," said Michael dejectedly as we rounded out fifteen more minutes of waiting time we would never get back.

"This sucks. Let's go get dinner. Last one to the car has to remove the iguanas from the roof!" As we drove away, we heard another thunderous "whoosh" as sea spray covered our back window.

From reading the guides and talking to locals, I gathered that many other attractions, activities, and events occurred on Aruba. Unfortunately, as I learned more about them I felt compelled to avoid them if possible. Some of the better opportunities we passed up included:

- Donkey Sanctuary –Arubans historically had a bad habit of abandoning their donkeys, leaving them to wander the island looking for water and gullible tourists with tasty sandwiches to share. In 1997, the "Save our Donkeys" foundation rounded up the lucky creatures and contained them on pleasant land to live out their days in four-legged tranquility. Tourists can now visit the sanctuary to watch the creatures stand around aimlessly. Also, the facility thoughtfully offers donkey-themed souvenirs for purchase to commemorate the experience. Everyone needs an ass keychain.

- Aruba Aloe Factory – In 1840 an Aruban native planted some aloe in his garden. The aloe liked the Aruban environment so much that it decided to overthrow the government and take over the entire island. For a while mapmakers called the place the

"Island of Aloe" because no one could find the beaches underneath this super-sized plant. The locals have been fighting back ever since, and created a factory to process the hoards of it they chop up every year, as burying or burning it just made the plant angry. After inhabitants realized that eating the plant was not a good use of the excess because it produced gastrointestinal distress, someone came up with the ingenious idea to wipe it on themselves, a practice that is still used today. The factory tour includes the secrets of how the leaf goop is squeezed into expensive bottles to produce a miasma of topical ointments, salves, gels, lotions, and other products to help tourists part with their dollars.

- Numismatic Museum – This is not the place where people with breathing problems go to study ancient inhalers, as I originally thought. The term numismatic means the study or collection of currency. This extravaganza houses 30,000 historic coins from Aruba and around the world. In an effort to protect these coins without using a vault the Arubans put the most boring name they could think of on the museum to deter any shred of interest or excitement about the place or its contents. The moniker is working so well that I hear they leave the doors unlocked at night.

- Youth Bowling International Tournament – Because when I think Caribbean island, I think bowling. Forget the beaches. Forget the sun and surf. Visitors go inside the Bowling Palace to watch kids roll balls down humidity-warped lanes for international fame and fortune. An opportunity to pursue when one just can't stand paradise anymore.

- Beaches, Beaches, Beaches – Arubans are enamored of their beaches, a fact which I can appreciate due to the sugary sand and turquoise water that grace the island's fringes. However, natives tend to list each beach as a separate experience when describing island attributes that seem suspiciously similar. "Baby Beach, now that has really nice sand. Another great thing to do is go to Eagle Beach, which has really, really nice sand. Druif Beach has super nice water, and sand." There are critical beach differentiators, like massive weekend crowds and occasional land mines placed long ago in less peaceful times, but Arubans frequently leave those petty attributes off the descriptions. We stuck to the beaches within walking distance of our hotel and enjoyed the super nice water and really, really nice sand just fine.

After exhausting the cultural opportunities on the island, we turned to the land-based activity the rest of the tourists pursued with vigor: shopping. I'm not sure why shopping became such a major sport in the Caribbean, but for many visitors to the region it's one of their trip highlights. Perhaps it's the sea air, the relaxing of inhibitions, or just the perception of a bargain, but the Shopping Superheroes just could not stop demonstrating their buying power. In that regard, Aruba was no different than many other vacation destinations.

We started our shopping tour at the market wharf in Oranjestad's harbor, where quality and crap sat side by side. Original paintings, island photographs, and hand made pottery lay on tables next to t-shirts, random aloe products, painfully fake designer purses, naked lady coasters, and carved coconuts imported from China. I was happy to see a unique specimen of island ingenuity, djuco nuts, carved, polished, and sometimes inlaid with precious metals by local craftsmen. The nuts did not grow on Aruba, but occasionally washed up on the shore from neighboring Venezuela, which made them even more unique in my mind.

The market pricing scheme, however, confused me. The Spanish arrived on Aruba's shores first. The Dutch took possession of the island in1636 near the end of the Eighty Years' War between Spain and Holland. Brittan borrowed the island for a brief stint, but other than that it has been part of the Kingdom of the Netherlands ever since, which explained the use of the Dutch Florin. A heavy visitor population from the U.S. and Europe accounted for the use of the Dollar and the Euro. Venezuela's proximity explained the occasional Bolivar use. But nothing rationalized which currency each vendor used to quote prices. Some focused on one currency, while some quoted prices in multiple currencies in a way that made me yearn for my calculator to see which denomination provided the best bargain.

One small painting had a "20" on its price tag, a reasonable cost in U.S. Dollars for the handmade art. But, if the vendor quoted Florins, then the painting cost eleven dollars, a super bargain. If the tag meant Bolivars then it offered a steal at nine dollars. If the "20" meant Euro, however, the painting actually cost twenty-eight dollars. The situation hurt my vacation-addled head with too many numbers. I thanked the vendor and left the painting behind before I passed out from the higher math.

Supposedly, the name Aruba means "red gold" a name given to the island a long time ago when explorers thought the rocky shores contained the mineral. These days, the only source of gold appeared in the numerous downtown jewelry shops. Intrepid explorers no longer braved the desert, stinky goats, and prolific aloe, but rather aggressive salespeople in the air-conditioned stores all over town. We left the marketplace and walked through downtown, stopping often to window shop.

Despite common visitor beliefs, Aruba isn't actually a duty free port, but the duty is pretty low. The jewelry stores had reasonable prices. In addition to the usual diamonds, semi-precious stones, and watches, Aruba also seemed to have an abundance of sea-themed jewelry. Starfish-shaped gold earrings, silver sea shell bracelets, and necklaces with dangling tropical fish, their eyes studded with amethyst chips, appeared in almost every store. If the significant stock was any indication, the vendors expected an imminent run on dolphin pendants. Not to worry, though, the cases overflowed with plenty of porpoise posh for purchase.

I recognize that some manly men like to wear heavy gold pendants from substantial gold chains around their necks in a display of wealth, testosterone, or both. The style does not do much for me, but judging by the number of men who pursue this fashion

> **"I think men who have a pierced ear are better prepared for marriage. They've experienced pain and bought jewelry."**
> **-Rita Rudner**

statement some females must be providing positive reinforcement. The Aruban jewelry stores obliged the style with rope chains, ranging from dainty to heavy enough to support a boat anchor. Creativity ruled the pendant selection; the usual eagles and crosses were eclipsed by an aquarium full of sea life. Some subjects seemed too dainty for the manly intended purpose, like starfish and sea horses, but others, like crabs and sting rays, looked appropriately masculine. My favorite was an evil octopus, ten ounces of angry cephalopod with glowing red ruby eyes and muscled tentacles that reached out two inches in either direction. What sort of guy would wear something like that? It would take a very special man to sport that bling. Maybe Poseidon needed a necklace.

On day three of our trip we moved from the shopping marathon to more aquatic sports. Since we planned to dive later in the week, we decided to break up our beach time with a popular Aruban activity, wind-surfing. The constant trade winds made Aruba an ideal place for the sport. Fisherman's Flats, the most trafficked windsurfing spot in Aruba, occurred offshore just down the road from our hotel. We booked a lesson with a company located on the Flat's beach.

The surf hut resembled a ski chalet in all but temperature and clothing. Rental equipment hung on the walls, well-used, water-absorbent carpet covered the floor, and tanned twenty-something guys hung around sporting sunglasses and egos. A not-so-faint whiff of "athletic" odor hung in the air. To complete the chalet look, an après-surf bar occupied one corner of the building to quench one's thirsts when the sun set.

Brad, our instructor, took us outside to the equipment room and issued us two sails to attach to our windsurf boards. I could barely walk carrying the enormous, rainbow triangles of thin plastic sheeting. The moment the wind blew, mine attempted to take flight requiring me to wrestle it to the ground like I roped cattle for a living. Under Brad's watchful eye we threw on our t-shirts to block the intense sun. Apparently the t-shirts contributed to the windsurfing uniform, though I suspected their primary function served to differentiate the tourists from the locals.

Brad gave us an overview of the gear and the basic process, and hooked our sails to our boards. We waded into waist-deep water where a cash crop of squishy algae grew on the sandy bottom. I held up the sail and waited for a good wind to come along and hoist the sail into the air with me attached. Wind came and went, my sail flopped around in protest, but I didn't budge. Perhaps the algae glued me to the bottom.

After a few more pointers from Brad, who managed to be encouraging yet infuriating with his deceptively simple directions ("Hang on. Lift!") I prepared to try again. I gave a good kick when the next gust came along and, lo and behold, I rose into the air. My triumphant view from the top of the board lasted only a millisecond as I then continued my forward momentum face-first off the other side of the board, landing on top of the sail flat on the water. Now I was mad. And stuck. Brad extracted me from the equipment, righted the sail, and set me back upright on the correct side of the board. Michael stifled a laugh, though not having made any progress himself.

The next wind blew along and I kicked, gently this time. The sail rose with me firmly attached and better balanced. Suddenly I stood on the board, sail in hand, looking like a genuine surfer. The wind filled the sail and the windsurfer took off like a shot. Wobbly but excited, a momentary thrill of victory filled me. I headed straight off the beach, bound for Venezuela. Only then did it occur to me that Brad had not shared return trip secrets with us yet. Out was good, but back was better...and necessary. I didn't want to be mistaken for a waterlogged refugee when I washed up on the South American coast.

I glanced back at the rapidly disappearing coastline to see Brad waving his arms vigorously to communicate the obvious issue that I had already noted. The wind died down which slowed my pace to a stop, but did not remedy the issue that I had sailed *really* far offshore. To my credit I still stood on the board with the sail in hand, maintaining a reasonable amount of balance considering my lack of experience and the ten pounds of wet t-shirt that hung off me awkwardly.

A wave came along, making me stumble to the other side of the board. The sail flopped with me, pointing us in a new direction. The wind picked up again and suddenly I sailed along, no longer to Venezuela but back towards our hotel a mile down the beach. Though this was an improvement from my prior international travel, it still did not return me to Point A. After several minutes of moving parallel to the beach, I began to get the hang of steering the thing, and started angling towards shore.

Ten minutes later I thankfully planted my feet on dry land. I had to return to the water, however, to drag the windsurfer back to the surf hut. Although not heavy, the contraption was ungainly, making me look and function like a rainbow colored bird with only one working wing. From time to time the wind picked up, pulling the sail and myself in every direction other than the way I headed. By the time I returned to Michael and Brad, the board had beat me about the shins so much that I could have made a successful claim for spousal abuse.

"Look honey! Brad taught me how to go out *and* come back using you as an example of what not to do," Michael said, using that spousal jovial yet sarcastic tone that is a significant driver of the high divorce rate in America. He managed to get up on his board as the wind picked up, then headed parallel to the shore. Just as he flashed me his triumphant smirk, the wind died down, he lost his balance, and landed in a giant seaweed patch. Served him right.

Our wind surfing adventure demonstrated that we excelled at aquatic sports only when under the water. Fortunately, Aruba is home to a wide variety of interesting dive sites including the largest diveable wreck in the Caribbean, the 400-foot *Antilla*. The island also has a wealth of dive operators to suit every diving need and interest. Prior to the trip I located a dive outfit that appeared professional and accommodating. They picked us up from our hotel early the next day and shuttled us to the dive shop located right near their dock. After only a momentary signup and payment process, we boarded the boat.

Aruba diving consists of a few reefs and a lot of wrecks. Conservationists placed some of the wrecks in the waters intentionally to act as artificial reefs, but other crafts just met their end a bit too soon. On the first day, we stayed on the island's south side to visit two interesting wrecks, the enormous *Antilla* and the disintegrated *Pedernales.* Sharp, rusty metal makes me nervous underwater; I'm usually more of a reef girl. But these legendary wrecks offered volumes of sea life and easy navigation, a combination that produced super diving.

On the short ride to the dive site from the dock, I began the gearing-up process. I've braved hungry sharks, roaring currents, and unidentifiable dive boat food. Michael has been known to push me in front of approaching predators with big teeth while he makes a quick getaway behind me. On the whole, I was a pretty adventurous diver, not easily intimidated underwater. But, I had never been able to conquer my fear of the great scuba diving beast: my wetsuit.

My concern fell into two categories: not having it on me and having it on me. First, similar to chocolate and my big brown dog, I _need_ a wetsuit. Without it, no matter how similar the ocean temperature is to bath water, I get cold and enter a shivering state faster than an octopus can strip a tasty clam. In a last ditch effort to warm up, I sometimes swim back and forth like a crazed tuna, a maneuver that has gotten me "rescued" several times by divemasters thinking I was out of my gourd.

Dive boat personnel frequently got a chuckle out of my space suit. "You don't need that thing," they say. "There are enough monsters in the sea already!" Easy there, buddy. I didn't make fun of your mismatched shoes or bad taste in tequila. I know my limitations, especially when it comes to body temperature, so I schlep my 4mm suit with me to all dive locations no matter how small my suitcase needs to be. One pair of shorts, two shirts, one case of M&Ms, one wetsuit, and two weeks: no problem!

Which brings me to my second category of concern: the suits are, by design, tighter than NYC rush hour traffic. They usually have a zipper, put there like bait to lure the diver into thinking they actually have a chance at getting into the suit. I have heard that powder can sometimes enable the process, but no amount of talc could help me win this battle of The Bulge.

Once on, the neoprene acts like kryptonite for a diver's positive image of their body. It is so tight, one would think it acts like a girdle. But, no. Every hot fudge sundae and grilled cheese (with bacon) transgression is highlighted by the silhouette of the black suit against the boat's white background. I'm pretty sure a *very* thin woman painted it white in the first place. I try to overcome the inner tube effect by sucking it in until I realize there are some body parts that will not appear smaller no matter how much I deplete the atmosphere.

But then, the other divers on the boat put on their vests, specially crafted jackets that can be inflated with air for buoyancy. Suddenly our looks equaled out, a uniform army of strange sea life covered in lumpy gear waiting to enter the water. We stopped first at the *Antilla*, which I spotted easily because part of the rusty wreckage stuck clear out of the water at low tide. The other end touched the bottom at 60 feet. On our way out to the site, the divemaster gave us some history.

"The *Antilla* was a freighter used by the Germans to supply their submarines during World War II," he said. "The allies called it the 'Ghost Ship' because it managed to elude detection and attack over and over. When Germany invaded Holland in May of 1940, the *Antilla* was moored just off the shore of Dutch-owned Aruba. The Aruban government gave the *Antilla's* captain one day to surrender, but instead he fired up the engine to full power, which basically set the ship on fire, and scuttled it. It turned on its port side and sank only 600 yards offshore. Hurricanes have moved it around, but for the most part it's in the same place it sank."

"Follow me, and I'll give you a good tour of the wreck. There are some really large openings, so we can penetrate it some. Oh, and be careful. There are a lot of parts of this ship that stick out in all directions, like the mast that's fallen over, so make sure you keep an eye out for stuff so you don't hit your head."

Once the captain moored the boat to a buoy attached to the wreck, I took a giant stride off the back of the boat into the water. With almost no current, I was able to get acclimated and descend without being swept out to sea. Boats frequently sink in the channels in which they run, so many wrecks are sitting right in the middle of roaring current, making it difficult for a diver to get to his or her destination accurately. It's not uncommon for a boat to drop divers off far up the current so they have time to descend as they are swept along, hopefully intersecting with the wreck at the right point in time and depth. The thought of missing the target entirely makes every diver wish he or she paid more attention in geometry class as a kid.

As our group descended, I could see the enormous wreck's outline. I always found approaching a wreck to be horror-movie creepy, as the dark, hulking mass appears out of the gloom looking more like something I want to avoid, rather than approach. Once we got closer to the wreck, the details became visible, and my interest piqued considerably. Thick marine growth coated the ship, especially the starboard side where crowds of knobby corals and finger-like sponges took up residence, fighting over every available inch like Miami Beach condo complexes.

The divemaster led us by the crow's nest, again encrusted in sea life, then down to the ship's side where one whole wall of a cargo hold was missing. We entered the shadow-filled hold then swam through the interior. I felt like Ahab, the ship's steel ribs towering around us, like floating in a whale's belly. Small damselfish and butterfly fish darted amongst the debris; piles of helmets fused together, machinery parts, and ragged pieces of rusting metal made a bizarre playground for sea life.

Our proximity to the shore and the waves overhead stirred up the bottom and reduced the visibility to 40 feet or so. As we exited the other side, I noticed a sediment cloud moving towards us that would surely reduce the visibility further. Other dive groups checked out the wreck, one of which may have stirred up the silt and unintentionally sent it in our direction. I had only a second to grab Michael, who fortunately hovered close to me.

The moment the sediment cloud enveloped us, I couldn't see a thing. The visibility dropped to near zero. I fought the urge to panic, knowing that the cloud would move on in a moment or two, but freaking out nonetheless. Fortunately, I had Michael firmly in my grasp. I find the complete loss of vision underwater, from sediment or mask issues, to be disorienting and scary. Although I know other divers are near, I get an overwhelming feeling of helplessness and loneliness, like I'm the only person on earth. The reaction is completely fueled by emotion and not by logic, and fortunately it passes as soon as I can see again.

A few kicks later the cloud passed, the panic subsided, and we continued on our wreck tour. The divemaster found one last treat before we ascended, a lumpy frogfish. The well camouflaged fish resembled a sponge so closely that I had to study the area for some time before I could even pick it out. The divemaster must have seen that particular fish in that area on prior dives, as finding a master illusionist like a frogfish could take even a pack of divers a very long time. We ascended after the find, watching the sunscreen-covered underbellies of snorkelers floating around the more shallow wreck parts.

Back on board we snacked and relaxed while waiting for our surface interval to expire. Our next site, the wreck of the *Pedernales*, lay just to the south of the *Antilla*. A German submarine torpedoed the *Pedernales*, an oil tanker, in 1942. The U.S. military carved the damaged ship up like a juicy ribeye steak, taking the bow and stern for parts and leaving the fatty mid-section behind for the fish. The wreck sat in shallow water and little current, guaranteeing a long, relaxing sea floor romp.

The divemaster led the pack towards the ruined metal heap on the sea floor that used to be the *Pedernales*. During the briefing he had encouraged us to find identifiable parts of the ship, like motors, pipes, etc. But, once I descended to the rubble, I recognized nothing. Coral covered the twisted

> Though the extent is debated by biologists, octopi are highly intelligent creatures. Tests have proved they have both short and long-term memory, which they use for a stunning variety of tasks. Some octopi can mimic other sea creatures. They can also be trained to differentiate shapes and patterns. Octopi can even use tools, for example by collecting broken coconut shells to construct a shelter. The sea creatures have been seen running around the ocean floor with the shells on their heads, like aquatic party hats, waiting for the need for shelter to arise.

metal bits and fish set up nice homes in the debris layers. Hurricanes had thrown the wreck around like a toy, scattering the pieces into a different order than they originally emerged from the boat yard. The only thing I could identify for sure was an upright sink that randomly appeared on the sand with fish swimming around in the basin like bath toys. I guess the U.S. military did not need to wash their hands.

Michael showed interest in a mound of coral, rock, and boat bits. He circled it, peering into the cracks. I swam over for a closer look, and noticed a pile of shell halves scattered around the base of the mound. It looked like someone held a "clams on the half shell" party on a boat above, and then threw the remnants overboard. I looked for an abandoned Tabasco bottle nearby.

Suddenly the center of the mound blinked. I blinked back, not believing my eyes. An octopus had made a home in the junk fortress, keeping its whole body tucked inside, but facing one eyeball out to watch the passing sea show. Further inspection revealed one sucker-covered, well-camouflaged tentacle wrapped around the mound entrance. Human partiers didn't cast away the shells, the octopus did, right after it ate them for dinner. I snapped picture after picture of the fascinating find, thinking all the while that it appeared a lot more interesting than its gold namesake in the jewelry store.

The day's diving made us ravenous and longing for something more substantial than a salad or fries. Some friends back home mentioned a unique yet tasty Aruban restaurant that specialized in ostrich dishes. Not to be discouraged by what seemed to be a strange thing to eat, we decided to try the place.

As we pulled up to the Ostrich Farm, the restaurant looked nice, though the grounds behind it looked awfully spacious for a place that served food. After a brief stroll around, what I should have known from the name became visually apparent: the place not only served ostriches, it also raised them. My stomach turned. The whole setup just seemed wrong. *Look at the helpless birds, milling about merrily. Don't worry, there will be fewer feathers when they are on your plate.* The farm even contained a hatchery, where visitors could see the cute little fuzzy ones cheeping away before they became full grown meals.

Westerners did not usually think of ostrich as a food source, which perhaps explained the place's popularity. I couldn't imagine a beef ranch having the same success. *While you wait for your scaloppini to cook, would you like to go pet the other calves?* Conceptually the "grow an ostrich, serve an ostrich" idea sounded grotesque, but in execution, the owners combined the two ideas tactfully, almost naturally. Though the scheme probably would not work in my home town, it seemed to do just fine in Aruba judging by the number of visitors.

Did I mention we were starving? Heaven help us, but we took a table after suffering only a brief moral dilemma at the front door. An eclectic fusion of Caribbean and international fare filled the menu. The ostrich came in many forms, raw, sautéed, wrapped in breads, and grilled. We each ordered ostrich steaks. The lean meat tasted like mild beef. When we focused on the meal instead of the surroundings, we enjoyed a pleasant evening. We did, however, decline the tour afterwards.

Aruba's wrecks carry a great reputation among divers, one that is well-deserved. In addition to oil tankers, one can also dive fuel barges, cement freighters, tug boats…all sorts of rusting metal requiring little more than a diving certification card, a tetanus shot, and a sense of adventure. The next day we caught up with our dive company again, this time to explore a unique underwater feature, an airplane.

Aruba's waters actually house several small airplanes. Local scuba diving and airplane enthusiasts placed some of the crafts; others took a more direct route to the ocean floor. Hurricanes took their toll on a few of the older ones, tearing them up into bits that don't really resemble planes anymore. We headed towards two that sat intact and near each other on the bottom.

Since Aruba is small, approximately the size of Washington D.C., and since most sites are along the southern and eastern shore, any diving destination is only a short boat ride away. After 15 minutes we arrived at the designated site and dropped anchor. Sensing our enthusiasm, the divemaster made the dive briefing...brief. Follow the leader, don't crowd, and don't touch any coral.

We entered the water via the swim platform. A slight current snaked along, so the captain threw a nylon rope off the back of the boat. Divers grabbed the rope to prevent them from drifting off with the current before the rest of the group was ready. Michael and I jumped in first, so we grabbed onto the line and waited, regulators in hand. We finally set out on the tour after everyone entered the water, adjusted their equipment, retrieved critical items (like masks) forgotten on the boat in the excitement of the moment, and got our bearings. After descending to the bottom, we swam only a short distance to the first airplane. Michael and I hung to the back of the pack, preferring a more leisurely pace that gave the opportunity to snap a few underwater sightseeing pictures along the way.

The plane sat in fifty feet of water not far off the coast. An environmental group cleaned out the seats, wires, and other items that would otherwise snag a diver, turning it into a playground for the aquatically inclined and a home for wayward sea life. In its former days, the plane carried 60 passengers. Now it hosted red star coral and the beginnings of some orange tube sponges along with a manifest full of tropical fish.

We entered the plane from the tail's door, which had also been removed for safety. My first view of the plane's interior was of the bathroom, which still had the toilet seat intact. I found it funny that on land a toilet got nary a second glance, but underwater the utilitarian item took on new significance, attracting considerable diver attention and a bevy of aquatic poop jokes (yes, underwater communication can convey even the shallowest ideas). Every diver stopped to take a good look, myself included.

The next step involved turning to my right and then swimming up the fuselage. When I step out of a dry airplane's bathroom there is always sort of this situation where I bump into the opposing wall or seat and have to squeeze myself back into the aisle. There never seems to be enough room for me to exit the facility in a dignified manner. Well, that same maneuver is necessary underwater, but made more difficult by carrying a large air tank on my back. I clanged my tank against every metal surface in the area, sending out nice clunks of sound that traveled to the other divers, making them turn in interest to my tin pan symphony. I smiled to them and waved, and then continued swimming towards the front of the plane.

The divers in front of me looked like astronauts floating through the plane in zero gravity. On either side I could see out the windows, some filled with voyeuristic fish. At the head of the plane, the cockpit door had also been removed, making it easy to take a long look inside. The controls looked good as new, though covered in corals and other sea life. I took a picture, my flash illuminating everything well because of the confined space. The light revealed a surprising sparkle of vivid purples, pinks, and yellows of corals and other sea life that now ruled the helm.

Finally, I made a left and exited through the hole where the front door once hung. I quickly turned around and snapped a picture of Michael doing the same; a surreal vision as he passed through the opening head first, then swam up and over the top of the plane. After our plane tour we circled the area, poking amongst the coral boulders for interesting animals while we waited for the rest of the group to complete their flight.

We swam along the reef towards the next airplane. I noticed an enormous anchor chain, each link a foot long, lying along the bottom. It intertwined with the coral heads, and sported a significant amount of sponge growth covering it entirely in some places. Either the anchor had gotten irretrievably stuck, or the ship left in a hurry, as that much chain would have been missed if someone had mistakenly dropped it overboard.

The aircraft's shadow materialized in the blue then became more detailed as we approached it. The plane was much smaller than the first, only a four-seater. It sat in 25 feet of water amongst soft corals that swayed in the current. The airplane looked like it had been in the water longer than the other plane, with plant life covering the fuselage as well as the wings. Red algae engulfed it. I swam over to peer under a wing, and found a family of red squirrel fish, their big black eyes goggling at me. I swam up to the front windshield, whose wipers were still attached. Organisms covered even the glass, obscuring the inside from prying diver eyes.

Our exploration of the second plane consumed the rest of our dive time. We ascended with the group then climbed back on the boat. As we returned to shore one last time Michael and I reflected on our Aruba trip. Usually the presence of man degrades reefs, but ironically in Aruba man-made wrecks actually enhanced the underwater world. In many ways we found the human presence underwater to be more authentic and engaging than the topside offerings. Just don't tell that to the goats.

CHAPTER 10

Federated States of Micronesia:
"You want to go where?"

"**Y**ou want to go where?" said the airline booking associate.

"Micronesia," Michael said.

"And in what part of the world may I search for that destination?" she asked. Apparently a map test was not a part of the hiring process.

"It's in the Pacific Ocean, somewhere near Indonesia," he said.

"How about Majuro or Kwajalein?" said the associate.

This stumped us. Our prior research on Micronesia had produced useful knowledge on the islands, including the 58 edible uses for a taro root and how to ask for a bathroom in Yapese. However, we had not committed all 607 Micronesian island names to memory and our knowledge of neighboring island nations was even more limited.

"We want to go to Yap. It's one of the Micronesian islands," said Michael.

"Huh?"

"Yap."

"How do you spell that?" asked the associate.

Fortunately my husband is a patient and resourceful man. After much discussion and dogmatic use of an atlas he procured us two tickets.

Though the Federated States of Micronesia occupies more than one million square miles of the Pacific Ocean, the scuba diving is concentrated in four main areas: Kosrae, Pohnpei, Yap, and Chuuk. Kosrae and Pohnpei are known for being pristine and mostly unexplored marine environments. Manta ray sightings are almost guaranteed in Yap. If a diver's taste tends towards the manmade, the Chuuk lagoon is famous for World War II wrecks of all shapes and sizes.

The unfortunate reality of our day jobs dictated that we only had time to visit one Micronesian island in depth (no pun intended). We were pairing this trip with a visit to neighboring Palau. Manta rays are on every diver's underwater Dream Team, so we chose Yap. We had not seen any rays since Bora Bora and Hawaii and were eager for more. Armed with enough diving gear to scare away even the most determined porter, we were off.

> "Long before time was recorded the story goes, Gusney and four other supernatural Spirits sprang into being from a fresh-water well located in the area now know as Tho'long, Colonia. ... Many moons passed and Gusney came upon a human family from the ancient place called Malaya. He liked them and sent them on to Wa'ab to let the other Spirits know of his whereabouts. Later he met another couple from India and sent them to Wa'ab as well. This couple, named Wan and Rayina, and a daughter of the first family, Ruliya, made Wa'ab their permanent home and, according to legend, are the ancient forebears of the Yapese people."
> -Yap Visitors Bureau

The name Yap comes from one of those "silly European explorer misunderstands the native" stories so common to island destinations. The original name of the island was Wa'ab. However, when the explorer pointed to the ground and made international gestures of "What do you call this?" he was told Yap, and the name stuck. Unfortunately, the legend says, the natives thought he was referring to a nearby oar.

There are four indigenous languages in Yap: Yapese, Ulithian, Woleian, and Satawalese. Fortunately we did not have to purchase the Woleian language tapes because English is also commonly spoken because of Yap's brief stint as a stepchild of the U.S. after World War II. This purgatorial time also accounts for the Yapese use of the U.S. Dollar and a 120 volt system. It's almost like being at home except with more grass skirts and less traffic. In 1986, Yap and its neighbors Chuuk, Pohnpei, and Kosrae formed the independent nation of the Federated States of Micronesia, but kept the currency, language, volts, and an affinity for American TV dinners.

The flight from Atlanta to Micronesia was long and tedious, with periodic bursts of excitement when our stewardess, Maria Andretti, crashed the drink cart into passengers' elbows. The airline had planned a game of Pacific hopscotch for us. We would fly from Atlanta to Los Angeles to Guam, then direct to Palau, then immediately backtrack to Yap. After our week-long stay in Yap, we would fly back to Palau for another week and then back to the U.S. Printing out our impressive pile of paper tickets contributed to significant global deforestation.

Despite our complicated flight plan we were surprised to hear the engines rev down indicating landing two hours before we were supposed to arrive in Palau.

"Please put your seat backs and tray tables in their upright and locked position. We will be arriving in Yap in fifteen minutes," said the stewardess. This was puzzling. Our tickets said the flight was direct to Palau where we would then pick up another flight to Yap.

"But I thought this was a direct flight to Palau?" I asked hoping for some clarity and another of those colorful little bottles of alcohol that had been my sustenance throughout the flight.

"No, this flight always stops in Yap en route," she said.

Several people around us, who had used a more stringent screening process when choosing their booking agent gathered their belongings and prepared to deplane. The man across the aisle from me happily packed his things, whistling and smiling the whole time. I hated him and his apparent expertise in local airplane stops.

The plane touched down and I wished the whistler a good trip, filled with bed bugs and bad restaurant service. Then I flagged down the stewardess and explained our intent on returning to Yap later in the day. She agreed to let us off the plane to discuss our plight with the gate agent.

Some airports, especially American ones, are large overwhelming places full of rules and TSA screeners stopping every granny with knitting needles. In other countries the rule of law prevails in airports, resulting in machine gun-toting men scaring everyone into doing the right thing. In Yap, the airport is little more than some thatch and a smile.

We deplaned to a tarmac that extended into the jungle in either direction. The only buildings were a festive, palm-covered hut and a small adjacent cinderblock building. We were greeted by a smiling woman handing out flower leis and dressed in traditional Yapese clothing – a long grass skirt, sandals and nothing else. It was at this point that my husband considered giving up his U.S. passport in favor of a more "traditional" lifestyle.

With my husband predictably distracted, I approached a small desk in front of a turnstile where a weathered but friendly man was stamping passports. Apparently the process was for him to stamp and us to walk through the turnstile in order to exit the airport. Since a turnstile is usually used to provide a way of egress from an enclosed space, the requirement seemed odd; there were no fences, no walls, not even a few fallen logs around the airport. I could have walked directly off the tarmac straight into the jungle, had I been so inclined. However, in the interest of avoiding an international incident in the first two minutes we were in the country, we obliged, passing through the little metal arms with a satisfying clunk.

We found the gate/hut agent in the cinderblock building. We explained our situation quickly, since the plane was taking off again soon. The seemingly teenaged manager of the "international gateway" was helpful, though absolutely devoid of useful suggestions as to what we should do. Apparently if we changed our flight plans and left the plane now in Yap the rest of our reservation might be cancelled and we would have no way home. My husband looked out the window at the woman with the leis and pondered the benefits of the situation.

We decided to re-board the plane and take the circuitous route to Palau and back. Upon our return to Yap, later that day, we were the only ones deplaning. This was presumably because everyone else deplaned earlier and used the past four hours in a more productive way. It was evening and even quieter than before. The lights in the cinderblock building were off, and the woman with the leis had gone home to find a shirt. Only the man with the stamp remained, and he looked frightened to see us.

"I know you," he said suspiciously. Belief in spirits is still alive and well on Yap. Most Yapese people are afraid of ghosts and conjure magic as a form of protection. Perhaps he thought we were the worst kind of devils: phantom tourists.

We reminded the man that we had in fact met him earlier in the afternoon in the flesh and explained that we had simply misunderstood our flight stops. We pantomimed our excitement at returning to his beautiful island. He softened then, noting our insanity. The long flight and bad airline food had clearly taken its toll. Again, in the continued support of treaties of the United Nations, we exited the turnstile with a second Yap stamp in our passport for the same day.

The dirt parking lot outside the hut was empty. We waited a few minutes for the appearance of a taxi that never arrived then started to discuss possible means of transport. The problem with remote parts of the world is that sometimes there is no one else there. Fortunately a van pulled up a few minutes later with the name of our hotel on the side.

"I'm James," the man said. "I'll be your driver to the hotel." We hopped in, happy to be over our travel challenges for a while.

The island of Yap actually consists of four continental islands. The four are joined by a common coral reef and fringed with beaches and mangrove swamps. The terrain is mostly hills with dense tropical vegetation. As Yap is only 38 square miles, our trip to the hotel was a quick one. The streets were not bad for the tropics, with quality asphalt and minimal potholes. However, in some places there were ravines on either side of the road that could have swallowed our van. The only evidence that we had ever existed would have been a loud burp from the crevice.

We arrived at the hotel tired, but excited. The place was perfect. Sort of a classy jungle lodge, but with running water and scented bath soap. It had a unique, multi-cultural history of its own; its foundations being a combination of a U.S. military building and a Japanese command post. Our room overlooked Chammorro Bay and the sparkling, deep blue ocean that beckoned beyond.

After checking in our porter introduced himself. "I'm James," said the familiar, multitasking man. "I'll help carry your bags up to your room."

The Federated States of Micronesia has a population of about 107,000 people. Yap Island claims only about 8,000 of those. A census in the 1990's identified eight whole Yap inhabitants as living abroad. Basically, there are not a lot of Yapese people. And since they stay close to home, they need to be resourceful and versatile. James was not just multitalented; he was representative of his countrymen.

The next few days we got down to the business of diving. We were visiting in the low season, which rewarded our gargantuan travel efforts with rain and bugs. More than one morning we awoke to monsoon-like rains and thought our diving opportunity was drowned for the day. We quickly learned that after a cup of coffee, some patience, and a sacrifice of my blood to the ravenous mosquitoes, the rain gods would usually let us go on our way.

Low season has its advantages, too. The dive boat was blissfully empty, so there was no need to mash anyone's toes with a tank to get a good seat at the back of the boat. We also had our choice of dive sites because of the small number of boats on the open ocean. This enabled us to easily pursue the reason for our visit: the manta rays of Yap.

Manta rays are the largest in the ray family, with wingspans that can reach 20 feet and more. They glide through the water by flapping their side fins like a graceful underwater bird. Although they are enormous, they are filter feeders, eating unfortunate plankton and other small ocean tidbits. In the Yap high season they are seen in large numbers performing acrobatic dances to attract mates and produce little mantas. In the low season they are equally as impressive, but fewer are seen, usually hovering near the coral heads and filter-feeding in the channels.

The first few days were spent diving Miil Channel and Goofnuw Channel. At these sites there is a good chance of seeing rays and a great chance of seeing other sea creatures if the mantas are away on vacation. There are also currents here that zip divers along past the beautiful coral scenery. Yap's secondary underwater attraction is its vibrant hard corals, which do not disappoint in any season.

We saw crowds of sharks, mostly white tips and grey reefs, throughout our dives. Some of these ferocious predators were embarrassing the rest of their kind by embracing the good life, lying on the bottom while eyeing us lazily. They posed no threat to us as we were too challenging of a snack. Also in view were UFO-shaped stingrays, red and white schooling snappers, and green moray eels in what seemed to be almost every hole in the reef.

The rainbow of small tropical fish reminded me of the tie-dyed shirts I made I summer camp every year, displaying every color and pattern imaginable. The celebrities were the clownfish made famous worldwide by Nemo, that talking orange guy in the movies. They can be found living within the branches of almost every anemone, which are stinging creatures that zap curious predators. The clownfish were a wily bunch, charging straight at me when they felt I got too close. Some were red-orange with one white ring, some brown-orange with two, others still were bright orange with a white stripe down the back. I had no idea Nemo had so many relatives who spent their summers in Micronesia.

There comes a time on every boat trip that divers hate: the dreaded surface interval. Even though the whole purpose of a dive trip is to be *in* the water, periodically one has to get *out* of the water to rest and reduce the unpleasant effects of deep diving on the body. For most, it is like putting a tantalizing birthday present in front of a kid and then asking him to wait for a full hour before opening it. On our fourth day, when we were the lone divers on the boat, the captain asked us if we would like to spend our

surface time on a small island near our next site. It seemed like a good way
to make the hour go faster, so we agreed.

"What's the name of the island?" I asked, wanting to enter it into my
dive log book where I captured the details of all of our dives with religious
zeal.

"It's the Forbidden Island," he said. Well, now that was interesting.
I felt like a Bond girl. "The local people say that spirits live there. Many
won't go on the island. Lots of tourists ask to go there, but no one wants
to take them."

"But we are going there anyway?" I asked, not wanting to anger the
spirits lest they take it out on my air tank midway through our next dive.

"Oh, yes. I know the guy who lives there. He and his wife are really
nice," he said.

We had to anchor the boat offshore and wade in the last few yards.
The island was long and thin, with piles of delightful, undisturbed shells
along the sandy fringe. This place hadn't seen tourists in a long time. On
one end of the beach was a hut cobbled together from the finest products
the sea had to offer: driftwood, dried palm fronds, and a giant blue plastic
tarp.

It was from this tropical hodgepodge hut that a man emerged. He was
tall and lanky, with a crazed afro and a rusty machete in his hand. I could
not decide whether he was a man possessed by a spirit, or was actually the
spirit itself. To my dismay our wading gave him enough time to intercept
us on the beach. I began to calculate the physics required for us to walk
on the water to get back to the boat if needed.

"Hey guys!" said machete man.

"Hey Ronnie!" said our captain. "Mind if we let our divers rest on
your beach for awhile? We brought beer!"

My husband and I laid a towel down on the beach, which attracted
several hermit crabs looking for a lift to the mainland. It was beautiful,
serene, and peaceful. Abruptly, the quiet was interrupted by a chopping
sound made by machete man swinging his sword against something near

his hut. We hoped it wasn't our captain's head. Fortunately, a moment later our captain reappeared.

"Ronnie split open some coconuts for us," he said. Seeing our look of big-city confusion he continued. "You drink the milk then scrape out the flesh with your finger nail."

"Of course," I said sounding confident. The coconut cart with the rusty machete comes by my office every day around 2 P.M., so I was already in the know. We nibbled at the gift and found it quite good: refreshing, tropical, and lacking any noticeable parasites. It was a better surface interval than we had had in quite awhile.

After a week of being underwater we became a bit waterlogged, like kitchen sponges used one too many times. We decided to embrace dry land and seek out some of the cultural aspects of the island. We arranged for an independent, guided tour. All land, except in Colonia, the capital, is privately owned by the traditional leaders and chiefs. One must ask permission in advance to visit, or risk death, dismemberment and other bad things. It made sense to hire a local guide to ensure we kept all of our limbs.

That morning we waited on the front porch of the hotel for our guide. A familiar man approached.

"I'm James," the man said. "I'll be your guide today." We were starting to see a trend here. In addition to James the driver and porter, we had also experienced James the waiter in the small hotel restaurant and James the room service runner who provided extra towels when needed. This was a man of many talents and loads of energy. And, we surmised, he was, aside from the owners, the only low-season hotel employee.

James was wearing the traditional men's dress of Yap, a *thu'us*, which is a colorful man-skirt that represents a way of life that is alive and well in Yap. Even with modernization creeping ever so slowly in, the island's culture and traditions remain strong. Earlier in the trip I saw several men walking towards town in their *thu'us* carrying modern, leather briefcases. They perfectly captured the Yapese appreciation for the new, but respect for the old.

Women too have traditional dress, as we saw at the airport. It consists of nothing more than an ankle length grass or woven hibiscus skirt. Bearing their breasts in public is perfectly acceptable. However, any exposure of a woman's thigh, even at the knee, is considered scandalous. Although my husband and I try to embody the "When In Rome..." concept of cultural experiences I thought it best to leave this aspect to the pros. I donned some pants and a tank top for our tour.

We climbed into the back of a small van as James started up the engine. As soon as we pulled away from the front of the hotel, James began our education with some thoughts on one of Yap's forms of currency, stone money. The circular carved disks of calcite range from three inches up 12 feet in diameter and require enormous change purses. They were originally carved in the shape of a fish (hence the local name for them, *rai*, or "whale") but not all carvers were budding Michelangelos and so a doughnut shape quickly became the form of choice.

"Most of the money was mined in Palau by the Yapese," he said. "They then brought it back by canoe." This impressed me, as it was 250 miles between the two islands, a long canoe trip for a big doughnut rock. I guess they did not have Krispy Kreme back then.

"The value is based mostly on the stone's history; how difficult it was to mine and bring back and how many lives were lost in its transport. No more *rai* is mined. We have a total of about 13,000 pieces and that is all there will be. That way the value never changes."

After studying economics for all those years in college, here at last was a supply and demand equation I could understand. The story made me think that here must be a Yapese relative in Ben Bernanke's family tree. Our car came to a halt and jolted me back to the tropical present as we pulled up to a clearing fringed in palms.

"Some pieces are kept in the villages to show their wealth, but most are kept here," he said, pointing to a shallow valley lined on either side with rows of *rai*. They varied greatly in size and the quality of craftsmanship. James pointed to one piece in particular that appeared older than most. The edges were jagged, indicating crude tools, most likely made of shell, were used to shape it.

"This one would be more valuable because it is older than many of the others. It would have been harder to carve and carry," he said.

"What about its story? Its history?" I asked.

"It's true that each piece has its own story that contributes to the value," he said. "That doesn't mean that the owners tell the story to anyone with ears. People keep the stone's history a secret so that no one steals the stone or can estimate the village's worth until it is needed." We sensed that the bank held not only currency, but also an exciting string of stories of the island's history.

No spear-wielding security guard was needed for that bank. It would be pretty obvious if a visitor tried to leave with one piece tucked secretively under their *thu'us*. Even in our Western attire, we left the bank no richer than before. Our next stop was a local village. On the way, James continued the stone money story.

"We use dollars to buy things like food and clothing. We get paid in dollars, too. But, stone money is still used to settle debts between villages and for more ceremonial reasons like marriages. When I started working at the hotel I wanted to move to a village that was much closer to my job. My old village had to pay stone money to my new village to allow me to live there."

Just then we pulled up to an enormous thatched hut with a steep pitched roof that sat on the bank of an ocean inlet. The hut was rectangular in shape and richly decorated with shells and various palm frond designs. In every inland direction we could see similar, but smaller dwellings between the trees. A man emerged from the large hut and greeted us. James introduced him as one of the village's elders.

The elder explained the building was a *faluw*, or Men's House. There the men gather to socialize and discuss village matters, such as how to make better use of the tourists and which other villages they want to eliminate. Women are not allowed to enter the Men's House, except when chosen to be the resident female, a position held in high esteem but mostly outlawed today because of the "services" they provided. As a guest in a village that was accustomed to visitors, I was allowed to enter the house only in the presence of my husband.

While seated in the house the elder told us many stories of the village. He shared tales of the various storms that destroyed the structures and how they always rebuilt, sometimes with the help of sympathetic neighboring villages. He talked of the traditional roles of women, tending the cultivated fields of taro and weaving baskets, and of the men, who fished extensively and were experts in canoes and sailing. Mostly, he ruminated on life while chewing betel nut.

I think it is important here to dedicate a paragraph to the art of chewing betel nut. The nut is a national addiction, and is the source of the frightening, red-colored smiles one sees across the island. To prepare a wad, you split the nut, add lime, and then wrap the package in a pepper leaf. Then, chew. This tasty tidbit produces a ten minute high and a tidal wave of red saliva that is expelled, often with surprising velocity. The serious betel nut snackers can be identified from the casual ones by their red-stained teeth, scary to us, but darn attractive to most locals.

This village elder clearly fell into the "serious chewer" category. By the time we took our leave of the village, the ground around him was littered with the juice. As we continued on to other villages during the tour, we found similar red-patterned ground at several of our stops.

In addition to the chewing habits of the locals, we caught other glimpses of village life and its integration into the modern world. Along one road we saw a boy walking in his *thu'us* with a woven palm basket in one hand and a portable CD player in the other. We saw groups of women and children socializing in open-sided huts wearing customary grass skirts with American style t-shirts, their Nike, Bart Simpson and Red Sox logos on proud display. Traditional building materials such as palms were used in conjunction with 20ᵗʰ century products such as concrete and plastic. I took away the feeling that these were a people who recognized some of the benefits of modern society, but also appreciated their heritage and fought to keep their culture alive.

As we were leaving the last village of the day, I heard a drumming sound coming from down the road. A woman was practicing a native dance in the clearing in front of her home. A young boy, an aspiring Ringo, provided the beat on an overturned plastic bucket. The dancer's movements conveyed a splendid story by using an alluring combination of graceful gestures and jarring outbursts of emotion. I had read that dance played an important role in Yapese culture. But, this impromptu performance in the middle of the jungle illustrated the point better than any book.

We had absorbed oodles of culture from the mainland, but after several days of diving, we had yet to see the famous manta rays. Of course, there is never a guarantee that the anticipated sea life shows up on a dive. I have long thought that the dive master's "you will see this when you get in the water" pre-dive briefing is a joke they play on the tourists based on a minimum of fact and a maximum of creativity.

"There is a 500 year-old lobster just after the coral head and a Volkswagen-sized clownfish if you swim north along the reef wall. Don't make any sudden movements or they will swim away before you can see them."

But I was determined. We had traveled too far to give up. My husband had come down with a cold, so he could not go with me. I thoroughly weighed my options, diving alone or sympathetically staying behind at the hotel, for about five seconds. I decided to go, not wanting to pass up our last opportunity to see the rays. When I got to the dive boat I found that it would be just the captain, Martin the dive master, and me on the boat that day.

Monsoon rains graced us again that morning. I huddled with my back to the deluge and a towel over my head as we sped towards the dive site. Cold drops pelted every exposed part of my body. I began to wonder at the soundness of my decision to go out in boat-filling rains with two strange men in hopes of seeing creatures larger than my garage. I closed my eyes and waited until rational thought passed, then got back to enjoying the day.

We went back to Goofnuw Channel, defining insanity by expecting a different result from the same activity. There were no other dive boats in sight. I put extra weight in my pockets to ensure I would not float away while waiting for our honored guests to appear. Martin and I dropped down to the sandy bottom at 60 feet depth and sat down. This was a cleaning station, a place where mantas would come to allow small fish to pick off parasites and other tasties. This sort of dive required nothing more than waiting at the bottom and sending out a come-hither vibe to the mantas.

So we sat. We waited. Forty minutes later we were still sitting and waiting. I had committed every grain of sand and miserable sponge in my vicinity to memory, having had little else at which to look. Then a shadow came overhead. And another. And

> "Sponges grow in the ocean. That just kills me. I wonder how much deeper the ocean would be if that did not happen."
> -Stephen Wright

another. The mantas were amazing, enormous but graceful. They appeared motionless in the current, exerting almost no energy to stay in one place. They made every move look effortless despite their full-figured bodies.

They took turns hovering over the coral head to get coiffed by the fish. While one was being vacuumed by cleaner wrasse maids, the other two floated nearby filtering the water for a snack. Their cephalic lobes-small fins on each side of their head-were unfurled, greedily guiding the plankton-rich water into their gigantic oval mouths.

All too soon we realized we were getting low on air. Sixty minutes had now passed. We needed to spend some time on the surface and get new air tanks. Time flies when one is having "close encounters of the enormous kind" fun. We ascended slowly, taking care not to make sudden movements and scare them off. We hoped they would still be there when we returned.

That 45-minute surface interval went slower than a politician admitting defeat. Usually the time goes by quickly as I play with my gear and trade exaggerated fish stories with the other divers. This time it was excruciating. To pass the time Martin and I discussed the manta ray phenomenon on Yap.

"Local fishermen have always seen the rays," he said. "Some thought it was a bad omen. The way the rays' heads are shaped sort of looks like horns. Locals call them the Devil Rays."

"To divers these manta rays are incredible to see," I said. "People are willing to spend a good amount of money to dive with them. That must be good for the economy."

"Yes, but some people here just don't care. They're superstitious. Some still believe the animals are evil and won't take divers out to see them."

Soon we were back in the water. The earlier vibe we sent out must have worked because two of the mantas were still there. We sat on the bottom for a while and watched the show. Then Martin encouraged me to creep around the coral head so I could get a better look. I came up around the side until I was about 12 feet away at eye-level with the creatures.

I could see the differences in each of the animals from there. From underneath they had all appeared white. From my new vantage point I could see their backs. Each animal had a unique, mottled design of white, black, and dark blue. Watching them was like an aquatic ink blot test.

Then, one swam towards me. Fortunately, the extra weight in my pockets prevented me from floating up as I started to breathe heavy from the excitement. My heart pounded and I thought about the meaningful one-on-one experience I was about to have with this creature. He drifted by me, giving me almost no notice, then floated out into the nearby channel, and went to the bathroom. I was clearly a lot less eye-catching to him than I thought: he just didn't want to soil his friends.

He did swoop in for a closer look at me on his way back from the Pacific port-o-potty. I stayed very still, resisting the urge to reach out a touch him, as I knew this would cause him to leave in a big hurry. He looked into my mask with his left eye, floating only three feet from me. It was a moment of acknowledgement and acceptance from him that I found incredibly moving. Most creatures that divers encounter will either swim away when approached or ignore the diver altogether. Rarely is there recognition, and even less frequently is there confident curiosity like I experienced with this ray. After a minute that felt like an eternity, he returned to his pals at the cleaning station.

They say that manta rays are solitary creatures, but their congregation sure looked like my colleagues back at the office gossiping around the water cooler. I could have watched them all day, hoping to pick up a juicy story on the octopus' new boyfriend and the tuna's poor taste in bait fish. Unfortunately, those of us without gills max out at about one hour of air at that depth, so it was once again time to ascend. Before I climbed up the boat ladder, I peeked underwater one last time to imprint a picture in my mind of their graceful silhouettes.

On the way back to the dock our boat passed under a bridge linking the two shores of Chammorro Bay. A large gap in the guardrail indicated a poor choice of direction by a prior driver.

"Glad I wasn't in that car," I said offhandedly.

"So you've heard that Martin's a star now," said the captain.

"What do you mean?" I asked.

Like any small island, paradise has its downside. An island, by definition, is surrounded by water, which means there are limited places to go and very limited things to do. A jaded friend of ours who grew up in Bermuda once told us that there were a lot of things for locals to do at night on the island, as long as those activities involved drinking, drugs, or sex. This is not to say that all islanders follow this lifestyle, but that it does occur, to a greater or lesser extent, almost everywhere.

Particularly affected are teenagers, full of raging hormones, a rebellious attitude, plenty of free time, and a lack of responsibilities. The prior week in Yap, the captain said, a car full of teens had tempted fate and lost. They had been out drinking and were driving home over the bridge when their car veered off the road, through the guardrail, and into the bay.

Martin and another dive instructor were at the dive shop working late on some gear. They heard the splash, saw the car sinking and grabbed their masks. By the time they got the skiff to the place where the car had landed, it was already submerged. The divemasters were able to get the two girls in the back seat out first by breaking a window. They went back down and struggled with the guy in the passenger seat who was stuck in the wreck of metal. They finally got him to the surface too. The driver wasn't so lucky.

"We had to help them," Martin said, unemotionally, like he had watched it on television. "They didn't know what they were doing. So drunk...they couldn't have gotten out on their own." I was struck by this stoic comment from a man who had joked with me all day. Perhaps his lack of surprise or outrage was born from a culture that was much more aware, or at least connected, to the rhythm of life and death than my own.

Our time in Yap had been enriched with the Yapese way of life and its ocean wonders. However, we had one last dive we wanted to do before leaving. It was a very shallow one, only 16 feet maximum, and had to be done right after sunset. At that time of night in the shallows of Rainbow Reef there is a special "adults only" show: *Mandarin Fish in Love*.

A mandarin fish is only two to three inches long, but sports a stunning, striped pattern of blue, green, orange, red, and yellow. They are shy creatures, and hide amongst the coral most of the time. But at dusk, the males hit on the ladies at the coral reef pick up bar.

"I'm a Pisces. I like slow swims and moonlit crustacean dinners. Turn offs include bright light, sudden movements and predators. But, jump on my pelvic fin and I'm yours for at least 30 seconds! No scales here, I'm covered in sexy slime. I've only got a 12-year lifespan, so I'm not looking for long term relationships."

Again it was just Michael, the dive master and me. We entered the water, floated to the bottom, and sat on the sandy floor facing a large boulder of coral. Tanks seemed like overkill; we could have used long straws for this shallow depth. I had put on a hood to keep me warm as I usually do on a night dive, but quickly realized my mistake when I started to sweat in the 80-degree water. We had bright flashlights to spot the fish, but if it was me at the bar, I would have found the beams to be poor mood lighting.

We did not have to wait long for the peep show to start. Soon the heads of females were popping up between the coral fingers, closely followed by the males. They met and then swam up together several feet off the reef. Their mating then culminated in a brief release of sperm and egg. Finally, in a fraternity house finish, the pair then quickly separated and disappeared among the coral.

It was an easy, but amazing dive, and a great way to end our time in Yap. When our plane took off, we were sad to leave this island that time forgot, but manta rays remembered year after year. However, our next stop, Palau, was beckoning with the promise of adrenaline-filled diving, historical highlights, and a real treat: air conditioning.

CHAPTER 11

Republic of Palau: Land of Day-Glo Sumo Clams

Schools of fish flash by me like shiny coins tossed in a fountain from the hands of hopeful lovers. Juan, my bronzed and Speedo-clad dive master, leads me gently through gardens of blooming coral that have grown for hundreds of years in anticipation of this perfect moment. My tank provides not air, but a steady stream of high-quality dark chocolate to sustain me through the dive. Miles of crystal clear visibility surround me. The water is blue-green glass that magnifies the beauty of the reef and minimizes my waistline. In my reflection, I look 30 pounds lighter in my wetsuit.

Suddenly, a great white shark (on loan from his usual habitat of much colder waters) appears from the blue abyss, a muscular torpedo crazed with the anticipation of an entire tank of chocolate. He rockets past Juan, who valiantly tries to defend me and loses his Speedo in the ensuing mêlée. The shark then turns his black marble eyes on me, sensing my fear in the water like an electric current of pure fright. He closes his massive jaws around my left arm as I feel a shooting pain in my elbow and hear the sound of glasses clinking...

"Watch your arms, please," the stewardess said as she rolled the drink cart down the airplane aisle and nailed my elbow with great velocity, precision, and enjoyment that only a professional demolition derby driver could achieve. I was reluctant to wake up and leave my diving dreams behind, but our plane was about to land in Palau, the second stop on our Pacific diving adventure.

From the time our plane touched down we could tell Palau was quite different than its Micronesian neighbor, Yap. The airport was a modern (lacking visible thatch), air-conditioned building with plenty of taxis out front. There was a greater selection of comfortable hotels, complete with doors *and* mattresses. It even had a "downtown" area, Koror, with several three-story buildings. While Yap's population could only fill a thimble, Palau's 21,000 people could at least fill a reasonably-sized bucket.

Palau, formally known as the Republic of Palau, or Belau to native Palauans, is an island nation in the Pacific Ocean about 2000 miles south of Tokyo, but with less baseball. Palauan infrastructure has leapt boldly ahead of Yap (which isn't really saying that much) because of the volume of people who have occupied it over the years. The Spanish, Germans, Japanese, and finally the Americans have all played Gilligan's Island in Palau, leaving a pinch of customs, language, and technology here and there.

Like Yap, Palau was a part of the Trust Territory of the Pacific Islands, which the U.S. headed at the end of World War II. In 1994 the Republic of Palau moved out of their parent's basement and became independent. Apparently they had the option of joining the Federated States of Micronesia like Yap, but decided they did not want to play with the other kids in the sand-box and chose to go it alone.

The island is now known for world-class diving, so that is where our fun began. Palau has a little bit of adventure for every type of diver, including majestic underwater walls, sprawling coral reefs, strong currents, and dives on historic wrecked ships. We started at one of the most famous sites, Blue Corner. Here a finger of land extends into the ocean, creating a unique outcropping of rock and coral. A wicked current whips around this point bringing tasty nutrients and hungry fish.

The other divers on our boat trip out to the site gave us a glimpse of what we would look like in 30 years. We were joined by a large group of tattooed, retired sailors bent on squeezing every last bit of fun and excitement out of their trip. They kept us roaring with tales of the "way it was" when scuba was new and unexplored and they were considered deviants for trying it. The gear of these mature, salty dogs was old school: a plain vest, mask, fins and air regulator. That's all. No fancy computers or other high-tech paraphernalia for them. Collectively these guys had logged more hours underwater than my husband and I had actually lived on this earth. It was comforting to dive in such good, experienced company.

At the dive site our gang dropped down through the water column to the reef shelf at 50 feet, then launched over the side of the outcropping to swim along the rock wall below that extended far down into the abyss. This dive is different for each diver, depending on the current, time of day, tides, and how much betel nut was chewed beforehand, which might lead to visions of tie-dyed groupers. On this day the current was moderate - enough to take us on a tour - not a high-speed train ride.

The current swept us along the wall past all sorts of sea life. Lobsters hid in the coral nooks, their antennae protruding to sense food and predators and to pick up reruns of "Seinfeld." We paused for a moment, finning gently against the pull of the current, to watch a turtle munch on a large red sea sponge. While it looked like a cheerless meal to us, it must have been caviar and champagne to him, because he never even noticed we were watching.

Near the top of the wall I spotted several nudibranch sea slugs. Normally on land a slug would have to tap dance and recite poetry to get me to notice it. Underwater, however, average creatures get fascinating fast. A nudibranch is a shell-less mollusk that looks like it swallowed a box of fluorescent Crayola crayons. They are colorful and often uniquely shaped, but are also masters of disguise so finding them can be a challenge. Best of all they *don't swim away,* giving a diver time to give one a good, nosy inspection and even point the critter out to other divers.

We then came up to the tip of the outcropping and tethered ourselves to pieces of dead coral with reef hooks so we could watch fish television without fighting the current. By slightly inflating our scuba vest and facing the open ocean beyond the edge of the wall, we were able to watch the activity unfold without getting tired and using up all of our air. Schools of horse-eye jacks flashed before us, endless mirrors of silver and blue that disappeared as soon as they arrived.

There were also many large tuna, but sharks were the stars of this show, measuring four feet and larger. They were mostly chunky grey reef sharks and white tip sharks with ugly faces that only their mama could love. A few inquisitive black tip sharks, the

> "Man, of all the animals, is probably the only one to regard himself a great delicacy."
> -Jacques Yves Cousteau

aquatic version of Curious George, were also thrown in for variety. Judging by their large size and the ease at which they navigated the currents it was clear they often drove this way to work. At any given time I counted ten or more passing by us. The most curious would swim right towards us, veering off at the last moment before we soiled our wetsuits. I imagined them picking each of us off one by one, in *Goldilocks and the Three Bears* style: that diver is too thin, that one's got too much gear, that one's *just right*. Chomp.

When it came time to release our tethers and drift back over the more shallow coral we realized we were not alone. A friendly and gentle 200-pound turquoise Napoleon fish had swum up between my husband and me, wanting to see what fish television channel we were watching. He became part of our underwater gang, swimming along with us until he found his Waterloo.

In the shallows we encountered some oddballs of the tropical Pacific. Bumphead parrotfish, their namesake heads obscenely bulging, munched at the coral. A leaf scorpion fish floating along the sea floor struck its best inconspicuous pose, but the lack of nearby trees gave it away. A resting anemone had curled itself up into a glowing pink beach ball with only a few lime-colored tentacles sticking out the top like hair on an overweight Muppet. In Palau, nature has a good sense of humor.

After several days of high-adrenaline diving we decided to take a break. Palau is also famous for its shitake topography, the mushroom-shaped islands. These are the most photographed locations in Palau, and can be found in almost every piece of literature on the place. It is possible to visit these islands up close via kayak, but it requires a guide. We booked a promising-sounding tour that touted "additional exploration opportunities" during kayak breaks.

We started with an easy paddle. These small islands are limestone remnants of coral reefs that existed in the area when the water level was higher. The limestone sides are easily eaten away by the ocean giving them their mushroom shape. Our lack of paddling ability became quickly apparent as our arms turned limp like sautéed portabellas and we dropped to the back of the small paddling group. We eagerly agreed to our guide's suggestion of a break.

Ulong Island, the westernmost rock island in Palau, has a long history. Thousands of years ago native Palauans lived on the island though now it is uninhabited. They left behind evidence of their settlement including building foundations and artifacts. They also painted bright red and white pictographs in caves and on the cliff faces at which we were now looking.

We admired the paintings and marveled at how high the artists had to climb to paint them. Our guide explained the climbing process, which entailed scaling an almost vertical limestone cliff face with only an occasional foot-hold of vines and small trees that took root in the porous rock material. I then noticed he started to refer to "us" and "now" in the climbing process explanation, an observation that began to cause me concern.

Against rational thought our "When in Rome…" mentality kicked in and we began to climb. Up was not so bad once I got over the fear of falling like a flightless bird to the rocks below. There were several people on the trip with us, some of whom were older than the cave paintings. Our fear of looking weak in comparison to Grandma Moses propelled us to the top. We were rewarded with breathtaking views of the mushroom islands and close-up inspection of the pictographs, which depicted people, animals and sea life.

What goes up must come down. I was hoping for a controlled descent. Instead I slipped and slid all the way, gracefully displaying my climbing inability. I had moss under my finger nails from clutching the rocks and mud splattered down my front from head to toe. I followed an ominous trail left by a deep gash on the knee of the man in front of me. The last part was supposed to be this Tarzan-like maneuver where I swung out over the water while grasping a tree limb and then dropped several feet to the boats below. Needless to say this did not go well. I'm no Jane.

Back in the kayaks we paddled on, now keeping a keen eye towards the sky on a lookout for plummeting tourists. The water glistened like crystal; so clear we could see the vibrant coral bottom in many places. After covering a particularly large expanse of water our guide suggested another break. We agreed a bit more reluctantly this time. The kayaks floated in the shade of a rock island as our guide explained our next adventure.

"Many of the stone money pieces in Yap were mined here in the islands of Palau," he said. "Would you like to see a piece that was not brought back to Yap?" Having seen the money at the Yap ATM, we were eager to see where they printed it.

The guide showed us a small opening in the side of the nearby mushroom island base. It was a 20-foot long tunnel about four feet in diameter. Apparently, the island was doughnut shaped. This tunnel would lead us to the center where we could see an inland saltwater lake and the tropical forest that surrounded it.

"Okay. First we are going to crawl through the tunnel. Watch out for the sharp rock on all sides. Bring your mask and snorkel because once we get to the other side we will have to swim across the inland lake. You'll want to look for the crocodile that lives there. You can't miss him, he's a big one."

"Watch out for the jellyfish. They are the stinging kind," he continued. "Oh, there are also sea urchins along the edge of the lake, so be careful when you get out on the other side. So, who wants to go first?"

Inexplicably, no one raised their hand. My kayak was closest to the tunnel, so he pointed to me and said "Let's start with you." This seemed to be a popular decision with everyone except one person in the group.

On the upside it required me to climb out of my kayak and wade to the tunnel which was a good strategy to wash off the mud from our last adventure. I crawled through the tunnel crab-style, providing the person behind me with a lovely, full moon view. I was careful to avoid the sea urchins on the other side. I was even more careful to let the person behind me jump into the lake first in case the crocodile was not only friendly, but also hungry.

In all fairness, I never saw the crocodile. I did see the jellyfish. They were beautiful, pulsating creatures with long iridescent tentacles that had a "come hither, I want to eat you" look. The swim to the other side of the lake was quick, fueled by the desire to avoid becoming something's lunch. Soon our group was on the far shore, ogling a round of stone money that did not make it to Yap.

"No one knows why this one was left here," the guide said. "We think it was mined on the main island and then brought here for safe keeping until the owners could return to collect it." Clearly they had forgotten their bank account number.

The trek back to the kayaks was more of the same routine: over the urchins, through the lake, avoid the crocodile and jellyfish, and crawl through the sharp coral tunnel. Thankfully, we spent the remainder of the trip gently gliding through the rock islands in our kayaks. After the rest of our adventure, paddling seemed like a breeze.

The pictographs had reminded us that there is more to Palau than great diving. Unlike Yap, Palau's traditions and history did not whack us in the face on arrival. There are villages with clans and a council of chiefs in Palau. Traditional ceremonies are still performed and Palauan is an official language in addition to English. Disappointingly, however, we did not get to immerse ourselves in much authentic local culture even when traveling around the island. Perhaps it is because of the large volume of visitors that the natives keep their secrets a bit closer to the vest.

However, we were still curious about the culture of Palau so we turned from the present day to the past. On the north end of Babeldaob Island are a series of primitively carved boulders, know as Badrulchau in Palauan. Carved by humans before Palauan history was recorded or even remembered, the stones' origin is a mystery. Just reading about them in our guidebook wasn't enough; we wanted to soak up some of their mystical air in person.

We rented a car so we could take our own tour of the site. This was our first mistake. Our second was assuming we could follow the deceptively easy directions provided to us by the helpful front desk clerk at our hotel. I had waited in the car while my husband asked for directions, so I did not hear the exchange between him and the clerk. The two men exchanged lots of confident nods and smiles, which I understood to mean the ride would be easy.

We took off down the main road and eventually came across a sign with the word "Badrulchau" and an arrow pointing left down a side road. Good, I thought. Then, my husband drove past it and continued going straight.

"Um, wasn't that the turnoff?" I asked.

"The clerk said to ignore that one because the road is washed out," he said. "We need to take a different road a little further down."

"What's the name of the road we are looking for?" I asked. This was a silly thing to say, I know. Roads in Palau don't really have established, published names, but I really wanted to believe we knew where we were going.

"I don't think it has a name. He said to take the second turn after the big boulder." Ahh. Now we were getting to the heart of the matter. We were going to navigate by objects, rather than maps or specific streets. Perhaps we could break out our sextant and read the stars if we really got lost.

I was relieved to see that a boulder really did exist, although skeptical that someone had not rolled it to a different corner in some twisted act of Palauan humor. *"They play that rock joke on all the tourists"* kept going through my mind. We continued on, making several more object-related turns: left at the three palm trees growing close in a row; right at the hut with the monkey painted on the side (it looked a lot more like a kangaroo to me); right again at the road that looks more like trampled grass than vehicle thoroughfare.

Unexpectedly we arrived at the Badrulchau site, albeit a significant amount of time later. It was deserted and filled with an eerie calm. Most of Babeldaob Island is covered in a lush tropical forest, and this location was no different. The clearing with the monoliths was bright green and dotted with periodic palm trees that rustled slightly in the breeze. The sight was on the side of a slight hill, with the dark blue ocean visible in the distance. A well-worn footpath wound its way through the stones.

Sitting in rows were 39 basalt monoliths carved roughly in the shape of rectangles. Archeologists have dated these formations back to A.D. 161. The current theory is that they were supports for a large structure, although judging by their placement it would have been an enormous building. Smaller stones, crudely carved with the unmistakable features of human faces, appeared throughout the site. Whatever the creators of this site intended, it was obvious that it had special meaning. The area had an aura of being sacred ground.

What is it about the ability of ancient places to transport the visitor to a different level of consciousness in a blink of an eye? I felt the same way in this field as I did at Stonehenge in England and Machu Picchu in Peru. I can only describe it as a combination of awe at the creators' vision and a spiritual connection to them through their site that still stands, even though they are long gone. Whatever the cause, I only know that the hair on the back of my neck did not go down until we had left Badrulchau far behind.

We were ascending at the end of a great dive at a site named Blue Hole. Fifty minutes before, we had started the dive by floating down from the boat through a gaping hole in the top of the reef, before descending vertically through a large cavern. A laser light show of beams from small holes in the reef had crisscrossed the darkness. Near the bottom we exited the cave through a small opening, which placed us outside the reef along a vertical underwater wall. We drifted along it, sighting a veritable encyclopedia of sea creatures. It had been a tremendous dive both for underwater topography as well as fish.

The divers bobbed in the water at the back of the boat, waiting their turn to climb up the ladder. Suddenly, a women floating near us shouted "Shark!" For many people this would have been an added incentive to get on the boat quick. But for many enthusiastic divers, like my husband and me, it was a great reason to put our heads back underwater and witness a really cool creature. Although we looked around thoroughly, we didn't see anything. I pulled my head back out of the water.

"Where?" I asked her, not wanting to miss it.

"Right in front of me," she said. Well, I saw how that could be a bit concerning. But, on further inspection, I still did not see it.

"He won't leave me alone! Help!" she said, starting to thrash about. I was starting to suspect a healthy dose of betel nut was at work, but then I noticed a fish, a remora about two feet long, chasing after her. Remoras are long brownish grey fish that thrive by attaching themselves with specialized suckers to other large fish and turtles. They can swim independently if needed, but prefer to hitch a ride on the Ocean Express, gaining transportation, protection, and bits of escaped food from their host's meal. It is probably a stretch to say they look like a shark, but their dorsal fin could be mistaken for the back fin of the toothsome predator if perhaps one's eyesight wasn't so good.

He had the tenacity of a vampire, wanting to suction himself to her and then to each of us in turn. Even the wave of a hand or a kick of a fin did not deter him. Although I was disappointed at the lack of a shark, this close up of the remora was still pretty intriguing. The sucker pattern on their uniquely flat and sloped head always reminded me of a sneaker print from a school yard bully. He finally gave up on us, swimming away to find more receptive mode of mobility and food.

My first thought upon climbing back on a dive boat is to put away my gear. If not immediately tied down or stowed, items tend to magically drift towards the back of the boat and threaten to jump off the swim platform. Masks, snorkels, towels, fins, and the like, all start to get suicidal thoughts the minute they part with the sea. On some boats it gets so bad that they station a crew member at the back to talk these items down from the ledge and return them to their rightful (and grateful) owner.

My second thought is always about food. The sport quickly makes a diver primitively ravenous. On occasion I have searched my bag after a dive only to find a flattened, expired snack bar and thought "Hey, that looks good!" Fortunately this time we had lunch included in our dive package, so I did not need to consume the usual lint-covered sustenance.

Lunch on a dive boat is always a sordid affair. It usually consists of some thin, mayonnaise-ladened sandwiches and hacked-up fruit arranged attractively on the boat table that only a moment before held rusty equipment and stinky wet suits. But, our dive shop was associated with our hotel. In a rare culinary opportunity, the shop had given us a variety of lunch options from which we got to choose using a laminated card with pictures of meals.

Our hotel tended to have a high percentage of Asian visitors. The lunch choices reflected this demographic. The only "Western" lunch was a ham and cheese sandwich, a sad comment on our gastronomic legacy.

Having lived in Japan for some time, I had developed a taste for Asian food, even for some of the more adventurous dishes. The pictures, however, did not look like anything I had seen before or wanted to eat now.

"What are some of these things?" I asked the dive master. The pictures on the laminated card looked less like food and more like those cartoon drawings used to explain seat belt use found in all airplane seatbacks.

"That's chicken, that's noodles, that one there is chicken and that one on the right is noodles," he said. I was starting to see a trend here. "That one on the bottom is egg and fish. I would not recommend it." That seemed to be sound advice. In my mind certain things just don't go together, like dairy and fish or reality and TV.

On the first day we chose the ham and cheese thinking we would start out easy and be adventurous later. Unfortunately, neither the ham nor the cheese looked or tasted like any ham and cheese we had ever encountered. It was paired with a decidedly un-American seaweed salad, which turned out to be the tastiest thing in the bag. I noticed that the rest of the divers on the boat were eating one of the chicken/noodles/chicken/noodles options, and looking pretty happy about it. I was determined to choose better the next day.

Day two I opted for Chicken #1. It appeared roasted. The avian hunk was covered in brown goo and snuggled next to some white rice. One bite and I knew I had made a mistake. I wasn't sure what area of the chicken it came from, but it certainly was the part with the most bones per capita. Each bite had to be inspected and dissected before eaten. I gave up quick, opting instead for the goo on the rice, which was actually pretty good. The other divers again chose well. They ate with such gusto that various bits of lunch became airborne, stuck to their wetsuits, and became fish snacks later in the day. Foiled again.

On subsequent days we tried each dish until we finally caught on that the noodles were the way to go. Watching me eat them must have been pretty funny; an awkward ballet of having to finesse chopsticks on a rocking boat while balancing the container on my lap. After that, we noticed that each time a new American diver came on the boat they first ordered the ham and cheese. My husband and I never said a word. We didn't want to spoil the gastronomic fun.

Our hotel was on the western shore of Ngerkebesang Island, on a shallow bay fringed with a wide ribbon of white sand. At the lip of the bay was a verdant, uninhabited island with several palm trees punctuating its emerald green ground cover. I spent many an hour daydreaming about being shipwrecked on that palm tree oasis, with a cold Red Rooster, the local Palauan beer, in hand.

But the bay was so clear and blue I couldn't pass up the opportunity for a swim. More than once I ditched the daydream and donned my scuba mask to go exploring. In the shallows, petite colorful fish swarmed the small masses of brain coral and strands of short sea weed, giving the overall impression of a classroom fish tank but without the kids fingerprints on the outside of my mask. My favorite underwater sightings, however, were the giant Tridacna clams.

Keep in mind, these aren't normal clams like the ones that bob in chowder and lie prone on linguini at home. These are clams on ecstasy and growth hormones with a bit of nuclear radiation exposure thrown in for good measure. They pulse and shimmer, their iridescent neon mantles glittering as they filter the water throughout their bodies in search of microscopic food. Measuring up to six feet across and weighing up to 500 pounds, they are the day-glo sumo wrestlers of the sea.

These clams were once plentiful, littering the equatorial Pacific seas. Their natural tendency to move as little as possible made them an easy target for food and ornamentation. Their numbers dwindled considerably, especially in the waters near humans. I was told that the original hotel owner had appreciated the clams plight and beauty and therefore had cultivated them in the bay, banning anyone from harvesting them. Sure, I had heard of oyster beds, but planting a giant clam seemed like a scene out of *Little Shop of Horrors*. The hotel eventually changed hands, but the bumper crop of clams were still coming along nicely in the shallow warm water.

The largest I saw was an electric blue, green, and white behemoth, measuring about five feet across. I think the hotel will need a bigger chowder pot.

We enjoyed several more days of diving at awe-inspiring sites such as Big Drop Off, Peleliu Express, and the unintelligible Ngercheu Garden. On the boat ride back from our dives on the fifth day, we stopped to snorkel at Jellyfish Lake. This is an activity that often inspires comments like "ick" and "ieeew," but it is not to be missed.

Jellyfish Lake is on one of the rock islands, Mecherchar. The lake is completely isolated, although the limestone allows for an exchange of salinity with the ocean. The lake is filled with mastigias and moon jellyfish. Because of their isolation from predators these jellies have lost their ability to sting, so they have adapted to feeding on symbiotic algae instead. It is an excellent study in evolution, an example of function driving form that Darwin would have loved.

Of course no adventure in Palau is an easy one. In order to get to the lake one has to hike 20 minutes up and over the lip of the island. In some places the trail is good and even has a rope to steady the climber. In others, it is just a mud slide. Along the route there are several instances of an indigenous tree that leaks poisonous sap. And, of course, every once in awhile there is the tour bus of saltwater crocodiles that seem to appear at all the good Palauan activities.

We started our ascent with misplaced enthusiasm, not realizing the climb ahead. We had our snorkeling gear, including fins, and an underwater camera. By the time we got to the top we were completely out of breath and roasting in the afternoon heat. Scuba diving is not allowed in the lake because of a toxic layer of hydrogen sulfide found at 50 feet. This is fortunate, as we would have likely abandoned our gear trailside before we arrived or sunk to the bottom of the lake from exhaustion.

At the lip of the lake we found a surprisingly well-built dock from which to start our snorkel. There were only a few other visitors so we had plenty of water to ourselves. At first we only saw a few jellyfish here or there and started to wonder if they had all gone on holiday. Then, we saw a few more, and a few more after that. Soon there were more jellyfish around us than water.

The jellies were amazing. They were swimming every which way, bumping into each other like crazed bargain hunters on the first day of a department store sale. Everything about them, their color, shape and size, warned me to stay away. "Do not touch, I found those sale shoes first!" But, I didn't feel any stings. My initial fear at touching them quickly turned to concern for them. I finned carefully to ensure I did not break apart their delicate forms. Swimming through the water was like pushing handfuls of Jell-O aside. After we had our fun in the desert-filled lake we reluctantly climbed out and trekked back to the boat.

By the end of each day our activities made us ravenous. We've never been the type to stay at our hotel to eat, preferring to branch out and see what intestinal parasites we can collect elsewhere. Palau is a melting pot of cultures from all over Asia, so we were hoping to find a variety of authentic food and drink.

Our first night we found a reputable-looking Japanese restaurant. Encouraged by the sheer volume of Japanese people in the place, we went in. The hostess took one look at us and promptly placed us in the "definitely not Japanese" back room for lepers with several large German families and a hippie couple from Australia. The

> **"If you reject the food, ignore the customs, fear the religion, and avoid the people, you might better stay home."**
> **-James Michener**

menu was disturbingly filled with reef fish we had dived with earlier that day including, as a special, turquoise Napoleon fish. We settled instead on an enormous mangrove crab, a meal fit for Poseidon and several of his sea-god friends. It wasn't very Japanese, but it was nicely tropical.

A fellow foodie on one of our dives had recommended a Thai restaurant down a side street in Koror. On a Tuesday night we went and found the restaurant completely empty except for 20 or so waitstaff attempting to take care of us. The food was excellent, but the abundance of attention was a little creepy. Because of the good quality of the food we decided to go back later in the week to try it again. Unfortunately so did the rest of the island. The crowd spilled out the front door and onto the street where a few makeshift tables were set up for those diners who just couldn't wait. Apparently Thai is a weekend thing in Palau.

There are not, to my knowledge, many people of Indian decent on Palau. There is, apparently, a great desire for Indian food. By far the best restaurant on the island turned out to be one that served southern Indian food. My husband and I do not frequently eat Indian food, but we got our yearly fill going back several times because of the clean, friendly environment. Suspect, however, were the highly spicy snacks served gratis at the start of each meal. Were they there to kill the bacteria or to kill our taste buds? We were not sure.

And there were the foodie mishaps. The sushi restaurant that advertised "Fruit Bat Pie," the flying rodent covered in pastry. Also, a Chinese food place that saw so few customers they kept the lights off to save money. Still, we were surprised at the wide selection of cuisines, presumably there because of the international nature of the prior occupiers and current tourists. We were also surprised to see a lack of Palauan restaurants. The doorman at our hotel explained it best.

"If I eat out, I want something different than what I get at home," he said. "And besides, did you really come here to eat a pile of taro?" He had a good point.

Palau is chock full of one-of-a-kind diving experiences. In addition to the reef hooks and the Jellyfish Lake there is a special diving opportunity at Chandelier Cave, named in honor of the gaudy stalactites that hang from the ceiling. Most cave diving requires an advanced diving certification that includes more than 20 hours of classroom and open water education in an effort to prevent the diver from expiring underwater. Chandelier Cave was an exception to this requirement because of its small size, straightforward shape, and available air chambers.

The entrance to the cave at Ngarol Island was in a small harbor where old boats went to die. Several littered the area in various states of decay and drowning. Reflecting on my last tetanus shot, I hopped into the hazy water. The sea floor was not much better. Random boat debris was everywhere; bottles, hunks of metal, even a toilet seat. At least nothing pretty or remarkable was going to detract us from our goal.

We swam towards the semi-circle entrance 15 feet below the surface. The cave had four separate air chambers in a row. The plan was to surface in each of them to take a look at the rock formations. The fourth, if we made it, had a space big enough to get out of the water and walk around. We took flashlights so we could see as we got deeper in the cave.

We swam into the cave, then ascended to the first air chamber. It was about ten feet by eight feet in size with four feet in between the water's surface and the roof. Long ago the cave was dry before the sea flooded it, so stalactites that once hung down from the roof into the air now touched, and sometimes even pierced, the water. The limestone rock island was permeable, which allowed fresh air into the cave. We were able to surface in the air chamber and talk, something a diver does not get to do too often in the middle of a dive.

"Long ago when the cave was dry, rainwater seeped in through the rocks," our divemaster said. "It carried calcium carbonate that dripped and built up over time, causing the stalactites." Some of the stalactites were large, indicating a very lengthy process of dripping and growth that impressed me. At home I can't even wait for a red light to change.

We descended again and went further back into the cave to the next air chamber. This one was smaller and lined with yellow sulfite deposits on the rock that looked like a mustard jar had exploded. When we dove back into the main part of the cave I had some trouble with my gear. I went back towards the air chamber to fix the problem. Unfortunately, I was so busy looking down at my scuba vest that I did not see the stalactite above. It got lodged directly between my back and all of my hoses.

All of my gear was hooked in some way to this fang of a rock. I was just plain stuck and dangling mid-cave like an upside-down popsicle, which was a bit embarrassing. The dive master and my husband were disappearing deeper into the cave not knowing of my frozen-treat predicament. I started to panic, envisioning the sea monsters, kin of the ones that hide under the bed at home, that were waiting to capitalize on my lack of coordination.

I started switching my flashlight on and off like a mating lightening bug, hoping that one of the Good Humor men might swim back and give me a tug. Then I waited. As I composed myself I started to sink ever so slightly. I noticed that I was a little less entangled than before. This may seem logical now, but at the time physics was not playing a big role in my thought process. My body said "swim away, swim away" not "sink down, sink down."

By the time the dive master and my husband reached me the popsicle had fallen off the stick. Feeling a bit self-concious I made a "broken" hand signal underwater and pointed to my light. When in doubt, blame it on the equipment. I made it to one more air chamber before deciding my cave diving experience needed to come to a merciful end. A fellow diver had told me that the last air chamber was the most impressive. I'll certainly never know. But I did have a strange craving for a popsicle that night for dessert.

There is something special about sunsets on tropical isles. It's the same sun, the same type of drifting clouds that one gets at home, only it seems somehow amplified. The yellow rays appear more golden. The ocean turns into a giant mirror, reflecting a thousand points of the saturated light on each ripple and wave. Back at home, I appreciate a sunset just a bit less, perhaps because the nature of travel inspires me to look and linger.

I was parked in a lounge chair on the beach watching the scene with a margarita, my drink of choice, in hand. Sad but true, our time in Palau and Yap had ended, but not before we had an incredible string of dives and adventures. Far from being satiated, my desire for traveling and scuba diving only increases after a great trip. Fortunately, we had already planned another adventure, and it was just around the corner. The massive whale sharks in Belize were calling our name.

CHAPTER 12

Belize: Patience is a Virtue,
Whale Sharks are a Vice

From the main terminal, an attendant directed us down a sketchy walkway towards a rundown building in the corner of the airport grounds. This, it turned out, was the "old airport" a dubious distinction since the "new" airport still looked pretty "old" to me. In the shed we found tourists, locals, children, chickens, and worldly possessions, all attempting to get onto miniscule planes flying to obscure parts of Belize.

After proving our identity to a frazzled man behind the only counter, he handed us two laminated pieces of blue paper. I couldn't tell if they were boarding cards or bathroom passes. We stood on the side of the room that seemed to hold a high percentage of people with blue cards, hoping that just out of sheer numbers someone would know what to do.

Eventually, the stressed-out counter attendant announced in Spanish that the blue card people should assemble. At least we assumed that's what he shouted, since the bulk of our blue card neighbors picked up their livestock and headed toward the door in a press of body odor and feathers. Another airport worker in an orange vest led us to a parked twin prop airplane, collected our cards, and promptly disappeared, presumably to gain access to the bathrooms.

Another man appeared in full aviation regalia, hoping to pass as either our captain or a member of the Village People band. He opened the doors to the plane's interior and to the baggage compartment. While two baggage handlers loaded various luggage and bundles, the passengers climbed into the cabin. The captain pointed at me then pointed to the plane's front.

"You will sit in front," he said. "You will like. Nice view!" What could I say? I shrugged at Michael and followed the captain as he climbed into the plane.

The twin prop held 12 seats, so the hike to the front was short. When I went to sit in the first row of seats, the captain grabbed my arm, pointing to the co-pilot's seat. Assuming the co-pilot would find it distracting to sit on my lap as he (or she) flew the plane, I politely declined, then continued to store my belongings under the first seat row. The captain persisted.

"No, this your seat. You sit with me," he said, sounding quite convinced. By now I could hear Michael laughing behind me. *Nice.*

I climbed into the co-pilot's seat, only then realizing that the plane was so small and the flight so short that it really didn't need a co-pilot. The captain showed me how to work the multi-strap seat belt, which reminded me more of a nylon spider web than a life saving device. I imagined in an accident, it would keep me snug in my seat whether I wanted out or not.

With an ominous warning, "Don't touch anything," the captain took the prop down the runway and into the sky. We flew low; the countryside details still visible from the window. It felt strange looking straight out the front window, the view unfettered by TV monitors and hairy heads of first class passengers. Before I knew it, we crossed over water and began our descent. I caught sight of a white strip of land, initially mistaking it for an abandoned road. As we neared, however, it became apparent that the captain planned to land our tin can on it.

As we touched down I noticed the strip wasn't paved, but rather covered with white gravel that I later determined to be crushed stone and seashells. As we taxied to the hut at the end of the runway, an old, dusty man on a rusty bicycle rode parallel to us. He kept pace for awhile until he veered off through a hole in the fence that surrounded the airport. Not only could one land a plane on the strip, but one could also use it as a short cut to the corner store.

After a brief but determined struggle I released myself from the Spider Man seat belt and climbed out of the plane.

"You did good. You no touch *anything*!" the Captain proclaimed proudly. Why no, I did not. While my survival instinct tends to fall short when it comes to street food and meetings with my boss, I'm pretty good at avoiding the more obvious sources of death, like causing an airplane to fall out of the sky.

We unloaded our bags and walked to our hotel, which perched on the beach a block away. We took the direct route. The locals were right, that hole in the fence provided a great short cut.

I awoke to a scratching sound coming from our hotel room's thatched roof. The rustling sounded not like something walking on the top, but rather crawling around inside, between the fronds. I lay there quietly, hoping that the critter would leave or I would fall back to sleep. Neither happened.

"Michael, wake up," I hissed, giving him a swat on his sleeping shoulder. He rolled over, grunted, and fell back into a soft snore.

"Michael, wake up!" I said, more loudly this time. "There is an animal *in* our roof!" He opened one eye and looked at me vacantly.

"You are in Belize," I prodded. "You are in very odd accommodations, and now the original inhabitants are coming to take the room back!"

"Let them. I'm sleeping. Wake me up if they try to climb in our bed," he said, closing his eyes and returning to his dreams of Mary Ann and that promised "three hour tour." I lay there listening to the creature do Lord-knows-what above our head. I expected it to come crashing through, landing (hopefully) on Michael. After an hour, during which the roof integrity remained unexpectedly intact, I finally fell asleep as the sun began to rise.

Thirty minutes later Michael woke me up. We were going to try to go diving again that day. Over the prior four days, an enormous storm parked itself offshore, making the ocean a choppy, hazy mess. Our hotel hadn't sent a dive boat out all week. Even if we could have found another dive company to take us out we would have seen very little in the cloudy, angry water.

Our hotel was a dive hotel. Dive, as in scuba, not dive as in poorly constructed and full of bugs. Although it was that, too. Never before had we booked a hotel so completely dedicated to the sport of diving. The dive shop resembled Christmas morning, overflowing with scuba toys. The dock and the dive boats could not have been more convenient, practically located at the footboard of our bed. But, what one gained in scuba amenities, one seemed to lose in others, such as consistent hot water and a hotel room ceiling containing indigenous creatures.

The hotel sat on the beautiful, sandy fringe of Ambergris Caye, the largest of several hundred small islands in Belize's northern coastal waters. The small strip of land once was home to Mayan, then pirates, and now Belizeans who make money primarily from reef-related tourism. Belize has the second largest barrier reef in the world, making it a haven for fish and divers alike.

After four days, the storm lost steam, so our hotel planned to send out a boat to mollify the visiting divers itchy to get wet. We quickly signed up for two spots, loaded our gear and camera equipment onto the boat, and swallowed a significant amount of non-drowsy Dramamine to combat the still-choppy water. While scuba diver opinions vary on taking any seasickness medication before diving, I am a true believer. I've never had the non-drowsy kind make me tired, but I have missed several wonderful dives as I lay prone in the back of a dive boat, green as a shamrock. Why chance it? I'm not Irish anyway.

Our destination, Turneffe Atoll, was located right outside Belize's barrier reef. It's the largest of the country's three atolls. Mangroves comprise many of its 200 islands, providing a great hiding place for juvenile fish, which in turn, feed the atoll's enormous fish population. On the extreme southern end sat our goal, the dive site named the Elbow.

I had to double back to our room to collect my mask, which caused us to be one of the last couples to settle onto the boat. Space was at a real premium; divers with weather-induced cabin fever crammed onto the boat in hopes of feeling better after aquatic submersion. I was pretty sure the desperate lot of them would have taken up an offer to dive in the hotel pool if it meant they could leave their room and stretch their fins a bit.

We located two full air tanks almost all the way at the front. The spot was inconvenient; six other divers sat between us and the platform at the back where we would enter the water. Having no other options, we began to set up our gear, attaching our vests and regulators to the tanks and putting our fins and masks within easy reach.

As the captain started up the boat's motors, two more people came bounding down the dock. Was this dive company kidding? No more divers could fit on the boat, especially these divers. The woman was a normal size, but the man was huge, almost seven feet tall and four hundred pounds. The physics and gear required to perform scuba activity at that size were unimaginable, as was the space he would require to suit up.

The man made a b-line, of course, for me. He took the last available full air tank between my gear and the front of the boat. His vest alone was so large that it extended past my tank, flattening my gear against the wall. His wife and her human-sized gear took up the last tank at the opposite side of the boat. The diver next to her smiled contently as she minded her personal space.

After getting an up-close and personal view of the giant's rear as he set up his equipment, I excused myself, escaping to the flying bridge before he crushed me. It would be a shame to die before seeing the Elbow. A barrage of Russian assaulted me throughout the 45-minute ride as the couple argued back and forth. I usually just take along a good book, but I suppose every diver has his or her own way to pass the time.

The captain cut the engine as the crew moored us to a buoy. The captain split the group into two, paring Michael and I with a family of four and the Russians. Our perky divemaster, Peter, gathered us at the back of the boat for our dive briefing.

"I'm so excited we came here!" he said. "This is a great site and the conditions are pretty good today. Here we have a convergence of several ocean currents passing by canyon-type formations. We'll descend along the buoy line to the sandy patch below the boat then we will swim over the side of the wall for awhile. Watch your depth. Once you go over the wall edge, you'll hit 100 feet pretty quick."

"The currents bring lots of nutrients to the water around this site, so there is plenty of sea life. We should see lots of schooling fish, like jacks. We usually see turtles and sharks here too. Yeah!" he shouted, as he gave a few stunned divers high 5's.

"Don't forget to look at the coral while you're down there. We'll pass some big barrel sponges, stands of staghorn coral, and a lot of other interesting parts of the reef. Alright? Let's suit up!" His genuine, ebullient enthusiasm was fun, but left me wondering what to do. Should we cheer? Perhaps yell "Break" and then slap each other on the ass before getting into formation on the oceanic gridiron? Even in neoprene that is sort of a socially awkward thing to do. So, I smiled, nodded in agreement, and moved away from the group in case anyone else got the ass-slapping idea.

Michael and I headed for the back and stopped at the steps to the flying bridge when we realized that Boris was already back there, putting on his gear. Michael was able to get to his stuff, but I couldn't even see mine behind the rotund Russian. In a moment of brilliant self-preservation, I decided to wait until he completed his activities before attempting to squeeze into my spot. If Boris decided to continue to pursue this scuba thing, he really needed to consider cutting down on the caviar, or his fellow divers were going to make him charter his own dingy.

Soon enough the Cossack finished his pre-dive routine, rose, and stumbled towards the platform at the back, frightening the other divers as he teetered along with the roll of the waves. His wife followed behind him, graceful and unfazed. As I donned my gear, I wondered how the two opposites ever got together in the first place.

Michael sat patiently next to me, all geared up and ready to go. I first put on my fins then opened my tank valve. Other divers amazed me when they forgot to do that, only realizing it when they were already in the water. One would think it would be *the* critical task when preparing for a dive.

I clipped on my vest and then reached down to get my mask when a dark shadow loomed above me. The giant returned to retrieve some forgotten paraphernalia. As he reached down next to me, the ocean kicked up a sizeable wave that caused the boat to lurch sideways. My life flashed before my eyes as he toppled towards me. Fortunately, he stopped his forward momentum by bracing himself against the boat behind me, but not before I got a good face full of large Russian crotch. An exploration of the Russian nether regions was not part of the dive itinerary, and I did not appreciate it being added.

He grumbled an apology to me as he walked to the swim platform. I flashed him my best stink-eye look, usually reserved for dog abusers and slow drivers. Finally geared up, I made my way to the back of the boat and joined the rest, already dangling from the tow line in the water. We descended as a group to the sandy bottom, where little eels danced at the entrances to their burrows, and then continued down a groove formation that intersected the wall. An enormous school of curious horse-eye jacks ogled us with interest.

We began a slow swim against the current along the wall. Not five minutes into the dive, an eagle ray pair rode the current past us on the right, flapping into the distance until I could no longer make out their fat little bodies. Barrel and vase sponges periodically protruded from the wall like chartreuse and orange construction cones. Peering down inside one, I found a dainty arrow crab staring back at me, trying its best to look inconspicuous.

We swam on a diagonal line, inching our way upwards to the top of the wall. The cracks and caves in the rock provided homes for a multitude of sea life. Lobsters waved their antennae at us and grouper eyed us lazily in from the shadows. After another few minutes, we reached the top of the reef, then turned around and drifted back towards the boat. Although I loved swimming along walls, poking through the reef top was my favorite part of a dive. With a little time and a lot of patience, I could usually find plenty of interesting creatures and coral to photograph.

Michael and I branched out from the other divers to scour the reef's nooks and crannies for eye-catching finds. I found a cork screw anemone with Pederson shrimp hiding between the fingers. A green turtle peeked out at us from behind a coral head then took off in the opposite direction to find more private accommodations. Green morays extended their heads from their dens, some even free swimming from hole to hole. The reef practically exploded with sea life.

As we swam towards the boat, the divemaster encouraged Michael and me to stay on the reef longer since we had plenty of air left. I located a forest of brightly colored Christmas tree worms attached to a boulder, and spent the rest of the dive blinding the poor creatures with my flash. The tiny hairs of their spiraled, feathery fingers provided a detailed subject matter on which I could practice using my new macro camera lens. Though the larger animals like sharks and rays are exciting, its often the small creatures like nudibranches and worms that contain the brightest colors and the most remarkable features, thus producing the best pictures. It doesn't hurt that they tend to stay put. My pictures always come out better when the subject can't swim away in a huff.

After a nice, lazy poke about the reef we returned to the boat. The other divers had already put up most of their gear, so the removal of ours was less eventful than the application. The rest of the day went pretty much to plan. We visited Calabash Wall and a little spot named Vicente, squeezing a greasy, dive shop-provided chicken lunch in between the two. The Turneffe Atoll diving was nice, not the most exciting we had ever encountered, but certainly filled with colorful fish and coral. Maybe our expectations were a little high, having heard about the wonders of Belize, the "scuba mecca," for so long from other divers. Ultimately any day is a good day if you are under water, as long as no one flattens you beforehand.

That night, we went down the beach to the main town of San Pedro, a ten-minute walk at a casual pace. Vendors set up makeshift tables along the way, selling various carved wood items and strung beads. In a nice change of pace from our usual travels, the friendly vendors had actually made the goods instead of importing them from China. The distinct selection from table to table reflected the originality of the goods.

The town felt different than a lot of other "tourist" destinations we visited. The line between visitor and local was completely blurred. Natives walked along with beach with us, enjoying their evening as much as we were. A group of teenaged boys whom I would otherwise classify as a "gang" said "Good evening" to us as we passed, polite and sincere.

We found a small open-air restaurant on the beach that served warm fish tacos and cold Belican, Belize's national beer. Although I would never order a fish taco in a restaurant at home, my trepidation vanished at eateries along Latin American coasts. There is something about incredibly fresh fish roasted over a fire and snuggled in a hand-made tortilla that makes the mouth water and is intensely satisfying. The authenticity makes me feel like I am one step closer to being a traveler, not just a tourist. And, on the less profound side, they are damn tasty.

We ate quickly. Our enormous diving-fueled appetites accelerated our usually unhurried dinner pace. On the way back the sky grew dark as storm clouds obscured the moon and stars. We returned to our little grass hut and fell into a deep sleep, dreaming about the next day's dive to the magical Blue Hole.

In a blink of an eye and a rustle from our ceiling the next day arrived, finally clear and bright. The ocean looked different, the white caps and milky water replaced by blue-green glass. The ride to the Blue Hole took over an hour, all the more reason to thank the Gods for getting rid of the big, bad storm. When we arrived at the site, I climbed to the boat's flying bridge to get a bird's eye view.

From the air, the Blue Hole looked like a dark blue ink spot on a sheet of textured aquamarine paper. Millions of years ago, the Blue Hole was a series of dry caves. Over the millennia the caves flooded and eventually their ceilings crumbled, forming an almost perfectly circular hole that is 1000 feet in diameter. The hole is over 400 feet deep, much deeper than the surrounding water, which causes its inky color. Coral and rock lined the circle and stretched to the ocean surface. Our boat was small enough to enter the center of the ring via a channel on one side.

"Can everybody gather 'round?" asked the divemaster. "I want to do a dive briefing. It's real important on this dive." The eight of us divers crowded around him.

"This will most likely be the shortest dive of your dive career. The most interesting thing to see in this hole is at 135 feet, so that is where we are headed. When this spot was still a dry cave, huge stalactites and stalagmites formed as water seeped through the porous limestone ceilings and left mineral deposits. At 135 feet there are overhangs and ledges where we can still see some of these rock formations."

"In order to stay within safe scuba diving limits we can't dive long at that depth. Once we all get in the water, we will need to descend at a fairly quick rate. When we get to 135 feet, we will level off. I'll indicate when we have reached our destination, but please keep an eye on your depth gauge. We will remain at that depth for six minutes then we will start our ascent. When we get to the overhang have a good look around, but please don't drift away from the wall. It can be very disorienting in the center of the deep blue."

"Oh, and talk about deep. If you drop something, it is gone for good. The Blue Hole bottoms out at around 450 feet. I imagine that if I could collect all of the gear and cameras that probably lie at the bottom I could open a successful second hand dive shop."

"One more thing. Diving at that depth can bring on a case of nitrogen narcosis. You will know if you are *narced* if you feel drunk, massively in love, or like you just bought a winning lottery ticket. If you experience euphoria in any of these forms, please ascend a few feet and the feeling should go away. If not, please let me know, so I can enjoy it too."

As a kid I watched Jacques Cousteau make the same exciting journey into the Blue Hole. I didn't have the French accent or skinny butt, but I was thrilled nonetheless. After we all entered the water the divemaster signaled the start of our dive. We descended quickly as promised, following the almost vertical slope of the inside wall. The wall was firm but porous, like a concrete sponge. As we went deeper, less light penetrated and less organic matter grew, until the walls were barren and the deep blue behind me turned a dark grey.

> Jacques-Yves Cousteau sung the praises of Belize's Blue Hole, including it in his list of top-five must dive spots on the planet. Interestingly enough, however, there is evidence that he used dynamite on a natural channel on the hole's side in order to get his boat, the *Calypso*, into the center.

Then, the straight wall turned out, forming a small cave containing the promised stalactites and stalagmites, pock-marked by corroding water and clingy deep-water bi-valves. Suddenly, I realized I loved diving. I also loved diving with Michael. And, I loved the things we saw underwater, like those wonderful stalactites and stalagmites. I loved them so much I wanted a picture with one.

I swam over to Michael and handed him my camera, indicating I wanted a picture with a particularly lovely stalactite. We had a bond, that piece of rock and me; we were friends of the sea. I posed with it, my arm wrapped around the back protectively, like I was embracing my best friend. Michael just shook his head and laughed, but took the picture anyway. Then, he indicated we might want to rise a few feet in the water so I could clear my head. After ascending only ten feet, sobriety hit me quick. I did love diving, but hugging rocks was probably exaggerating my feelings just a bit.

Our six minutes elapsed. The group began to ascend, following the vertical path back up the wall. At 20 feet, we paused at the wall's lip for a safety stop, hovering for 10 minutes at that depth so our bodies could expend their built-up nitrogen. A small school of electric-blue midnight parrotfish in the shallows gave us something to watch as we waited for our safety stop to end. Finally, we returned to the surface, the whole unusual dive taking only 25 minutes from start to finish.

The southern coast of Belize is not an international tourism hotbed. For 9 months of the year, the few people who visit enjoy the peace and tranquility of the sugary beaches with absolutely no crowds. Then the spring comes, and everyone goes crazy because of the fish sex. During the April, May, and June full moons, whale sharks dine on the spawning Cubera snapper eggs, bringing excitement to the sleepy waters of the offshore formation known as Gladden Spit. Divers from around the globe overrun Placencia, the largest town near the Spit, using it as a base from which to search for the nomadic, majestic animals.

I first found out about Placencia's whale shark phenomenon in a diving magazine. The key, apparently, was to be in the right place at the right time, since the exact dates and times of whale shark viewing were based more on the whim of the fish and less on the exact calendar. Although the full moon's arrival is well documented, the appearance of the snappers and the whale sharks is less precise, varying up to a week before or after. We decided to add a stop in Placencia with this variable timing in mind, with the understanding that we might miss the sharks no matter how much planning or praying we did.

We flew from Ambergris Cay to Placencia in a six-seater plane that made the trip two times a week. I actively chose to sit in the co-pilot's seat this time, like deciding to watch a scary movie even though you know it will keep you awake at night for weeks afterwards. The plane took us over miles of jungle with little evidence of human existence. Then, the disorganization of jungle growth turned into neat rows of tidy trees where man made order of the chaos in the form of orchards.

"Naranjas," the captain said, pointing to the endless fields of oranges. I didn't even know that Belize grew the fruit, never mind enough to end world hunger. At least the Belizean people would never have a vitamin C deficiency.

With the coast in sight, the plane began to descend, which wasn't saying much since I could have achieved more altitude from the observation deck on the Empire State Building. The landing strip, which looked more like my driveway then an aviation right of way, was barely paved; the asphalt cracking in places. We touched down smoothly then taxied over a road (complete with cars waiting on either side) that bisected the runway. The captain turned the plane, driving it up to the tiny airport building. The few of us deplaned, and helped the one lone airport worker unload our bags. Worldly possessions in hand, we entered the building in search of our ride.

There were three main hotels in Placencia, in addition to a few questionable "guest houses" that resembled the Bates Motel, based on their Internet pictures. Francis Ford Coppola, the film director, owns one of the hotels, which is both environmentally friendly and super swank. Though visually stunning and very private, the establishment cost more per night than I made in a week. Hotel option No. 2 offered pleasant accommodations and reasonable rates, but was completely sold out due to the whale shark season. This left option No. 3, a new hotel/condo combo for which I could not seem to find many pictures or reviews online. Not seeing any other acceptable options, I booked an oceanfront room that included a kitchen area in case we wanted to save money by cooking our own dinners. The hotel included pickup from the airport. Our booking agent promised to have a van waiting for us.

The other passengers passed through the terminal and sped off in family-owned vehicles, leaving us to stand alone between the shriveled potted plants and the pleather-covered seats that filled the room. From a window

I saw the captain and the baggage handler climb into a pickup truck and leave also.

"So they said they would pick us up?" Michael asked dubiously, as he peeked around the lone ticket counter to see if anyone hid from us in the "Employees Only" area. "I think we're the only ones here."

"Well, we could call the hotel or we could start our own airline," I offered. "We have a plane, a ticket counter and a crackly intercom – what more do we need? I don't think anyone would notice if we used it. Maybe the orange farmers need a lift?"

I picked up the phone behind the ticket counter and was pleasantly surprised to find a dial tone. I successfully dialed the phone number gleaned from my Internet research. The front desk clerk assured me that a vehicle had been sent to pick us up. He offered to try to call the driver to verify his location and suggested we wait outside in the meantime.

We rolled our ity-bity clothing bag and our enormous scuba gear bag out the front door to the terminal's dirt lot. Outside, there were no signs of life. The only car we saw was a dusty, beat-up van circa 1970 parked at the far side. It was possible that someone abandoned the relic there before the airport was even built. As we stood in silence and waited surrounded by jungle and heat, I began to wonder if adding Placencia to our trip had been a good idea.

Suddenly, I heard a faint ring coming from the Mystery Machine parked in the corner. It sounded electronic, like a cell phone. Up popped the van driver's head, who, by the look of it, had been napping across the front seat. He quickly started up the van, drove over to where we were standing and popped the trunk open for our bags. After confirming in broken Spanish that he was indeed heading our way, we loaded our luggage, climbed onto the stained cloth seats, and rolled down the windows as far as they could go. The driver pealed out of the lot and sped towards our accommodations faster than I would have ever guessed the van was able. I kept looking behind us for engine parts we might have left along the road, especially when the asphalt ended and the pot-holed, dirt road began. I would never complain about my municipally-maintained, curbed road at home again.

The intrigue thickened as we drove deeper and deeper into the jungle. The houses grew farther apart, their scrubby front lawns containing more and more farm animals. Live chickens and goats, with the occasional bovine tied to a tree, seemed to be staple lawn ornaments. I swear I saw a pig wandering down a side street. Then, a stone and stucco wall began on the right-hand side of the road; its modern and sleek appearance was a stark contrast to the slow jungle decay behind it. An equally modern housing development appeared to our left along with a bay. The asphalt had started again, clearly laid by the owners of the property.

I began to catch glimpses of the ocean to my right behind the wall. Through the trees and in front of the ocean, a strip of stone and stucco buildings appeared. In the center was a large stone house, reminiscent of Portofino, Italy. Pink bougainvillea overflowed from large pots placed throughout the grounds. In the center of the parking area out front was a large, lillypad-filled pond with a tinkling fountain in the middle. The taxi driver stopped the van and got out to remove our bags, pretty much cementing the fact that this was our hotel. I climbed out, took a good look around at the fairytale setting and thought, *so this is a bit unexpected*. Since so little Internet information was available about the property, I expected to find Gilligan's Island vs. Fantasy Island.

After a brief check in, the porter led us to our room, which was a condo rented out when the owners were not there. The furnishings leapt straight out of a decorator's magazine; the chairs, tables, and even the four-poster bed were made of hand-carved hardwoods. The advertised kitchenette turned out to be a full kitchen gleaming in stainless steel and granite. And, there was the balcony that stretched the length of the condo, overlooking the beach and the blue water a few feet away. If this was my last-minute hotel pick I needed to start procrastinating when planning all of our dive vacations. It put my Ikea-clad abode to shame.

We quickly unpacked and went down to the hotel bar at the end of a long dock. It was quiet. We didn't see another guest for at least an hour. As we lay on lounge chairs sipping Belican, another local beer, we listened to Wilson Picket's "Dock of the Bay," piped in from the stereo behind the bar. From our perch over the water we looked back towards the land, watching the pink and purple sunset. Just down the beach from our hotel, the white steeple of a local church stood in contrast against the pastel sky. That night, tucked in the four-poster bed I dreamed of the beautiful sunset and the whale sharks that would hopefully come to play beneath it.

The next morning it was sunny with blue skies and minimal wind and waves: perfect diving weather. During whale shark season, the Belizean government regulates how many boats can enter the Gladden Spit Marine reserve at any given time in order to reduce the impact on the whale sharks and also to make a little money in the process. Dive boats wanting to bring divers to the site had to apply for permits months before the season, and could only hope to obtain one or two time slots per day.

The time slots were strictly monitored by local authorities who parked their boat on the Spit's edge. From the time we entered the Spit we had exactly one hour before our boat had to leave. If our boat went beyond the allotted time frame, the hotel would be fined and, even worse, might lose its privileges to enter the Spit again. To strictly adhere to the rule, we donned our scuba gear before we reached the marine park, and prepared to jump in the minute the captain located his desired spot. The six of us divers sat against the sides of the boat, ready to backroll into the water at the divemaster's direction.

The captain steered the boat alongside the authorities' boat. In a barrage of Spanish we obtained clearance to enter the area. The captain sped to his predetermined location. With a brief countdown of "3-2-1" we all rolled into the water in unison, then gathered at the waterline near the bow to descend. Gladden Spit is a deep trench that does not bottom out until 6,600 feet. We were diving in open ocean, a first for Michael and me, which meant there would be no fixed point of reference to guide us visually. We could easily sink too deep or float off course if we did not watch our depth gages and stay within the divemaster's eyesight. With a few final warnings, he gave the thumbs down sign to descend.

We planned to descend to 35 feet where we would wait to see if the snapper and whale sharks showed up. Since we would be remaining at that shallow depth, we could easily stay underwater for the full hour, hoping to catch a glance of...well, anything really. I fought to stay at 35 feet, alternating between floating up and sinking down, with absolutely no self-awareness until I glanced at my depth gauge. I never realized how much I relied on the sight of the reef, a wall, or the bottom to guide my underwater navigation.

Throughout the dive we saw only one or two snappers. You know those people who show up early to a party before the hosts are even done getting dressed and plating the canapés? These snapper were those guests. I began to yawn into my regulator (yes, it can be done). The highlight was a series of small iridescent jellyfish that floated past my mask, their bodies pulsing with glow-in-the-dark light. After 60 minutes we ascended, climbed aboard the boat and left the Spit. It was a disappointing dive day.

The next day we boarded the boat again, this time accompanied by two other divers instead of four. The second couple had been diving there for a week in hopes of seeing the whale sharks, but had not met any luck. They decided to take a day off and explore the area instead. We headed back to the Spit to try again. Similar to the prior trip, we geared up, the Spanish flew, and before I knew it I was back in the unending blue depths, staring at my depth gauge, waiting for Godot.

Several dive boats leaving the Spit as we were entering shouted to us about promising "activity" underwater, although no one had seen any whale sharks. The other dive boats were right; more fish appeared, including snapper. Several schools swam by, igniting our excitement until we realized they were groups of individual fish, not one large one. Several times the divemaster pointed in the distance and made the "small shark" hand signal, indicating interesting sharks were present, but not the big daddies we were after. Although I strained to focus on the fleeting fins, I couldn't make out any of the sharks.

We surfaced after another 60 minutes without whale sharks. I climbed on the boat first and reached over the side to help the next person with their fins.

"Get out of the water now," the divemaster said calmly to Michael and the couple still in the water and then placed his face back underwater.

Michael climbed on to the boat. Before the couple could start up the ladder, the divemaster pulled his head out of the water again.

"Climb up the ladder now," he said, a little more firmly. "Don't waste time taking off your gear." He put his head back into the water.

As the other couple quickly climbed out of the water, I watched the divemaster turn in the water, clearly keeping an eye on something circling our boat. I could see a dark shape, maybe ten feet long, slowly swimming in an arc. After everyone was safely in the boat, the divemaster practically leapt from the water, landing squarely on his flippered feet in an impressive ballet maneuver.

"Bull shark," he said, as he removed his gear and the captain started up the motor. "They come to eat the snapper, but there's not enough here yet to eat. They can be aggressive towards divers sometimes. This one was coming too close." My eyes must have looked like dinner plates. Sharks don't scare me because I know they are private, introverted creatures that prefer to avoid humans unless provoked. I had never been stalked by one before. I couldn't wait until more snapper arrived and we were off their dinner menu.

On our way out of the park, we came across a small dive boat filled with commotion. The divers were running back and forth from one side of the boat to the other, pointing to the water excitedly. A brief discussion between our captain and theirs provided the explanation: a whale shark was swimming near the surface. Suddenly, the water surface erupted as a large, squared head peaked out from beneath the waves. Whale sharks have beady little eyes underscored by huge oval mouths. He or she turned an eye towards us, then retreated back underwater until the coast was clear.

Although we were not in the water with the shark, the sighting was still thrilling. Although it lasted only a few seconds, it was enough to excite me for the following day's dive, which could potentially involve another hour of seeing nothing, or might produce an opportunity to actually swim with a whale shark. The boat carrying the local authorities pulled up alongside ours, threatening to revoke our park permit if we did not leave immediately. With a wave we pulled away, energized for the next day.

That night we decided to have dinner in Placencia. Our hotel gave us three options to get a bite, but wouldn't go so far as to recommend any of them. Determined to see something besides the dive boat and the hotel room, we hopped in a cab and bounced down the road towards town. At the airfield, our driver slowed and looked both ways before crossing the landing strip, a necessity I both appreciated and found disturbing. He dropped us off in the town's "center," a loose cluster of commercial buildings and homes.

We instantly saw the three restaurants the front desk clerk mentioned. His dining suggestions turned out to be not just *a* list, but *the* list; there were no other restaurants. We entered the first one, an empty restaurant combined with an Internet café in a strange open-air teepee-shaped building. Our clerk had deemed it "some good food there." A scraggly man who looked like Jimmy Buffett after a bender sat behind a desk in the corner, idly clicking on a computer.

"Are you still serving dinner?" I asked.

"Sure thing," he said, surprisingly chipper and alert. "My wife is in the back. She can cook you a hamburger or a hotdog, if you'd like." I glanced at Michael, throwing him my *no way* look.

"Thanks!" said Michael. "We are going to walk around town a bit, then we'll be back."

We walked out the front door then down the road a piece to the next place. It looked well lit and clean, but again, no one was there, not even a proprietor. We shouted "Helloooo!" several times before giving up and moving onto the final restaurant.

The last place was welcoming and lively, with several tables taken up by families. I think we managed to find the only Chinese restaurant within thousands of miles. At least I believe it was Chinese. The proprietors were Asian and the menu pictures looked faintly like New York City's Mott St. delicacies. On the downside we did not speak Spanish or Chinese, and the proprietor did not excel at English. In an effort to order, I pointed to several pictures on the menu, but she kept shaking her head negatively, indicating they were out of the ingredients or she just didn't want to cook it for us. The plates she could prepare seemed to involve mystery meat and lumpy sauces.

After several minutes of back and forth between the proprietor and me, Michael and I finally gave up and found ourselves back on the street with growling stomachs and no dinner. Dejected, we hailed a cab (again, *the* cab) and returned to the hotel, intent on cooking up a bowl of macaroni and cheese, which we dragged along in our suitcase for such an occasion. At least we would be able to enjoy the immense cooking resources our room had to offer.

Michael called the front desk to see if we could get milk and a pat of butter while I raided the kitchen for a pot and some plates.

"Can you ask them to send a pot as well?" I asked Michael after finding a bizarre lack of cooking equipment in the gourmet kitchen. A long, frustrating conversation ensued.

Apparently people had just bought the condo and had not fully furnished it yet with all of the comforts of home. While they had gone overboard in the furniture department, they had yet to stock the kitchen cabinets. Furthermore, they had requested that no one be allowed to cook in the kitchen until they had time to test out the effect of cooking odors on the expensive furniture. So, nice kitchen, but no cooking. It was like salivating over a beautiful desert only to find out it's only the display and they have no real ones. To add insult to injury, room service was not available that late at night.

We gave up and went to the main building to find the hotel dining room. As we walked up to the restaurant entrance, a waiter clicked off the lights. Either they were about to sing "Happy Birthday" to the busboy, or everyone was going home for the night. I needed to leave the building as Michael explained our plight. I can only be rational for so long before hunger steals all logic and runs off with it into the night.

After several moments I returned to find Michael seated at a small table in the corner overlooking the beach, with two glasses of red wine.

"The chef has gone home," he said. "But they promised to find someone who could cook something for us. I have no idea what they are going to serve, but I'm pretty sure I could eat this table cloth right now, so...I guess we just go with it."

After about fifteen minutes our wine was mostly gone. As I started to wonder if they had gone home and forgotten about us, a young man approached our table with two plates.

"My mom works here with me, but she's a good cook," he said, setting the plates down and leaving us to gaze at the contents.

So there we were in southern Belize, sipping red wine by the light of the moon in a corner of a deserted restaurant, staring at two perfectly executed plates of...spaghetti carbonara. The pasta was perfectly al dente, the sauce thick but not pasty with a smoky bacon sprinkle mixed in for flavor. I have no idea why that was the chosen dish, but I do know I was full and content by the time the plate was empty.

The next day dawned sunny and clear with a small wind raising a slight chop on the water. It was our final day to see the whale sharks before leaving. We would be the only divers on the boat, the rest having had given up after numerous fruitless tries. The couple we dove with the first day saw us off at the dock and wished us luck. They were colorful characters from the U.S. Midwest, outspoken, friendly, and fun. As a special treat, they offered to do a "Good Luck Whale Shark Sighting Dance" for us.

As we pulled away from the dock, each one had a hand on their straw hat-covered heads representing dorsal fins. They danced in a circle bobbing their heads and wiggling their free hands behind them in a sort of tail-swishing pantomime. It is a shame what prolonged exposure to the ocean does to some people.

We motored out to the Spit then geared up in anticipation of our entry. In we went, down we drifted, and there we waited. In the first few minutes I could tell conditions were different than the prior days. Thick groups of fish swam below us, some in schools so large that their scaly parade continued for several minutes. In between the schools, bull sharks roamed, their dark shadows all but unnoticed by the large groups of flirting snapper. I, for one, was just happy the bulls now had other tasty tidbits to pursue.

Then, as the dive guides and Nostradamus predicted, an enormous shadow materialized from between a large school of snappers. Our divemaster began waving and pointing like he was having an embolism, a clear validation that the whale sharks had finally arrived. At first their distant shapes faded in and out of view, leaving me wondering if they were actually there or if the mushroom content of the spaghetti carbonara was playing tricks on my mind.

> "Noble and generous Cetacean, have you ever tasted Man?" "No," said the Whale. "What is it like?" "Nice," said the small 'Stute Fish. "Nice but nubbly."
> - Joseph Rudyard Kipling
> "How the Whale Got His Throat" *Just So Stories*

Michael pointed wildly to a spot behind me, apparently experiencing the same embolism attack as the divemaster. Because of all of the disorienting gear, a diver just doesn't have the same awareness of what is going on around them, or in my case, right behind me. I turned to find a whale shark swimming towards me, all 30 feet of him resembling a transit bus more than a fish. He ignored me as he swam lazily downwards, passing right below my feet. I drifted downwards with him as I clicked picture after picture, leveling off only when the divemaster called attention to my all-but-forgotten depth gauge.

Still stunned from my encounter, I demonstrated the embolism maneuver as two whale sharks materialized behind Michael, making a slow b-line towards each other. We watched in awe as they bumped into each other, causing one to quickly swim off with a flick of its massive tail. I found it incredible that an animal that large could move so fast with such ease.

The large snapper schools were swimming through the water column like individual fish rivers. The bull sharks sneaked in and out of the mêlée, periodically snatching a passing snack. Amongst all the activity, the stars of the show, the whale sharks, continued to fade in and out of view, appearing from all directions as they gobbled up the fish eggs. Though a diver can't really talk through their regulator, I was speechless anyway.

Our time was up, our tanks were empty, and it was time to ascend to the boat. We climbed back up the ladder in silence, having nothing to say that could even begin to do justice to our experience. On the way back to the hotel the sky opened up and the rain poured down in monsoon proportions. I huddled under a towel looking off the back of the boat towards the Spit with an enormous smile on my face that no amount of precipitation could wash away.

CHAPTER 13

Cayman Islands: Hammerheads on Harleys

Santa Claus ice cream pops lined the convenience store's frozen food shelves. The icy cases displayed an impressive selection of the winter treat considering it was July. Had the pops sat there since Christmas, or was the shop owner anticipating the next holiday rush? Either way, I was pretty sure that Santa wasn't meant to sit around that long, especially on a tiny tropical island like Cayman Brac. It would take the small number of patrons a long time to work through the jolly stock.

Palm trees outnumber every two and four-legged creature on the island. Only 1,600 people call the Brac home, many of whom belong to one of the five main family lines on the island. Everyone knows everyone, whether by kin, marriage or just plain neighbor nosiness (though they are an incredibly friendly bunch). Few restaurants, fewer hotels, and little industry exists on the island. Anyone with a social agenda or a need for electricity past 10pm would do best to head for Grand Cayman, the Brac's more industrious and lively big sister.

But, for those who enjoy scuba diving, the Brac is an ideal destination. Michael and I visited the Brac not for the nightlife, but for the sea life. What the island lacked in vacation amenities, it made up for in abundant coral and fish. The lack of significant amounts of tourist traffic enabled the reef to blossom; it was the healthiest one I had seen anywhere in the Caribbean.

Our hotel catered to divers with a well-equipped dive shop and a sturdy boat dock right off the beach. Our room sat on the main floor of a two-story bungalow. Usually I preferred a loftier perch, but with a ton of dive gear and no elevator, the location was just fine. The room layout made good use of the constant trade winds that blew across the island. A screened-in porch that contained the kitchen, sitting area, and a hot tub surrounded a hermetically sealed, air conditioned bedroom. When I turned in at night the bedroom door's swoosh made me feel vacuum packed into my bed.

Outside of the bungalows that lined the beach, the rest of the hotel was in need of repair. A two–story, crumpling building housed the bulk of the rooms. A cracked rectangular pool retained its water by sheer will. The closet-sized sundry shop offered a random collection of useless items (think single flip-flops and the skull of some dearly departed quadruped) that had undoubtedly washed up on shore over the past few years. The hotel needed a facelift.

When we showed up at the dive shop on our first full day on the island, we were happy to find a solid program with quality boats and gear. It was clear where the hotel had spent its money. Our divemaster, Paul, came to the Cayman Islands on vacation and fell in love with their beauty and relaxed way of life. When a divemaster job opened up on Cayman Brac, he jumped at the chance to work there. He lived a quiet life on the Brac, but his work was also his passion. He was friendly and knowledge-able, and we liked him immediately.

We boarded the boat and drove out to our first site, Green House Reef. Usually the dive community christens sites with interesting names to get divers excited. Location names like Champagne Cork, Octopus Alley, and Sharks' Dining Room are all meant to elicit an adrenaline response from potential visitors. Apparently, the folks on the Brac were not so tourism-minded. At some point a resident diver thought: *This is a great reef. And, I can see that pretty green house on the shore from here. I'll call this place Green House Reef.* I wondered what would happen to the reef's moniker when the owner decided to apply a new coat of paint.

But the Brac did not always have such laid-back inhabitants. In the 1700s, pirates partied on the island. At that time, the Brac had no permanent local population though there were plenty of fresh water wells and plants and animals to eat. Caves littered the island, making great hiding places for stolen loot. Pirates and their crew could rest on the idyllic isle undisturbed by laws, governments, or people who were not so keen on their heathen ways.

Pirates, turtles, and the British have all significantly influenced Cayman Island culture. Nowhere can one see a better representation of these three inspirations than in the unofficial national mascot, "Sir Turtle," the cartoon drawing that appears in many Department of Tourism communications and even on the tail of some Cayman Airways planes. Sir Turtle is a jaunty, smiling fellow with a shell on one side and an arm with a sword on the other. To add to his confused yet inspired look, he sports a British navy hat and outfit, finished off with one peg leg.

"During this dive you should keep an eye out for the pirate anchor imbedded in the coral," Paul said as he delivered our briefing. "We have several of them scattered in the waters around the island."

"Did the ships sink here?" I asked, eager to hear the sordid tale.

"Nope. The anchors are here because of pirate ingenuity. The ships they wanted to rob had plenty of firepower and were frequently faster than their own. So, the element of surprise was the pirates' best weapon."

"When the pirates would see a ship passing around the other side of the island, they would hide in this bay, dropping anchor and unfurling their sails to the fullest. When the other ship finally rounded the point, the pirates would chop their own anchor line, which would in turn send their boat flying towards its target. The other boat, unprepared for full speed or a pirate attack, would be easily overcome."

The old "chop and go" was a nifty trick if one didn't mind losing an anchor from time to time. The pirates couldn't always recover the anchors, especially when they became embedded in the coral like the particular specimen we prepared to visit. We geared up easily on the nearly empty boat and took a giant stride off the back into the clear aqua blue water.

Michael and I planned to navigate the dive on our own, relying on our compass and sense of direction, rather than have the divemaster show us the way. Based on our not-so-successful attempts at underwater navigation in the Bahamas, we knew we needed to improve our skills. The underwater terrain was covered in spur and groove formations. Determining direction would not be difficult, just follow a spur out to the deeper water, turn around, and then follow a groove back to the shallower water.

We descended to the bottom, picked a spur, and then started a slow swim away from the island. Unconcerned about the impact of my slow speed on other divers, I felt liberated going at our own pace. Almost immediately I found a four-foot-long snake eel entwined in a stand of elkhorn coral. Its thick body was mustard yellow with white dots. Our slow, quiet approach paid off: the snake paid us almost no notice, opting instead to continue its lazy rest and allow us to study him at close range for a long time.

We swam on, rounding the spur and starting back up a groove. We located the enormous coral head that held the embedded pirate anchor. Over time the coral grew over the edges, engulfing the pirate's castaway. The parts of the relic that protruded from the head looked surprisingly intact considering it had been there for hundreds of years. It must have really frustrated the pirates to leave something behind of such quality.

We continued on our tour, our unhurried pace enabling us to find even the smallest creatures such as peppermint-striped coral-banded shrimp and frilly yellow lettuce sea slugs. The site's inhabitants weren't all cute and benign, however. A cash crop of brown fire coral poked its stick-like fingers out from all over the reef. A bristle worm, an aquatic caterpillar on steroids, offered an intriguing subject for photography but promised a nasty sting from its "fur" that would last for hours if touched. Two agitated stingrays flapped their wings vigorously at me, annoyed at being disturbed from their seabed nap.

Our time and air ran low. We made our way back to the boat, which, miraculously, appeared where we thought it would. Michael and I had completed a successful foray into underwater navigation and found our way back to tell about it.

After several more days of diving at creatively-named places like School House Reef and Sandy Beach Point, we exhausted the island's supply of sites. Paul offered to take us to a "special" spot that he liked to keep secret because of its abundance of tasty residents. He called the site the Lobster Pot. Our minds and stomachs quickly agreed to the dive site selection, though we wouldn't be harvesting any dinner. Local conservation laws only allowed fishermen (lobstermen?) to collect lobsters at certain times of the year, which did not correspond with our visit. Even without the opportunity to put one on my plate, it would still be fun to see that particular type of sea creature.

For me, our next dive was a big one, No. 100. Michael's 100th dive would be the one after mine, due to the manta ray dive I did in Yap without him. Somehow we had gone from scuba newbies to frequent divers.

"At this site there are three large coral heads in a triangle, with many smaller ones in between," Paul said. "Your dive plan is to start at the coral head below the boat, then visit each of the other two in turn, returning to the boat after circumnavigating the site."

"The lobsters here are Caribbean reef lobsters, which don't have

> The Spiny Lobster (*Panulirus argus*) is common throughout the Caribbean, being found as far north as the Carolinas and as far south as Brazil. These blue and brown crustaceans lack the fearsome claws of other lobsters, instead sporting long, thick spiny antennae for protection. Prior to the 20th century, eating lobster was considered a mark of poverty since these critters are bottom scavengers, eating unpleasant sea floor invertebrate and decaying matter. But oh, have times changed. Now humans see lobsters as a delicacy, fishing them almost to endangered levels in some parts of the Caribbean. Unfortunately for these bugs, humans are not the only ones looking to turn them into dinner: sharks, rays, groupers, triggerfish, moray eels, sea turtles, and octopus also consider them tasty tidbits.

claws but do have really sharp long antennae to scare you off. Just be careful, the antennae can give you a good cut. Oh, and take a good look at the second coral head," he said as he gestured off the back of the boat. "There is another nice pirate anchor there."

With a splash and a smile Michael and I were back in the water, hovering over the bottom. I handed Michael my camera and took out a small plastic underwater writing tablet where I had scribbled "100." Michael laughed and took my picture as I displayed my accomplishment to the camera. Paparazzi duties complete, we headed towards the first coral head.

The site quickly lived up to its name. Never before had I seen so many lobsters in one place. Some hid in nooks in the reef and many wandered around on the sea floor. All were huge, some so large I doubted they would fit in anyone's pot. One particularly robust specimen, maybe five pounds or so, sat on a coral shelf looking like a crustaceous king holding court over the reef. Being enormous, he had no reason to hide as there were few animals that would even consider challenging his reign. He waved his three-foot-long antennae at me like a royal scepter, just to remind me to steer clear.

We rounded the first corner of the coral triangle and headed for the second. I found the pirate anchor, though the years and the elements had not been kind to it; little of it remained. Near it sat a nice brown eel with small white spots that watched us with interest. The top of the coral head was a fish hatchery, where juveniles swam in thick schools that, from a distance, looked like hazy clouds.

We couldn't see the third boulder, but we aimed for shallower water where we knew it lay. The visibility, which had been great the prior few days, had reduced by half to 50 feet, owing to a strong wind and resulting waves. Sailfin blennies and other bottom-dwelling creatures peered at us from the rubble-filled sea floor in the shallower water. We finned some more then consulted our compasses when the promised boulder didn't materialize. After a few minutes of underwater bickering that included lots of head shaking and pointing with many different fingers, we agreed upon a new course. Yet even with our fine-tuned effort, no boat appeared.

Finally, we had to give up as time and air were getting short. When we reached the surface, we realized with embarrassment that we were nowhere near the boat. Our brand new navigation skills were no match for water with reduced visibility. The captain saw us immediately and gave us the "okay" arm gesture to check our status. We returned a positive "okay" gesture to him, as we weren't injured, just directionally challenged.

"Stay where you are," shouted the captain, his voice carrying on the wind. "The boat will come pick you up after everyone else gets back onboard."

Our scuba vests were well inflated with air, so we bobbed like two tops on the water's surface. The wind kicked up a current, which in turn, began moving us even farther from the boat. Every once in awhile I put my head back in the water to ensure no evil sea creatures snuck up on us, a phobia for which I can only blame Hollywood. Over time I noticed that we were drifting farther and farther into deeper water.

I reflected on the two greatest hazards to our situation, sharks and passing boats. Since I hadn't seen a single shark in our entire week of diving, I felt certain there was little risk of Jaws joining our floating party. We were, however, moving into the shipping channel. We would be hard to spot; the waves and our black suits would challenge even the most eagle-eyed captain if his boat and speed were great enough. We floated patiently but uneasily. What else could we do?

Finally the rest of the divers climbed onboard our boat, the mate retrieved the anchor, and the captain drove out to us. I expected substantial ribbing from the guests and crew at our attempt to impersonate buoys. Instead, everyone offered support and praised us for not panicking, which we appreciated. Diving can be a humbling sport; even after 100 experiences, we were still just learning how to survive.

We sat on the rickety barstools of our hotel's outdoor watering hut, sipping margaritas and listening to the bartender's tales of prior famous hotel guests. Story highlights included a seasick socialite, a politician and his bikini-clad "assistant," and a guitarist who woke up naked in a rowboat filled with coconuts.

"It's all ending, though" he said, wistfully. "If they don't find a buyer for this property soon, the owners are just going to shut it down. They say they are losing too much money."

Buying the hotel would cost more than the initial purchase price. Cracks in the walls, variable water and electrical supply, and the obvious lack of guests indicated the hotel needed significant investment to patch things up and attract clientele. Though way beyond our means, Michael and I daydreamed about buying the place and turning it into a boutique dive hotel. In the process, we came up with eight things a great dive hotel must have, based on our experiences.

Eight Dive Hotel Requirements

1. **A good bar** – Even beyond the adult beverage benefits, a good hotel bar provides a great place for divers to socialize and bond, two things they do naturally due to the idiosyncrasies of the sport. Finding a sea horse underwater is wonderful. Showing off the picture to anyone who will look at it is even better. Showing it off to people who actually know what it is and want to discuss it, is sublime. Discussing it with a margarita in hand is, well...priceless.

2. **Warm towels** – Even in 90 degree water, a diver will eventually turn hypothermic because the water temperature is below a human's body temperature. A warm, dry towel is not quantum physics. Heat it up, store it someplace insulated then hand it over to the diver when they get out of the water. I have seen divers actually swoon when receiving warm towels on a dive boat. It is a rare but appreciated service.

3. **Creatures in the ocean, not in the bedroom** – Abundant, interesting ocean critters within easy reach of a dive hotel is a "must." Abundant, creepy critters *in* a dive hotel is a "must not." Just because divers embrace the outdoors does not mean they want to take any of it inside with them.

4. **Air** – Without a tank of air, a diver is just a snorkeler with questionable swim attire. Without clean, properly-filtered air, a diver is just a hospital visit waiting to happen. A reliable onsite air compressor is a must. No borrowing air tanks from the next hotel down the beach. No jury-rigging the compressor with tape, cooking oil and a strategically placed flip-flop to make it work.

5. **The ability to wash** – This requirement includes washing one's body and one's gear, both of which will grow quickly ripe if not rinsed with fresh water after a sea-water soak. A freezing cold squirt from a garden hose is not a suitable substitute for a clean, comfortable outdoor shower near the dock.

6. **Sustenance** – Just because a diver breathes canned air doesn't mean they prefer canned food. Divers who have eaten well will have enough energy to swim back to their dive boat when they become hopelessly lost underwater and have to surface in a boating channel. Or, maybe I'm just blaming my compass issues on the hotel food. Either way, our hotel would not leave the diver hungry for dives or dinner.

7. **Surroundings that harmonize with wet things** – Divers are, by definition, wet. Wetness continues to follow them long after they leave the dive boat. They drip as they walk through the lobby to their room, making slip-resistant flooring a must (marble is nice, but life-threatening). Their clothes and bathing suits need a friendly place to dry other than a balcony railing that quickly facilitates the garments' flight to the ground below. And, the entire hotel décor needs to be able to withstand wet rear ends and sandy handprints.

8. **A good bar** – No, really. Don't underestimate it. Perhaps we would build two.

The gift was a slice of heaven from the tropics, a rum cake, the *Cadillac* of rum cakes: a Tortuga. One bite and we knew we must go visit its birthplace, the Cayman Islands. Or, at least that's what we told the clerk so we could get some free samples. Not that we needed to exaggerate our interest in his drunken desert, almost every store in downtown George Town, the capital of Grand Cayman, sold them aggressively. A rum cake was undoubtedly a vacation purchase that created wonderment the moment one returned home. *Why did I buy this thing? Who do I dislike that I can give it to?* I once worked in an office that reused a Tortuga for a whole year, leveraging it as a recurring birthday gift, door stop, and Frisbee with no noticeable change in the shrink-wrapped cake's appearance.

Downtown George Town offered something for everyone. Besides copious rum cakes, one could easily locate jewelry stores, handbag shops, and the usual vacation kitsch. Vacationers rubbed elbows with bankers, there to enjoy the fruits of flexible, tax-friendly banking laws. And in between them all were the Camanites, friendly and gregarious people eking out an impressive living from tourism and banking alike.

During our visit four cruise ships sat in port, making the downtown area a sheep herding experience rather than a pleasant stroll. After only a brief visit to the mayhem, we decided to walk back down Seven Mile Beach to our hotel. Many buildings perched along the five-mile strip of sand (someone had gotten over-enthusiastic with the "Seven Mile" name). Some advertised the opportunity to purchase a condo, many of them newly built. Hurricanes had severely damaged the island, especially in 2004. The storms, though destructive, had a rejuvenating flip side: they drove significant new construction.

One particularly attractive new building offered a range of layouts depicted alluringly on its glossy front-door signage. Though we were not in the market for a tropical hideaway, we found ourselves compelled to enter the lobby and find out more. Just inside the door, a tanned, buxom woman manned a desk labeled "Condominium Sales." Her coiffed blond hair and vague European accent gave away her status: non-native imported by the developers to move condos.

"How may I help you?" she asked, cheerfully. I felt for her; I'm sure she had to repeat her spiel 1,001 times a day, staying upbeat with every potential customer.

"Well we were looking to buy a Honda," my husband said, jokingly. Why does the sight of a good-looking woman turn men into babbling brooks? The woman eyed us, now a bit confused and very skeptical.

"We were interested in learning more about your condos," Michael continued. I could see light dawning on the saleswoman's face. We were back in comfortable territory now.

"We've got several layouts to choose from," she said.

"We're looking for a two-bedroom," I offered. She pulled out some paperwork including diagrams of room layouts and lists of amenities. As she fanned out the documents with great expertise, she gave us a lovely eyeful of plump cleavage, guaranteed to close the sale with any straight man with money. I strained in my seat to look into the office behind her, hoping they kept a Brad Pitt look-alike back there for female buyers like me.

"As you can see," she said, "The bedrooms radiate off the central living room…" she continued on with her tale, but my attention trailed off as I caught a look at the pricing sheet. Apparently if one wanted to purchase even the least expensive of the condos, one would have to either win the lottery or mourn the passing of a wealthy great aunt with a generous will. The smallest two-bedroom, which overlooked the street from only the second floor, cost $1.5M. As the view grew more impressive and the floors got higher, so too did the price. The penthouse, a three-bedroom wonder of glass and inspiring ocean views, cost $15 million.

We feigned interest for a bit longer then graciously took our leave. That same $15 million could probably buy us the dive hotel on Cayman Brac, though the condo would undoubtedly be less fun. We walked in silence back to our hotel, rendered speechless by the price of paradise.

"Hurricanes affect us every year," the divemaster, Rico, said. Not that we asked him, but he seemed intent on sharing anyway. "That last one washed through the first floors of most of the hotels on Seven Mile Beach. It did some damage to the reef too, but it doesn't matter; we've got miles of great diving here." Ah, a real conservationist. I wondered if he planned to break off bits of coral underwater and hand them to me for souvenirs.

After a week of diving in Cayman Brac Michael and I thought we would need some land time once we reached Grand Cayman. But, like a good margarita, the more one drank, the more one liked the taste. From the time our plane touched down in Grand Cayman, we hungered for more underwater exploration. Unfortunately, the dive company I selected via the Internet a few weeks before had only sporadic availability on their boat throughout the week. If we wanted more than a few dives, we would have to locate another company. On the upside, there were plenty of dive operators from which to choose. It seemed that every native with a boat promised some sort of scuba experience, abundantly advertised in local brochures, newspapers, and the phone book. I chose an operator that belonged to PADI, the Professional Association of Dive Instructors, a mark that usually indicated a reasonable level of quality.

The company operated off of a pontoon boat, a first for Michael and me. While it did offer plenty of space and a sun-blocking canopy, it lacked the scuba sexiness of a sleek craft, looking more like a giant floating day bed. The boat was moored off the beach a short walk from our hotel. Since there wasn't a dock, we had to wade out to the ladder with our towels, shorts, and shoes piled on our heads like pilgrims crossing the Ganges.

Rico introduced himself as the divemaster and boat captain. The introduction was helpful, as otherwise we would have mistaken him for a crazy old pirate. The gray curly hair on his bare chest made a nice nest for the pounds of gold chains and pendants that hung from his sinewy, tanned neck. His salt-dusted, cut-off jean shorts and ponytail of grey hair only contributed further to the look. Sadly, he lacked and eye patch and a parrot. Perhaps after a few more customers he could afford an avian accomplice.

Rico (I'm sure his name was really Hubert, Leslie or some other less testosterone-infused name) appeared to like hearing himself talk more than he liked to help the divers on the boat set up their gear. While we acquired appropriate scuba paraphernalia from a pile at the bow, he jabbered on about the island, and more importantly, himself. After living for some time without any obvious means of employment, he said, he became a certified dive instructor so he could earn money for beer and meet "lady divers."

When all six scheduled divers were onboard, Rico started up the engine, chugging us slowly to our first dive site named Hammerhead Hill. The dive was disappointing, producing neither hammerheads nor a hill. Once in the water, we fought a raging current that tired us quickly. When I climbed back on the boat, my tank was absolutely empty of air because of the exertion. Most dive companies will check the current first, moving the boat to a different site if the water moved along too strongly. Rico's already shaky popularity dropped dramatically with the exhausted, frustrated divers.

Next, we put-putted to Blue Peter Reef. The other divers threatened to mutiny if Pirate Rico did not guarantee the dive site would have a reasonable current. After checking it thoroughly, he deemed the "Pool Open." Blue Peter was a shallow reef with plenty of nooks and crannies to explore, so Michael and I agreed ahead of time that we would go off on our own.

The moment the noise and commotion of the group moved away, the reef came to life. Angelfish came out of their homes to inspect us, while a big green moray eel stretched his head into the gentle current to take a good sniff. Barely five minutes into the dive Michael found a rare adult spotted drum, a black and white polka dot and stripped fish that is always celebrated by divers when spotted. I found that the longer I hovered over an area of coral, the more creatures came out to greet me.

I closed in to take a picture of some blue bell tunicates when suddenly a big black eye surrounded by spikes filled my macro lens. A porcupine puffer emerged from a coral overhang right in front of my camera. He ignored me and my blinding flash in favor of a tasty snack affixed to the reef.

We swam on a short distance, finding so many things to look at we needn't go far. I was surprised at the volume of flamingo tongues, which are sea snails with an orange leopard-print pattern on their backs. They hung from almost every sea fan and stalk of upraised coral. Since they slithered rather than swam, I could get my macro lens up close without my subject disappearing. I snapped photo after photo of the fingerprint-sized mollusks.

One flamingo tongue, a large one perched on a bright purple piece of extended coral, caught my interest. The color contrast between the animal and its background produced an eye-catching tableau. With no fire coral or other hazards around, I had a clear shot at the animal. I used the opportunity to work on my photography skills, changing the shutter speed, aperture, and flash brightness to get different pictures and perspectives.

Back on the boat, the other divers asked to see my photos. I passed around the camera, explaining how to work the digital buttons to flip through the range of pictures. The first woman flipped through only a few before quickly handing the camera to the next person and running off to the opposite side of the boat. The next two guys who looked snickered and poked each other in the ribs.

The camera made the rest of the rounds, landing back on my lap with a lot of "Nice photos" comments and winks. I looked at the viewfinder to find out what all the fuss was about. The flamingo tongue on the purple branch wasn't fat; it was actually two separate creatures engaging in adult activity. I was so busy playing with the settings on my camera I hadn't even realized the R-rated show playing out on the reef in front of me. I had inadvertently become a snail pornographer.

Cayman taxis were blindingly expensive, so we decided to do our island touring with a rental car for a day. Michael managed the left hand side of the road quite well, though we steered clear of the crowded downtown, not wanting to add a cruise passenger as a hood ornament. We made our first stop at a small but well-known restaurant that overlooked the flats of the West Bay. Sumptuous plates overflowing with freshly-caught grilled fish and roasted local vegetables made us forget to talk until we cleaned our plates. While digesting contently, we engaged the proprietor in a little conversation about the place.

"We've been here for a long time," he said, proudly. "The hurricanes keep washing our deck away, but we keep rebuilding. Each time we make it bigger than the last!" I admired his enthusiasm for what must have been a discouraging situation time and time again. Clearly he made the most of the opportunity, expanding at a time when most people would have given up.

After topping our fantastic meal with some sinful deserts, we continued on our island tour by going to Hell. This destination was the best use of unusable land I had ever seen. A long time ago, an enterprising Camanite looked at the barren, black fields of eroded limestone and dolomite on the northwest side of the island and thought "Well that's ugly! Now what could I possibly use it for?" He deemed it "Hell," stuck a souvenir shop at one end of it, and voila, the kitschiest tourist spot in the Caymans was born.

We stopped and took some pictures, which a surprisingly large number of people were also doing. I proudly bought an "I went to Hell" mug for my office and even got a few postcards mailed with the "Hell" postmark on them, as the government considered it an official town. Twenty minutes later we continued down the road, $20 lighter and thrilled at the ridiculousness of it all. The spot represented true tourism ingenuity at work.

I had debated the sensibility of our final stop. The Cayman turtle farm had enjoyed popularity since its inception in 1968. It was the only turtle farm of its kind in the Caribbean, housing over 11,000 green sea turtles that ranged in size from mere ounces to over 500 pounds. Everyone we asked said we had to see it for ourselves.

We joined a tour, a necessity to make sense of the acres of pools, ponds, and buildings housing the little green wonders. The guide repeated the conservation message over and over. Saving turtles in the wild, reducing poaching, and maintaining the turtles' habitat was, happily, all a part of the farm's mission. The little kids on our tour clapped with joy when the guide showed us a video of the farm releasing adult turtles into the wild.

But, of course, the owners named the place the Turtle *Farm*, a term that usually indicates a bit of earth reserved for the cultivation of something people eat. While conserving naturally occurring turtles was a mainstay of the business, the owners accomplished it by providing a consistent source of farm-raised turtle meat to satisfy the worldwide demand. It reminded me of the Aruban Ostrich Farm where the plucky creatures were grown and admired, then eaten for lunch. Though I had an iron stomach and a belief that every dish should be tried at least once in lifetime, this was just one protein source I couldn't swallow.

My new underwater camera strobe fired intermittently. Over the prior few diving days I missed several nice shots because, when I took a picture the flash failed to work. A famous island underwater photographer had a large shop on the other side of George Town. More so than almost anywhere else in the world, I knew this place could help me get the strobe working right. We hopped in a cab with my gear in tow and headed out to the photo studio.

Photo gear and Cayman trinkets filled the store, which was nestled in the basement of an old plantation-style building. The artist's underwater photos were for sale on lots of different items: large wall prints, posters, note cards, and even mugs. The breathtaking photos captured realistic underwater life scenes. I recognized her subjects from my own Grand Cayman dives; the still life shots reflected points in time during my prior week underwater.

A salesman in the store helped me figure out the problem with my camera. Due to the awkward shape of my waterproof camera housing, the strobe sensor couldn't consistently pick up the camera flash. He outfitted me with a fiber optic cord with one end attached to the strobe and the other unceremoniously taped to the front of the camera flash with black masking tape. It wasn't sexy, but it would do the job. Twenty-five bucks later we were on our way with my new and improved gear.

Outside the photo shop stood a famous hotel built for the sole purpose of housing divers. Even more important than the hotel itself was an enormous bar attached to the back that attracted dive enthusiasts from across the island. It being late afternoon, the place overflowed with two-legged sea life looking for a cold beer after a long day of work or fun (depending on what side of the credit card they were on).

We settled onto the last two available barstools and flagged the bartender down. I ordered my usual margarita, pleasantly surprised to see that it arrived in a plain plastic cup without the usual tacky glassware and fruit topping that many high-end establishments assumed I wanted. This bar offered a no-frills experience.

Just as we toasted to another nice day in paradise, a loud roar almost knocked me out of my seat. A man in a fishnet shirt and holey, cut-off jeans pulled into the parking lot on a Harley, looking oh-so-80's and quite ventilated. As the waning rays of the sun peeked out from a passing cloud, his familiar array of gold chains momentarily blinded me. Oh yes, I knew this man. Rico, our divemaster, had arrived.

We ducked down in our seats, hoping to avoid eye contact. But, like a car wreck on a highway, we couldn't help but look. He crossed the room dramatically and joined a group of fashion-challenged, older men who looked comfortable in their seats, as if they sat there often. Many people in the bar seemed to know each other, the Harley guys included.

"Is this where most of the dive community comes after work?" Michael asked the bartender when he refilled my drink. "It looks like a lot of people know each other."

"Well, this is where a lot of folks *start* their night," he said. "Most move on down the road to a few other places. It's like a nightly pub crawl." I couldn't imagine diving all day and drinking all night. They must have hammering headaches. I bet pharmacies on the island did a brisk business.

"I've been a bartender on some other islands," he said, looking out over the crowd and waving to someone as they passed behind us. "Usually people who work in the dive community come and go pretty quickly. But Grand Cayman is different. It has a lot divemasters and dive shop owners who have been here a long time. And the divers are really loyal too. They come back over and over."

Michael and I nodded our heads in understanding as the bartender went back to his job. We talked with divers perched on either side of us about the week's dives, comparing stories and sea life sightings. We picked up some good pointers on a few more reefs to visit before we left, and I absorbed some underwater photography tips from a diver that took professional photos for one of the dive companies on the island.

Just as I finished my third margarita and the room began to sway, someone rang the large ship bell above the bar.

"What's going on?" I asked a Brit next to me who had been diving in the Caymans for the past two weeks. Judging by the number of men who came by to say hello to her, she appeared to have figured out the social network on the island.

"It's time to go to the next bar!" She said tipsily as the crowd stood up en masse, paid their tabs, and headed towards the exit.

The Hammerheads on Harleys led the charge, leaving the parking lot with a loud roar and a puff of smoke. They stopped only a few blocks down at the next bar. The rest of the crowd followed along on foot; Michael and I embedded in the throng. We blended in well, just two more scuba fans in a sea of divers.

EPILOGUE

I knelt on the sandy bottom as a hammerhead shark circled me; with each new pass he swam closer and closer. Just when I thought the shark would knock me over, it veered away, perhaps spooked by the shadow of the whale shark gliding overhead. A stingray with a four-foot diameter fluttered its wings in the sand next to me, as if laughing at my awkward, two-legged form amongst all the graceful fish. But, the sea creatures weren't the only curious ones; a group of school children on the other side of the glass ogled me, prompting me to wave. They clapped and waved back, though I'm sure a few would have found their field trip a lot more interesting if the diver in the tank was eaten by the hammerhead instead.

My quest for diving adventures had taken me around the world, eventually bringing me right back where I started in Atlanta. Each place I had visited was interesting in its own right, but made even more so by the opportunity to explore the sea. Even Atlanta, my land-locked home town (not exactly a diving Mecca) suddenly offered more to do and see with my newfound skills. Now, I was looking out from inside the tank of the Georgia Aquarium instead of the other way around.

Over time my scuba skills have grown, as has my confidence in my abilities. As I stood at the lip of the aquarium tank about to enter, I realized with pleasant surprise just how much my comfort level with the sport had evolved. I eagerly surveyed the tank, excited to jump right in. My self-assured approach to the dive was a far cry from our first efforts in Bora Bora when I flailed helplessly, both above and below the waves. As I climbed down the ladder into the tank and slowly sank into the water, I felt peaceful and at ease in my aquatic surroundings. I had come a long way.

The divemaster waited until all six of us were in the tank, then began a long, slow tour of the 6.3-million-gallon facility. Before jumping in, he described the simple rules for our visit: don't touch any of the fish and don't scratch the Plexiglas with our gear. This dive was easy compared to my open water experiences, with no chance of getting lost and every chance of seeing some amazing creatures.

Incredible animals lived in the tank. The whalesharks, used to periodic two-legged visitors, paid us little notice as they swam in graceful arcs. Hovering near the bottom were enormous grouper, so large they looked like pool toys. Bizarre looking species, like woebegone sharks and saw-snouted fish swam by modestly, seemingly unaware of their eccentricities. On the outside of the tank, walls limited the visitors' experience to the fish swimming past the viewing windows. From the inside, I had a clear view of all of the fish activity in the tank and the exceptional opportunity to swim alongside the creatures like one of their own.

This dive did have one thing in common with many of my prior dives: the time elapsed too quickly. Soaking in my last few moments with the hammerhead, I ended up being the last diver to leave the tank. As I sat on the deck removing my gear, I realized the dive had been ideal, filled with incredible sea life and not with worry about my scuba skills. It had been a long road to get to that comfort level, though I had learned invaluable lessons about the sport and sometimes even myself. These knowledge nuggets include:

No one looks good in neoprene – Neoprene is not a forgiving fabric. A dive suit has the uncanny ability to accentuate a diver's least attractive areas, while at the same time minimizing body parts that might draw prestige from looking large. I've given up worrying about what I look like while on a dive boat, focusing instead on what's going on under the waves.

If you thought the shark was scary, you should have seen the diver – I'm pretty sure the chances of getting electrocuted by a toaster are higher than getting bitten by a shark. Although the media wants people to believe otherwise, the purpose of sea life is not, for the most part, to eat people. If a diver gets bitten by a shark or other creature, it is usually because he or she did something frightening or aggressive, such as fondling, harassing, or chasing the animal. Most sea life chooses one of two paths when they see a diver: swim away or simply ignore. If the diver gets injured, it is usually because of his or her own actions, not the dastardly intent of the fish.

If it smells fishy, pick a different dive operator – It seems everyone with an oar and a smile wants to call himself a dive operator. Sometimes a large kickback is the determining factor between a hotel recommendation for Poseidon the Sea God's Scuba Company or My Cousin Vinnie's Row-n-Go. Some questions to consider when choosing a dive company are:
- Is the dive equipment older than the sport itself?
- Is the dive shop taking reasonable safety precautions such as heeding boating laws and plugging leaks before heading out to sea?
- Is anyone walking around wearing their gear backwards or inside out?

Depending on the answer to these questions, it might be time to locate other diving opportunities.

The only difference between a diver and a lobster is sunscreen – In all the excitement that comes with diving, one can sometimes forget that an ability to assume personal responsibility (and opposable thumbs) are the only features that set us apart from animals. A diver shouldn't rely on the dive boat staff and the pity of other divers to get them back home unhurt, or even alive. Check the gear, remember to apply sunscreen, and educate yourself about the sport in order to live through situations you can reasonably expect to occur.

S.N.A.C.K (Sustenance Necessary Although divemaster Cooking Kills) – Few dive companies provide snacks. Most prefer to deliver a fare of diesel fumes and lively banter on the way to the next dive site.

Frequently, the shops that do offer something to eat season the nibbles with rusty cutlery and plates covered in sea residue that is impossible to dislodge. Though I have found that toting around a full turkey dinner is best avoided, I always throw at least one small snack in my dive bag. I have also learned several helpful head lock maneuvers to pry my food away from starving divers who did not have the foresight to pack tasties.

You can lead a horse to water, but you can't make it put on a wetsuit – Scuba diving is like religion: once you find it, you want to tell everyone about it. But not everyone is ready to embrace the sport, and many people may think you are crazy for even trying it. I've had sky divers, race car drivers, and even politicians all tell me they thought that diving was "too risky" to even try. The scuba diving experience is different for everyone – but for me it's been sublime.

AUTHOR BIOGRAPHY

Author Karen Begelfer has been an avid scuba diver for 10 years, logging more than 200 dives in 20 countries. She holds an Open Water certification with PADI, the Professional Association of Diving Instructors. Karen has been in love with the ocean since she was a child, and is threatening to sprout gills any day now.

She is also a lifelong foodie, taking on the challenges of gastronomy from fish eyes in Tokyo, to alpaca in Peru to treacherous Manhattan street hotdogs. A self-taught cook, Karen's food delights those around her, including friends, family, co-workers, and the local fire department, recently called in to assist in an unfortunate exploding pound cake incident.

Karen has requested additional pages for her passport so frequently that she has gained celebrity status at her town's post office. She uses her excitement for diving and hunger for tasty tidbits as valid excuses to travel the world extensively. When not traveling she resides in Kansas City, Missouri with her husband, daughter, and two salty dogs.